About the author

Unity Dow is Botswana's first and only female High Court judge, and has a long record as a human-rights lawyer. She was the plaintiff in a ground-breaking legal case in which Botswana's nationality law was overturned and that led to passage of legislation through which women were enabled to pass on their nationality to their children. She has also written about the link between the Convention on the Rights of the Child and children's legal status in Botswana. She lives with her family in Lobatse, Botswana.

T0096586

Also by Unity Dow

Far and Beyon'

The Screaming of the Innocent

Unity Dow

Published in Australia by Spinifex Press, 2002
Reprinted 2013, 2017

Spinifex Press Pty Ltd
PO Box 5270
North Geelong, Victoria 3215
Australia
www.spinifexpress.com.au
women@spinifexpress.com.au

Copyright © Unity Dow, 2002
Copyright © typesetting and layout: Spinifex Press Pty Ltd, 2002

Copying for educational purposes: When copies of part or the whole of the book are made under part VB of the *Copyright Act*, the law requires that prescribed procedures be followed. For information, contact the Copyright Agency Limited.

All rights reserved. Without limiting the rights under copyright observed above, no part of this publication may be reproduced, stored in or introduced into a retrieval system, or transmitted, in any form or by any means (electronic, mechanical, photocopying, recording or otherwise), without the prior written permission of both the copyright owner and the above publisher of the book.

Edited by Deborah Doyle (Living Proof – Book Editing)
Typeset in Times by Palmer Higgs
Cover design by Deb Snibson

National Library of Australia cataloguing-in-publication data:
Dow, Unity.
The screaming of the innocent.

ISBN 1 876756 20 9.

1. Missing children – Botswana – Fiction. I. Title.
823.92

This is a work of fiction, and any character's resemblance to any person, living or dead, is purely coincidental.

DEDICATION

*I dedicate the book to my parents
and my daughter Cheshe.*

ACKNOWLEDGEMENTS

I want to acknowledge my husband Peter Dow and my friend Johannah Stiebert, both of whom read the manuscript in its early stages and took the time to offer their very valuable views: *le ka moso*. I also want to acknowledge my editor, Deborah Doyle, through whose comments I was stimulated to devote additional creative energy to the writing when I thought I couldn't write even one more sentence: *ke a leboga*.

Unity Dow, December 2001

CHAPTER 1

He bore her no malice. He simply wanted her, needed her. Surely, in needing and wanting, there's some affection, even if not quite love. And she was, by all accounts, available. He watched her as she laughed with her friends: throwing her head in the air, making flapping movements with her arms. She was telling her friends a funny story, imitating a bird, perhaps, and they too were laughing; perhaps, though, she was just being silly, as kids can be sometimes. Whatever she was doing, she was oblivious to his watching, appraising eyes. This was the second time he'd driven past the little group of children. He'd had no problem singling her out – he'd watched her before.

No, he bore her no malice: not by way of hating her, and not by way of wishing to cause her or her family members pain. He simply wanted her, needed her – the pain was inevitable.

He was, by all accounts, a good man. He'd been married to the same woman for twenty-five years, and there was no indication that he wanted out. He was twenty-three when he married his twenty-year-old bride, Rosinah. Over the years, she'd evolved from being a slim young woman to being a matronly, mature woman. Her friends envied her for her professionally braided hair: each braiding cost P250, which was equivalent to the monthly wage of a housemaid. They envied her for her ballooning, brightly coloured Ghanaian outfits and fancy matching headscarves. They envied her for her stockings that never had a run in them. Rosinah was perfect at every funeral, wedding, church gathering, PTA meeting and political-party gathering. She wore only a hint of lipstick: not enough to shout 'Cheap!' – just enough to whisper

1

'Polished'. People said, repeatedly, that Mr Disanka was, indeed, a good husband.

He was also a good lover. He'd just bought his mistress, Maisy, a single-cab Toyota Hilux two-wheel-drive van. He'd bought the vehicle having already paid for an extension for her house. A more reckless man, and there were plenty of reckless men around, might have bought his mistress a double-cab four-wheel-drive – but not Mr Disanka! He understood it was important to maintain boundaries. His wife drove a double-cab Toyota Hilux, as did he; it wouldn't do for his mistress to drive one as well. When his mistress had almost been allocated a business plot next to his wife's takeaway-food business, he'd intervened in the appropriately swift way.

His mother had been the first person to find out about the proximity problem. She'd whispered to him, urgently, 'Rra-Lesego, you can't put one woman on top of another: there'll be war.' She always addressed her son as Rra-Lesego – father of Lesego – as a mark of respect. She herself was addressed as Mma-Disanka – mother of Disanka – and was proud to be. A mother couldn't always be proud of her child, but she was happy to say that she honestly was.

'What do you mean?' he'd asked, reluctantly looking away from the TV: Manchester United, his favourite football team, had been playing, and he hadn't been happy about being dragged away from the match.

'Mma-Betty says she heard from her brother, who heard from his friend, that Maisy's getting a plot two businesses away from your shop, by the post office. She says the Land Board was there only yesterday, measuring out the plot. This can't be allowed to happen: you can't put one woman on top of another! Even the nicest of wives would object. You must do something!' Mma-Disanka had moved and planted her ample figure between him and the TV: a deliberate ploy to ensure she had her son's undivided attention. She had a stake in keeping the family unified; after all, her daughter-in-law, Mma-Lesego, was good to her and made her welcome in her home. Mma-Disanka had no intention of going back to her own home, although she'd originally come to her son's household under the guise of paying a short visit. She was

2

enjoying seeing her grandchildren growing up, and wasn't prepared to look the other way when the peace in her son's household was being threatened by way of an avoidable act.

He'd heeded his mother's advice, and made quick and urgent representations to the Land Board chairman, who duly allocated the mistress a plot on the other side of the village. It wasn't the best place for a seamstress's business, but at least a possible war had been averted. Mr Disanka had then owed the Land Board chairman a favour. The man had wanted to remain in the position of chairman for an extra four-year term. He'd needed votes, and expected the businessman to help by lobbying behind the scenes. Many people had agreed that Mr Disanka was a good husband who hadn't let his mistress make him forget his responsibilities at home. The Land Board chairman had understood the reason for moving the mistress's plot and duly approved the move. He'd wished that more men were as sensible as Mr Disanka, the good man who was on many committees and who earnt much respect for being committed to facilitating community projects. Indeed, when a delegation was sent to the Office of the President to protest that the police investigations in the Neo Kakang murder case were sluggish, Mr Disanka was naturally selected to be a member of it. That was how respected he was: a good community man, indeed.

He was also a good father. You couldn't say he was a great and regular smiler, but neither was he a great and regular shouter. His countenance was stern but gentle; 'civilised' was a word that people very often used to describe him. His handsome face; his straight bearing; his tall, lean frame: all suggestions of kindness and dependability. He loved his four children, and showed his love in many ways – the marital children, that is: he was expected to neither love nor not love his extramarital children. And being the good man he was, a man who lived within society's boundaries, he neither loved nor didn't love them. They benefited from his association with their mother: if he was sleeping with the mother, the children – both his and any others the mother might have – benefited financially. Occasionally, he returned to an old mistress and enjoyed a few weeks, sometimes months, of intimacies. During those weeks or months, the mother and children had extra food and, for an especially lucky child, perhaps even a new pair of shoes.

3

He loved his four marital children – two boys and two girls – in many ways. He drove them to school, whereas most children either walked or rode on a rickety bus. And he loved the littlest one, Morati – or, as she was affectionately called, Debaby: 'The Baby', 'Daddy's Baby' – so much she was threatening to burst out of her tracksuit even as she sat next to her daddy in the slow-moving vehicle. However, she couldn't actually jump; rather, she jiggled and wobbled from being loved in the form of endlessly being given ice cream, chips, fatty cakes, chicken, sodas and gum. If anyone insisted she do a minimum of chores around the house, an arsenal of hugs and objections was trundled out, even though she was all of eleven years old.

By way of contrast, the object of her dad's attention today could jump, skip and flit like a little antelope.

By most standards, then, Mr Disanka was a good man. He had businesses that were thriving, a good wife, a good mistress who knew to keep her child to herself, good marital children, and good ex-mistresses who kept their extramarital children to themselves and were occasionally available to break the monotony of the wife and the current mistress. After all, didn't people say often enough that a man can't possibly live on porridge alone?

By all indications, Mr Disanka was a successful Motswana man. He wanted to remain so, and was planning to ensure he remained so. He was planning to expand his business as well as to buy a new car within the next year. He was even thinking about installing a hot-water geyser at the mistress's house – and the lumpy bed there had to be replaced. Just to make sure his wife remained ahead, he was thinking about also replacing the bed at home – not that it needed replacing, but he didn't want there to be any doubt about who was the wife and who the mistress. He was planning to remain involved in community projects by chairing the various development committees and being on committees for neighbourhood crime watch. He was intending to push for the local school to be expanded so more children could attend it. And perhaps, during the Minister of Health's next visit to the village, he could urge the minister to consider putting more money into the local hospital.

Throughout the village, people were circulating muted rumours about him – but then, people circulated rumours about any successful man. It was common for people to suspect that a man attained his political position, business success, academic kudos or professional promotion – any type of success, for that matter – by devilish means. Mr Disanka had decided that the people who circulated these rumours were motivated by malice and envy.

Now the little group of children started playing a skipping-rope game. The one who Mr Disanka was focusing on skipped expertly as her two friends swung the rope, in harmony with a song: '*Moloi, tike; tike, moloi! Moloi, tike; tike, moloi!*' ('Witch, hide; hide, witch! Witch, hide; hide, witch!') The good man watched – fascinated, enthralled, absorbed. As the girl skipped, her skirt was caught by the wind and went up, exposing her impala legs: firm, muscular, a dark brown: the colour of a polished *moselesele* tree. Not a lump of fat in sight. Sleek. She grabbed her skirt and tucked the hem into the legs of her panties. She did so not out of modesty but to make sure she successfully completed the task at hand: the skipping. It was a gesture through which the watching man, the good man, was provided with an uninterrupted view of the brown legs, right up to her crotch, where a pink area, her undies, was visible. She was bare breasted, naturally: it was a hot afternoon, and she was skipping with her friends in her own neighbourhood – of course she'd be bare breasted.

'God, she's perfect,' he whispered to himself. The body was just right. She had no bulbous protrusions yet – he could barely make out the two nodes, just ready for his purposes. And what a tight little butt she had. He was sure that when she was skipping, under her flailing arms was exposed fine fur, not yet hair. Although he was too far away to see it, he was sure it was there. He was sure no one had been near this one yet. They didn't let their skirt fly up in the air if they'd lost their innocence. Then, they didn't skip bare breasted; in fact, they usually didn't skip any more then. She was just right for harvesting.

'God, she's perfect; just right,' the good father, husband, lover and businessman whispered under his breath. He'd stopped the

Hilux now and was watching her openly. As he watched and his mind went back to the previous harvesting, memory crushed into anticipation, and a pool of pleasure spread through his body. He was heady and dizzy, and could barely wait. His body trembled so much he couldn't hide the sight of it from his beloved daughter sitting next to him, the little girl who couldn't skip because she'd been loved into being a blob of fat. He needed the little, skipping girl so he could continue to love the little girl inside the Hilux by giving her hugs, ice cream, chips, fatty cakes, chicken, sodas, gum and few chores to do. Sweat gushed out of his pores, as if a million tiny bridges had collapsed all at once, and a cyclone of emotions began erupting, out of control. For a second, he even thought he'd wet himself: a warm moisture had spread between his legs and under his armpits. He experienced having to catch his breath as a sprinkle of fear. The feeling seasoned the pleasure, and in its wake was left sweetness spiked with a touch of bitterness. The bitter-sweet feeling led to another bout of trembling, and the cycle was set in motion again. For a second, he felt a wave of madness come over him. He considered sprinting into the hot afternoon, from the comfort of his air-conditioned van, and simply grabbing her, right there and then. However, his sanity quickly returned and he realised that option would have been pure madness. It had to be done right; it *would* be done right. It'd been two years since the previous one, and he was more than ready for the next experience. His body ached with anticipation of it. His heart was threatening to explode from the furious thumping that had seized it.

'Dad, are you feeling sorry for them because of their falling house? Will they go to the school you're building for poor child-ren? Daddy, why don't we go home? Daddy, I want some ice cream!' Debaby's concern ended up as a whine, and the good father knew he couldn't refuse her. He loved this spoilt daughter of his. He grabbed her and hugged and kissed her, and promised her he'd buy her an ice cream and whatever else she wanted. She beamed back at him, knowing she had the best daddy in the entire world: a kind, sweet daddy, who hugged, kissed and protected her. She bet that none of the half-clad, filthy kids skipping their knotted rope could produce a comparable daddy.

As the van purred into life, a small boy, about four years old, looked up at it. He raised both his hands in a jerky wave and in a childish voice shouted, 'By four! By four! Toyota Hilux! Toyota Hilux! *Mo-Japan! Japaneeeeese!*'

Yes, even by a four-year-old's standards, Mr Disanka was a successful man.

When the skipping girl heard the little boy's praise, she became distracted from her skipping. She subsequently lost her rhythm, whereby the rope looped around her ankles and caused her to stumble. Her friends whooped with excitement, whereupon she moved from skipping to swinging the rope. She looked up and saw the almost brand-new van, and the man and young girl inside it. She smiled at them out of politeness. She was a trusting village child, proud that a big, successful man was finding her worthy of a glance, and she mistook his interest in her entire being as an interest in her skipping prowess. She was an impala that wasn't noticing the poacher for what he was, an impala that was mistaking the poacher for a game warden.

'Neo!' The girl whose turn it was to skip was calling out to her friend impatiently. The impala girl looked away from the good man and started to help swing the rope for the new girl, who began skipping to a new song: '*Phuduhudu, thaisa! Phuduhudu, thaisa!*' ('Duiker, trap it! Duiker, trap it!') The new girl skipped expertly, pretending to be a duiker avoiding a snare. They were village children having fun and feeling safe, carefree in their neighbourhood, dodging imaginary snares.

The good man shook himself out of his trance. He drove off thinking about how to get the task done: the task of harvesting fertility before it erupted into public view, before men started interfering with it and polluting it. He headed for Maun, leaving behind the village of Gaphala and the little girl, and silently promising himself he'd return.

As he drove into Maun, he checked his mobile phone to see whether it had a signal. It did have one, so he decided to call a friend. 'Good afternoon, chief. This is Disanka here. Can we meet? Yes, tonight is fine. Yes, there's one I think you'll like too. A very perfect one indeed. Good. Good.' Mr Disanka, the good man, pressed the red button on his mobile phone, and the line went dead.

7

He needed a third man, perhaps even a fourth man, but definitely a third man.

He drove into Maun, and before he headed home, he stopped at a supermarket to fulfil his promise to his younger daughter, who by then was fast asleep on the seat next to him. And he had to pick up his elder daughter, Lesego, from school. He was aware that even at her age she wanted to be seen with her doting father. There'd been a time, a couple of years ago, when she'd put some distance between them, but she was now being the old Lesego again. He'd decided her quietness had been due to mood swings as a result of her growing up. He was happy she was now back to her old self again, so he obliged her with his company and decided to pick her up from school as much as possible rather than send a driver. He was suddenly hungry now, and was looking forward to eating a good meal with his lovely family – at least that was one urge he could satisfy openly.

CHAPTER 2

The man who Mr Disanka – the good husband, father, lover, businessman and community leader – had chosen to be his second man was Head Man Motlababusa Bokae, a man whose arrogance was evident in the way he walked, talked and bore himself. However, it was perhaps unfair to blame Head Man Motlababusa Bokae for being arrogant: one stormy night forty years before, he'd slithered out of his mother's womb, purplish and bruised from the effort of being born, the umbilical cord wrapped around his neck, whereupon he'd been encased by a waiting arrogance. While he was taking his first breath, the arrogance was claiming, owning and shaping him. The same thing had happened to his father before him, and to his father's father, and it would no doubt happen to his son.

And he did plan to have a son soon. The son born to one of his many women friends didn't count; it was the son he'd have with his wife who'd count. He planned to have a wife soon, too, so he could have a son so he could ensure that the Bokae lineage, a lineage of men who would be chiefs, was perpetuated. Unlike him, his son would bear a name through which all and sundry would know that the war had been won. He'd be a son who'd wear the leopard skin as a sign of his birthright: the ultimate public sign of being a chief.

Many people understood that Head Man Bokae's swaggering walk, bullish voice, and near- and actual rapes of young girls were simply the result of having been born almost a chief – or rather of having been born not a chief but a should-be chief. Although 'should-be chief' didn't have the same power as 'chief', people allowed the man who should have been chief to display a large measure of arrogance. Naturally, the arrogance was spiked with liberal doses of anger and bitterness at what the should-be chief viewed as being an inferior house's outright theft of his family's throne. The arrogant man was therefore also a bitter man.

It was hardly surprising that after three generations, the anger continued to rise rather than ebb. The job market was becoming more and more competitive, and every man was looking around, within his own circles, to challenge his competitors. With renewed energy, Head Man Bokae was therefore challenging his third-generation cousin's right to be chief. His methods of challenging his cousin's right were of a dark, quiet, secret nature, whereby he paid nightly visits to witchdoctors. He wanted to topple the chief and take over.

Being a chief meant having a good job for which no training was required. It was a job for which there was neither an entry age nor an exit age. Also, when a chief died, his son took over – no questions asked. Whereas applicants for other government jobs had to have a medical examination in order to ensure they were fit for duty, a chief didn't have to be subjected to so intrusive a procedure. Therefore, it was conceivable that a mad man could be a chief. And people existed who argued that quite a few mad men had indeed been chiefs.

As a chief, Mr Bokae would be the head of the tribe, a judge and an adviser to the legislator. The only required qualification was that he be the son of some specific man and the man's wife. The wife's lineage was inconsequential. Unfortunately for Head Man Bokae, someone had successfully challenged the validity of the marriage of his great-grandfather and great-grandmother, and as a result, three generations later, he wasn't the chief – just because one cow too few had been paid as bride wealth and the tribe hadn't supported the marriage. The tribe hadn't been swayed by the fact that five strong boys had been produced in the marriage. Naturally, although five strong girls had also been produced in the marriage, that fact had been irrelevant: each girl's identity had long been obliterated when she'd married.

Mr Bokae wanted the right to wear the leopard skin and was forever thinking of ways to do it. He wanted to get it back for both himself and his son after him – the son he was going to father as soon as he married the right woman.

He hated his title: Head Man; *Kgosana*; 'Little Chief'; 'Sub-chief'; 'Not Quite Chief'. He hated even more the rather meagre salary he was being paid by the central government. He hated the fact he was receiving a salary from a government that was populated by non-entities. He imagined a young woman working in Gaborone, her fingernails and lips painted an ugly red, sitting behind a desk, making out a cheque in his name and smirking at the amount she was writing.

He was given to paging through *The White Paper*, an official document in which the government published civil servants' salary scales. He was compelled to look at his salary figure and then at the chief's. He was driven to paging through the document and noting how much all sorts of inferior people earned. How anyone could justify that a social worker, lawyer or doctor deserved a salary higher than that of an authentic chief he could never understand! Even the headmaster of the local school earned more than he. To start with, these people were commoners who had no right to be where they were. He was accustomed to becoming filled with anger at the thought, and the person who bore the brunt of his anger was the next unsuspecting litigant seeking justice from the head man's court – he was, even as a head man, a type of judge.

Although in law his powers of punishment were limited, the fact wasn't obvious from his judgments. He hated women, chiefs, lawyers and parliamentarians.

He hated women because they wanted more than was their due traditionally and because they shouted crazily for women's rights.

He hated chiefs because he should have been one of them, and especially hated chiefs who were from what he considered to be an inferior tribe. Hearing the shrill shouts for recognition that emanated from the inferior chiefs, he believed those chiefs to be almost as bad as women.

He hated lawyers because he considered them to be arrogant. He thought they were a bunch of crooks bent on polluting the population by offering up crazy and foreign notions such as the right to be represented by a lawyer.

He hated parliamentarians because they ruled without having

the right blood coursing through their veins, and he hated the British for having allowed the situation to develop.

In general, he hated any person who he thought shouldn't have power but either had it or sought it. He was a bitter and unhappy man who went through life characterised by a fierce expression, sharp bark and sadistic laugh. He was a mean man, by any definition of the word.

Few people liked him, and even fewer loved him. Even his mother feared him and avoided him whenever she could. However, many people laughed in his presence, and the gesture was merely a mechanical baring of teeth, the result not of mirth but of duty. To his face, many people called him chief, not sub-chief or head man; some even shortened his name to Babusi: 'those who rule', rather than use his full name, Motlababusa: 'he who was born when other people ruled'. In public and with other people, people called him sub-chief – after all, they had the real chief to contend with.

The real chief was also a man who people crossed at their peril. He was aware of the malice the head man harboured towards him and was forever on the lookout for any one of his subjects who sided with his enemy. Many people walked a tightrope between the warring children of the house of Kgosikubu, and many chose to avoid Head Man Bokae and the cloud of nastiness that hung around him. For years, his father hadn't been sober enough to care what happened one way or another: he'd been given to muttering to himself about leopards, fat cattle and full granaries. However, no one had listened to him. They'd dismissed him as being insane, bewitched, or both, although most would have voted for 'bewitched'.

When the government increased all civil servants' salaries by 15 per cent, Mr Bokae again consulted *The White Paper*. Armed with a calculator, he confirmed to himself that the margin between his salary and the chief's would widen. On reading this, he span out of control, and began cursing everything and everyone. As he was putting the document away, a young police officer, Mosika Mosika, hesitantly knocked on the door and announced that a man who had a complaint against his wife was there to see him. The man had been waiting for two hours for the doors of justice to open. Head Man Bokae barked at Constable Mosika to give the man four lashes with a cane for failing to keep a woman under control: 'Give him the udder of a cow!'

'Four?' The young officer was surprised that the number of lashes he was to administer was rather high.

The could-be chief barked back, 'Do you know any cow with three tits? Perhaps *you* have three tits!'

'The udder of a cow it will be, sir,' the officer responded, humbly. Slinking away to fetch the cane, he thought that if any number of lashes had to be meted out, it would have been more appropriate to reflect the udder of a goat, or even to deliver only one lash. However, the head man had ordered four lashes, and four lashes it would be! The lashing would be a preliminary procedure before the head man heard the complaint itself.

As the head man watched the lashing, he scowled and nodded at every hit. Although blood was drawn as a result of at least two of the lashes, the man seeking justice neither winced nor showed any sign of discomfort. The lashes must have stung, though, because the head man insisted that when the canes weren't being used, they be buried in a bed of salt. Constable Mosika had hoped the head man would administer the lashing himself, as Bokae often did. Mosika hated this part of his job, and believed it was just a matter of time before someone challenged these pre-trial procedures before the High Court as being unconstitutional or in some other way unacceptable: these days, a growing number of lawyers were being brave enough to ask questions about procedures that no one had ever dared to challenge.

Once the lashing was finished, the man rose hopefully, expecting that he'd be heard. However, the head man simply stood up abruptly, walked to his car, got in it and drove off in a cloud of dust. He didn't bother to say where he was going or when he'd be back. It seemed the lashed man would have to come back some other day for continuation of justice. Constable Mosika was unable to tell him when; justice was to be meted out in irregular and unpredictable instalments.

The could-have-been chief was fuming, and needed something to calm him down. He headed for the nearest secondary school: the surest place to get a woman – a girl, really – without facing too many hassles. Also, he'd calculated that if he wanted to use his cramped, little, 'head-man salary' vehicle, he couldn't go and fetch his regular, rather large, sexual partner. And even a should-be chief couldn't always persuade a mature woman to agree to engaging in a mid-morning, cramped-car bush escapade. This morning, a student was a more appropriate candidate for his purposes. By engaging in the escapade, she'd have to miss a few hours of school, but he'd have her back within a reasonable time. And he could trust the headmaster to look the other way; after all, the headmaster was a foreigner, a Zambian who was keen to keep his job. It wasn't his place to question his hosts' ways; it wasn't his place to care. He wasn't about to do or say anything whereby he might end up back in Zambia, with its economic woes. He had a wife and children to think about.

Unlike his friend the good man, the head man didn't have to pay for non-marital embraces – at least not in material ways. He paid by offering himself: surely being touched by the-man-who-should-be-chief was payment enough.

The head man's dark mood was only marginally improved as a result of the bush encounter. Constable Mosika, reading his boss's mood from the way the man yanked the door open, tried to make himself small and invisible by sliding most of his body under the table. His boss wasn't beyond verbally abusing him for no apparent reason: a convenient target was what the young officer very often was.

The head man huffed past Mosika without uttering a word. The girl had been too experienced, and the whole thing had felt more like a match than a taking. He regretted not having instead taken the fourteen-year old girl, the younger of the two. However, he'd had little time for enticing the younger child away. At sixteen, the older one had known what he wanted, and because he'd had only a couple of hours or so to invest, she'd been the obvious choice. Nevertheless, he now continued to feel heavy with a burden he needed to offload. His head throbbed, his shoulders were stiff and his upper lip was curled in a snarl.

Therefore, when his friend the good man phoned him to say he'd identified a candidate, his mood improved dramatically. He called the next case and awarded the plaintiff damages without even hearing the other party. He delivered a tirade about lawyers and how they were all crooks. The speech's relevance was lost to the Sello Motlapa: the court recorder, so the young man pretended to record everything and omitted the part about lawyers. Court recording was a tricky thing: a good recorder had to know what to record and what not to. Should the head man get into trouble because of what the recorder had said, the recorder would be in even deeper trouble.

The head man had spoken, and the defendant went home muttering to himself. He only very briefly considered appealing the decision. However, he was a practical man. He 'factored in' that the next court in the hierarchy would be presided over by a cousin of Head Man Bokae. The cousin judge's office was next door to Bokae's, and the cousin would have heard the head man shout his judgment. Were an appeal mounted, the two cousins would be pitted against each other and the appellant would be the 'grass'. The court higher still in the hierarchy would be presided over by the cousin's relative, albeit a distant relative. The defendant therefore decided not to lodge an appeal; he'd accept justice as meted out by Head Man Motlababusa Bokae, 'the man who could have been chief'. For the defendant, unlike the man who had the wayward wife, justice had been swift and certain, if unsatisfactory.

CHAPTER 3

'Why don't you take the afternoon off? You're not looking well. I'll take care of things – really: I don't mind,' Mr Molatedi Sebaki, the deputy headmaster of Maun–Moseja High School, urged Mr Lotsane Mosi, the headmaster. The neck wanted the head off so the neck could assume the head's position. The neck hated the head.

The head knew the neck hated him: only the previous night, his diviner had warned him that a hostile takeover was in the planning stage. However, the head smiled, and feigned ignorance and gratitude. 'Thank you, Mr Sebaki, but I think I'll stay on until end of school.' The headmaster returned his attention to the papers on his desk, a gesture intended to convey to his deputy that the discussion was over. The deputy stood up to leave.

However, Deputy Headmaster Sebaki wasn't finished. He'd wanted the headmaster out of his office so he could work on it using potions from his witchdoctor. He knew that if the headmaster didn't leave during working hours, the headmaster would lock his office at the end of the day. Mr Sebaki simply *had* to have access to the office. The headmaster had no plans to have a day off, even though he had a terrible cold, so Mr Sebaki decided to use 'Plan B'. Before he moved from the headmaster's desk, he dropped his driver's licence under it. Several days before, he'd acquired a duplicate key to the office – an easy matter in itself because the lock was a cheap one. The difficult part was formulating a reason to go into the office when the headmaster was absent.

'I thought I had my driver's licence with me when I came in here. Did I? Did you see me holding it?' he asked, feigning a puzzled expression.

The headmaster looked up sharply and answered, 'No, I don't think so. No, I'm sure you weren't holding it – I would've seen it.' The headmaster was keen to deny having seen the licence: he didn't want any suggestion to arise that so important a document had mysteriously disappeared in his office.

The deputy smiled back, shaking his head as if trying to figure out what could have happened to the document. 'Well, I guess I didn't have it. I could've sworn I did. I most probably left it in my office. Well, I hope you feel better. I'm off to class, then.'

Mr Sebaki worked late that day. His colleagues eyed him suspiciously, because he worked late so rarely. It was such common knowledge he was lazy that he'd earned the nickname Lumpy. 'Did you see Lumpy trying to be the good boy? As if the head could possibly recommend he be promoted,' the school's head of science, Ms Khakhia, commented as she and her colleague and neighbour Mr Molaodi were heading towards the teachers' housing complex, located behind the school.

Mr Molaodi, who taught Setswana, replied, 'He could recommend it if he also decided to recommend Lumpy be transferred to some remote village – that's a common enough way of getting rid of sneaky and ambitious deputies. I hope he does it, too.'

Ms Khakhia replied, 'I dare say this village is already remote! Then again, though, things have indeed improved since the tar road's been finished. Maun's a buzzing, growing town. Then again, though, I guess he could send him deep into the delta; or better still, he could send him to one of those sorry schools in the Kgalagadi Desert – that'd be no great loss to us. That man gives me goose-bumps!'

Mr Molaodi was on a roll now: 'The guy's dangerously am - bitious – the way he attaches himself to every visiting official from Gaborone! And the letters he writes – thanking the government for this and that; always pretending to be assisting the headmaster when in actual fact he's undermining him most of the time. I've never met a worse *lelatswa-thipa*.'

Ms Khakhia laughed, despite herself. When she heard Mr Molaodi call Mr Sebaki a *lelatswa-thipa*, which literally means 'the one who licks the knife', she recalled an incident that had occurred during the previous year, when a group of students played an April Fool's Day trick on Mr Sebaki. The Regional Education Officer had come to tour the school, and address the students and teachers. Mr Sebaki had manoeuvred things so he'd be the person who gave the vote of thanks. On his insistence, the teachers had bought the officer a present, which Mr Sebaki had had someone elaborately gift-wrap. However, when he presented the gift after he'd delivered his long-winded vote of thanks, what the officer retrieved from the box was a red-stained knife and a note on which was written, 'I'll do more than knife-lick; I'll even brown-nose.' Mr Sebaki's humiliation was only marginally mitigated when the assembled students shouted, 'April Fool!' He stuttered and stammered and seethed, and then tried to smile in the spirit of April Fool's Day humour. However, in playing other minor pranks on other teachers that day, the students did little to blunt the message they'd delivered to Mr Sebaki; in fact, behind his back, they called him 'Mr Brown'.

This evening, when everyone had left the school, Mr Sebaki sneaked into the headmaster's office and quickly did what he had to do. It was essential he work fast: a security guard was doing the rounds and would no doubt be coming around to check the locks. Since a group of boys calling themselves the Smoke Pipers had broken into the science laboratory to steal and liberate some lab mice just for the fun if it, the security guard had been instructed to take his job more seriously. Mr Sebaki dipped his fingers in a jar he was carrying, and quickly dabbed the concoction on the underside of the chair and desk as well as on the filing cabinet. Then he used it to mark a cross where the headmaster's feet would rest as he sat on his chair. Then he used it to mark a cross on the opposite wall, where the headmaster would look as he raised his eyes. Then he rubbed all the marked areas down so the crosses wouldn't be obvious. Sure he'd dabbed the concoction on all the important places, he left the room and locked the door behind him.

Just as he was settling back into his chair, the security guard knocked on the door and gave it a push. He addressed Mr Sebaki. 'Good evening, sir. I'm just making sure all the doors are locked. Please let me know when you do go.'

'Thank you, Kabelo. In fact, it's a good thing you've come by. I've been looking for my driver's licence and I can't find it any -

where. I think I might have left it in the headmaster's office. I was in his office this morning, and it might have dropped out of my pocket then. Do you have the keys to that office? Please check to see whether the licence is among the papers on the desk as well.' Naturally, he knew that the guard had access to all the keys. He also knew that if he'd indicated he wanted to look for the licence himself, the guard might have been reluctant to open the office. He finished his spiel: 'Could you go and look? Check under the visitors' chair as well.'

The security guard went off, and a few minutes later came back with the licence.

'Oh, thank you!' Sebaki gushed. 'Where did you find it? I did tell the headmaster I thought it was in his office. Well, thank you. You know the police these days: I would have gotten into trouble – roadblocks everywhere! They can't catch thieves, but forget your driver's licence and from their reaction you'd think you'd killed someone. I want to go to Mosuke Bar for a few beers, but they always have a roadblock just outside it. Mean bastards, these police. Anyway, thank you for finding the driver's licence.'

The security guard replied, 'I found it under the desk. It must have fallen out of your pocket, like you said. Anyway, don't forget to lock your door when you leave – and please close the windows as well.' If he thought Mr Sebaki was especially garrulous that evening, he didn't show it. In constructing the licence episode, Mr Sebaki had intended to hide the fact he'd entered the office earlier. He expected that the headmaster had a way of knowing whether anyone had entered his office when he was absent: the headmaster was a suspicious man and was aware that Sebaki had designs on his job.

Months later, when the headmaster died in a car crash and Mr Sebaki became the head, he decided that the security guard had to go. He made arrangements for the man to be transferred to a school located near his home village. The man was grateful to him. Mr Sebaki was happy to have removed a pair of eyes that he believed were forever searching his face. He hadn't been able to shake the feeling that the security guard knew that he, Sebaki, had engineered, through witchcraft, the headmaster's fatal car crash.

CHAPTER 4

How Mr Sebaki, the deputy headmaster, became the third man is evidence enough that there are more than only five senses. Then again, though, it was perhaps simply evidence that Mr Disanka had long viewed Mr Sebaki as being a potential partner on account of the fact that among the region's network of witch-doctors, it was reasonably well known that Sebaki harboured an ambition to be headmaster of Maun–Moseja High School.

Walking past the corner of Mosuke Bar in which businessmen regularly sat, Mr Sebaki was heading towards the toilet when he came upon the businessman and the head man. Many times before, he'd seen the businessman, Mr Disanka, sitting with one or another companion just like he was this evening. However, this evening, as Sebaki passed the corner table, he felt as if he were being pulled towards the two men. He suddenly felt a recognition he was unable to ignore. Although his bladder was uncomfortably full, the power of the recognition was so great he was willing to postpone res - ponding to its demands; beer bladders usually aren't known to be obedient and patient. In every fibre of his body, he felt as if he were crossing a bridge in order to join the two men. Perhaps the magnetism lay in their eyes: the deep, dark pools that now looked at him, drawing him in. Perhaps it lay in the fact that the air around them was perfectly still in an otherwise noisy, bustling place. He knew, from the body language the two men were displaying, that they weren't simply two regular bar patrons discussing the results of a football match. 'Good evening, chief. Good evening, Mr Disanka,' he said.

'Sit down.' Mr Disanka, the businessman, was clearly the boss.

Sebaki sat down: it wasn't an invitation; it was an order.

The two men looked at him for what to him seemed to be a very long time.

Disanka finally broke the silence. 'What kind of man are you?' He'd locked his eyes into Sebaki's, and now he wouldn't let go of them. The deputy headmaster wanted to glance at the sub-chief but couldn't disengage from the businessman's eyeballing. 'What's the nature of your heart?' came the second question.

The man whose bladder was willing to wait felt ensnared. He delivered his response in a whisper. 'A hard heart.'

'How hard?' As the good man asked the third question, he yanked the man who had the waiting bladder towards him.

'Hard enough to do what has to be done,' came the words in response.

'Do you have a brave heart?' Question four.

'Yes.' Again delivered in a whisper.

'Do you have a man's heart?' Question five. Again the pull.

'Yes, I have a man's heart; I'm the son of a man.' Strength could be detected in the deputy headmaster's voice, a hint of boasting, perhaps a hint of challenge: he wanted to cross the bridge in order to join the men on the other side.

'We're looking for a man with a hard heart, a heart of stone, a heart of a real man.' The selection criterion.

'You've found your man, sir.' He was a confident applicant.

'What is this man I've found willing to do?' Question six.

'Anything. Everything. The ultimate thing.' He was firm.

'The ultimate thing?'

'Yes, the ultimate thing.'

'We're hunting a lamb.' Mr Disanka paused and watched his captive's eyes. 'What kind of lamb are we hunting?'

'A hairless lamb,' came the whispered answer.

A pause ensued as the two men looked at each other without blinking. Even during the confrontational stare, there was a leader and a follower, the yanker and the yanked. The yanker broke the spell. 'Go and have your piss and come back. We have business to discuss. We don't want you pissing on yourself like a little frightened boy.'

The deputy headmaster had been dismissed and now almost felt as if he'd been physically de-linked. He almost expected to fall back, as you'd feel if you'd suddenly been left holding on to the end of a rope. His bladder couldn't wait any more, and he hurried away. He had a frantic fight with his zipper, and as his urine finally oozed out, so did his fear; hot fear. However, more fear pooled inside his head, his chest, his belly, his knees, his waist. He briefly considered jumping the fence and disappearing into the night, but gave himself a reality check: he'd just been offered the opportunity of a lifetime. It was the kind of offer he couldn't walk away from; indeed, it was the kind of offer it mightn't even be safe to walk away from. He then realised that the deep whispers he'd heard about Mr Disanka were true. And he, Sebaki, had just been invited into this special, super-secret circle. He felt privileged.

As anticipation came to replace his fear, the frustrations of his day lifted. Soon he'd be sharing in an experience he could never make public but through which he'd acquire strength and power beyond belief. He conjured up a mental picture of the perfect candidate: no face, just tiny breasts – the type that hurt if you held them too tightly; a small, delicate chest on which the ribs were clearly marked out through the skin; a perfect V shape where the legs met the flat tummy. The deputy headmaster realised his bladder had now been emptied for a long time but that he'd been too absorbed in his dream to register the fact. He shook his member to get rid of the leftover pee, put his friend away, zipped up his pants and walked purposefully to the two waiting men. He wiped his wet hand on his jeans. Without even thinking about washing his hands, he ordered and tore into a piece of roast chicken: he had more important things to think about than stopping himself from recycling beer and urine. He guzzled the beer Mr Disanka now offered him. Then he guzzled another.

By the time the meeting ended, the three men had drawn up a broad plan. All three agreed it was far from perfect and that they'd still need to work on it. This would be their last meeting in public – the good man, the could-have-been chief and the deputy head - master, three pillars of the community. Each man's head was swollen with the knowledge he'd succeed, not only at completing the task at hand, which was only a means to an end, but at attaining the end itself. None of the three had any way of knowing that in five years' time, a box would be opened and out of it would spill a scream that couldn't be ignored. They had no way of knowing that darkness isn't always courageous enough to keep evil to itself.

CHAPTER 5

As Amantle Bokaa approached the Gaphala Health Clinic compound, she was both apprehensive and excited. She looked at its pale-yellow buildings and wondered who was responsible for deciding the colours of government buildings nationwide: the colours always seemed to be at odds with their surroundings. The rest of a village's buildings were a brown-earth colour, but all its government buildings were either yellow or white – and it seemed the government had a thing for blue doors.

Amantle was wearing a brown scarf to neatly hold back her recently braided hair. The only jewellery she was wearing today was a pair of plain silver earrings and a watch. That morning, she'd been very careful not to dress up too much. She hadn't wanted to seem glamorous or in any way frivolous, and she'd been mainly concerned about being taken seriously in her new job. She was planning to learn as much as possible and make herself useful in the community she'd just joined. She had no way of knowing she was soon to be instrumental in stoking the fire of five-year-old fears and waking up a five-year-old ghost.

This morning, every time she took a step, the mini-heels of her shoes sank into the sand, and she made a mental note not to wear that pair again during the year-long position in which she was about to commence: 'flatties', although less attractive, would be the more sensible choice. She'd also have to ditch the stockings she was wearing, because a section of the road she had to walk along was rich with grass-bearing seeds that seemed to have been waiting for her to disperse them – they were clinging to her ankles with a singleminded tenacity.

She watched smoke rising from the various compounds and caught the sound of children laughing behind her. She looked back, and just then saw a hawk swoop down from the sky. Before a mother hen could lead her chicks to safety, the hawk grabbed one of them. The children shouted at the hawk, but it was too late: the predator and its prey had disappeared into the distance. The group of children – six boys riding donkeys – went back to laughing and talking as they rode towards Amantle. One of them fell off his donkey, whereupon the other five boys doubled over with laughter: children being a bit mean, a bit playful; children being children. A woman came out of one of the compounds and shouted at the boys for not warning the mother hen in time. The boys apologised, but if the woman had taken a closer look at their faces, she'd have noticed mischievous eyes. Exasperated, she threw her hands up in the air, sighed and walked back into her compound.

The boy who'd fallen off his donkey dusted himself off and pulled himself back up on to the waiting animal. His exposed bottom came into contact with the donkey's back, and whereas Amantle would have expected him to wince, he merely chuckled triumphantly. He seemed to be totally unaware that the seat of his encrusted shorts hardly remained: he was a proud rider who'd just reclaimed his magnificent mount – the smile he flashed Amantle said as much. He gave his mount a gentle nudge with his knees, waved to Amantle and galloped off past her. When Amantle saw the gesture, her view was reinforced that she was at the right place for her year of Tirelo Sechaba: national service. *I'm going to like it here,* she thought to herself. She loved the remoteness; the lush bush; the chance to see Botswana at its wildest.

For her first day of work as a Tirelo Sechaba Participant – a TSP, or national-service worker – she was wearing a skirt that covered her knees. She'd worn the same skirt on the first day she and some other TSPs had been in the village and she'd been one of the ones to be picked by a family. She and the other female TSPs had discussed how they'd dress during their first few weeks of service. For all kinds of reasons, families were often reluctant to host national-service workers. Married women usually preferred to host a boy to be their TSP: it was common knowledge that they also assigned the abbreviation the meaning 'temporary sexual partner' for their husband. Because placements were for one year, sexual liaisons between husbands and female TSPs, who were fresh out of high school and had been thrust into the world of work, away from their parents, were indeed of a temporary nature. It was known that quite a few girls had returned home pregnant.

Generally, host families considered male TSPs to be unhelpful in the home and burdensome on the family's female members. It was unlikely that a swaggering eighteen-year-old boy, away from home for the first time and carrying a bit of money to spend, would be willing to cook and clean up for his host family; also, compared with a female TSP, he was more likely to be trying out cigarettes, alcohol and sex. A good, well-mannered and well-behaved girl could therefore be an asset – if she could just keep away from the man of the house. If a family could get a good girl, it would benefit by having an unpaid domestic worker for a year.

Amantle had long ago decided she wouldn't have any sexual liaisons, temorary or otherwise, during her TSP assignment. She'd decided to concentrate on leaving the position having earnt a glowing recommendation from her supervisors at the clinic. She wanted the government to award her a scholarship so she could study medicine and be the best doctor the country had ever known.

At twenty-two, Amantle believed she was already three years behind schedule. She'd lost three school years between the ages of fourteen and seventeen because she'd had to leave school when her parents were unable to raise her school fees. As a result of a drought that had lasted three years, most of her family's cattle had died. After that, her older brothers had lost their jobs in South African goldmines, so the family had had even less money. During those lean times, Amantle's parents as well as her six siblings had scrimped and saved so she could return to school to repeat Form 1, at age seventeen, in 1994.

The youngest of the seven children, Amantle had been the first member of her family to go to school, and when the family dream had been threatened due to lack of money, all the family members had banded together. It had taken them two years to mobilise their resources, but they'd finally succeeded. Over the years, each of them had remembered Amantle's first years at school and had often used them as the basis for the fireside stories they told. No doubt, they'd exaggerated aspects of the stories, whereby each person had mainly remembered how he or she had participated in Amantle's education. Her sisters had remembered proudly washing the baby of the family's school uniform, whereas her brothers had remembered sending money home to pay for her school shoes and fees. Her mother had remembered leafing through her daughter's exercise books to look for ticks and then to count and re-count them. Her father had remembered how his daughter taught him to write his name so he didn't have to put his thumb print on papers at the post office when his sons sent money from South Africa.

Amantle herself remembered her first day at school as vividly as if it had been a few days ago. That first day, she'd been unable to sit still as she and her mother waited outside the principal's office. In fact, she'd barely been able to sit down at all; she'd sat down, and then stood up, and then sat down again. She'd squirmed and fidgeted as she sat on the hard, wooden bench. She'd swung her small legs back and forth and winced as she felt a splinter from the rough bench jab her calf. She'd brushed imaginary dust off her new black and white uniform. She'd pressed a pleat she imagined was losing its sharp crease. She'd tightened and then loosened her belt. She'd kicked off a pinch of sand remaining on her right shoe. She'd held on to her mother for reassurance but let go so people wouldn't think she was a baby. She'd adjusted the empty cloth bag hanging from her shoulder.

She'd been excited about starting school. She'd poked at the girl sitting next to her outside the principal's office, and when the girl looked back at her, she'd smiled conspiratorially. However, the girl hadn't smiled back: she'd been holding her mother's hand firmly, and clearly been unhappy about being there. Two mother-and-child pairs had been waiting ahead of Amantle and her mother, and she'd wanted them to hurry up and shorten the queue. From where she and her mother were sitting, she'd been able to see a large desk, and behind it, a large woman.

'Next!' The large woman had finally shouted it from across her desk. Amantle had scrambled to her feet and hurried through the doorway, ahead of her mother. She'd almost collided with an exiting man and his young female charge, and for a moment wondered what had happened to the girl's mother: she'd been being raised to believe that school matters were 'mother' matters.

'Good morning, Principal Modiega,' her mother had announced as they'd entered the small room.

They'd found themselves standing in front of a swirl of green seated behind the desk. Mrs Modiega had been wearing a tent-like, puffy-sleeve green dress and a green headscarf, and her neck had been encircled with loops and loops of green beads. Large, green-plastic earrings had dangled from her ears. 'Name of child?' she'd asked, neither responding to the greeting nor even looking up.

'Irene,' Amantle's mother had replied. However, similar to half of her eight siblings, she'd been unable to pronounce the letter *r*, so the name had come out as 'Igene'.

Amantle had looked up at her mother and wanted to object; she'd wanted to say she was Amantle, not Irene or Igene. Then she'd panicked, though: perhaps it wasn't she who was to start school – perhaps her parents had changed their mind. '*I* want to start school!' she'd whispered urgently, squirming and twisting.

The principal had looked up briefly, as if annoyed, and asked, 'Surname of child?'

'Bokaa,' had come the answer.

'Age of child?' the principal had asked, moving down the list in front of her.

''76,' had come the reply.

The green swirl had then rustled as the principal looked up at Amantle, who'd felt the appraising eyes on her. 'Stand up, Eileen.'

Amantle had obeyed promptly, although she'd wanted to object; she'd wanted to shout, '*My name's not Irene, not Igene, and not Eileen!*' However, she'd decided not to, because children don't contradict adults, even if the adults give them a name they don't like.

'You look very small for seven.' The principal had addressed Amantle, and had been frowning when she made the comment. She'd then turned to Amantle's mother and asked, 'Are you sure she's seven?'

Amantle's mother had replied, 'She was born in the year of the black sorghum, Principal Modiega. Yes, she was born in 1976, the year the dam wall was raised by the Malekantwa Regiment. I know this for a fact, because it was on the third day of the –'

'Okay; okay,' the principal had assured her. 'Do you know the month and date of her birth?'

'I know it was at the beginning of winter,' Amantle's mother had affirmed; 'early June, it was – but then, perhaps it was the end of May; around that time, I'd say. The moon was waxing – I know that for sure.'

'All right,' the principal had responded, and then addressed Amantle. 'Eileen, you're in Mrs Seme's class. See those children over there?' She'd pointed to a cluster of children under a *morula* tree, about 100 metres away. 'Go and join them: you're in that class.'

That January day in 1984 had been Amantle's first day at school. She'd been seven and a half, and she'd just acquired an English name – two English names, actually: one after another. She'd cast one last look at her mother, smiled with gratitude, and skipped off to join her new class.

At first, she'd run towards the group members, but as she'd approached them, she'd decided to slow down. She'd searched for a familiar face, and then smiled when she'd seen the happy face of Moshi, her neighbour and best friend. They'd known each other since they'd been babies, and many times they'd played together and eaten from the same bowl. On just as many occasions they'd fought together as a team against a common enemy, as well as fought each other. They'd competed in many peeing contests, to see who could pee for the longer time and the further distance, and who could pee to make the deeper hole in the sand. They'd even shared their pee, when one of them hadn't been able to produce enough liquid to make the sand sufficiently wet to build sand huts.

The two friends had loved to *thaka* – to drape an arm over each other's shoulders when they were walking; they'd stayed linked for long periods while they were looking for something new to do. They'd made friends with a colony of ants, which they'd continued to secretly feed grains of sugar. Sugar is precious, so they'd been careful to avoid being caught sneaking handfuls of it out of the house. They'd loved watching the ants carrying the sugar grains into their little nest and greeting each other briefly whenever their paths crossed. They'd laughed while they were chasing butterflies and grasshoppers, and smashed each other's sandcastles and mud pies in anger. They'd kept each other's secrets and also told on each other. They'd made joint wishes whenever one of them had lost a milk tooth. They'd been good friends.

'What's your school name? What's your English name?' Moshi had now whispered as Amantle joined the group.

'Irene – no, no: Eileen. I think it's Eileen.' She'd known that her mother had meant 'Irene', but thought the principal's name would be the one to stick with: it had been the one written in the school register. Her older cousins who'd attended school had told her that whatever got written in a book stayed there forever. 'What's yours?' she'd asked her friend.

'Moses – and my surname's Montshiwa, so my full name's Moses Montshiwa.' He'd obviously been proud of his new name.

Before today, none of the children had had to worry about adopting a surname: they'd always identified themselves by referring to who their older siblings were. 'I'm Amantle, the younger sister to Mmadira, who's the younger brother to Molemoge,' had been how Amantle had routinely introduced herself. To older people who weren't from her ward, she might have added, 'I'm the child of Motsei and Meleko of Rampedi Ward. Meleko is a member of the Machama Regiment – Meleko, who's the son of Rameroko, Rameroko who killed a lion when he was young man.' Mrs Modiega had entered none of this information in the prin‑cipal's book.

Amantle's large, dark, expressive eyes had now begun to sparkle with feeling. She'd grabbed Moshi's wrist and whispered urgently, 'I want to keep my name; I want to be Amantle . . . You? You like your English name?'

Before Moshi, the younger brother of Mainane and who'd now become Moses Montshiwa, could answer, the teacher had started shouting above the hum of the students' introductions and excited chatter. 'My name is Mrs Seme. I'm your mistress. First, I'm going to call your names out. When I call your name, you'll move to my right.' She'd paused for emphasis before continuing. 'Okay. Mary Agang; Silas Binang; Apollo Botoka; Boyboy Chaba; Daniel

Dibui; Doctor Disang; Teacher Kokong, . . .' She'd progressed through a list she'd written in an exercise book she was holding. '*Eileen Bokaa!*' she'd shouted, and no one had moved. '*Eileen Bokaa!*' she'd shouted again. This time, Amantle had scrambled over to Mrs Seme's right. She'd made a mental note to remember her new name.

Amantle had then recalled a day about a month earlier, when she'd paid a rare visit to the cattle post and seen, for the first time, a calf being branded. The little animal had bellowed as the hot iron was searing its rump. Satisfied with their efforts, her brothers had untied it, whereupon it had scampered away to freedom. Just then, their father had arrived and announced that the boys had used the wrong branding iron. The animal, he had explained, belonged to his sister, not to him, so Amantle's brothers would have to re-brand it using the correct branding iron. They'd had to catch the animal again, tie it up and re-label it.

'*Irene Omphile!*' Amantle had heard Mrs Seme shouting. A girl wearing a new pair of shoes had stepped forward, and Amantle had been drawn to look at her own shoes. She'd brought her feet together and re-aligned the tips of the shoes so they were together. However, when she'd looked behind her, she'd been able to see that the right shoe was jutting out. She'd decided to stand so her feet were apart in order to hide the glaring fact that her right shoe was a whole size larger than her left. Although her mother had tried to clean and buff the left shoe, it had been impossible to conceal the fact that the right one was brand new whereas the left was very old; in fact, both shoes had been too big for Amantle, but at least the left one had been only a size bigger. The shoes had been standard school shoes, so at least they'd been the same make. Amantle had inherited them from two of her cousins. One cousin had been going through left-foot shoes at a rate much faster than he'd been going through right-foot ones, and the other cousin had had a deformed right foot for which he'd been requiring a specially made shoe, so she'd always had a right shoe to give away.

'Are you Irene or Eileen?' Before Amantle had been able to respond to Moshi, who'd now become Moses, he'd whispered, 'I like Irene better.'

'I don't want to be either!' Amantle had whispered back in frustration. 'I want to stay Amantle! Why can't I be Amantle?'

'But we all need a school name, an English name. It's for baptisms, when we're ten years old. You need an English name for the big book at the Dutch Reformed Church!' Both Amantle and Moshi had been attending the Dutch Reformed Church on most Sundays, although they'd sometimes been attending the Roman Catholic Church, which had been closer to their homes.

Amantle had kept the issue going. 'But Neo kept her name – and Matshediso as well! Why can't I keep my name? And I don't like the surname: I don't want to be Eileen Bokaa!'

Moshi had picked up on the mention of Neo. 'Neo's grandfather hid in the hills during the war: they're a family of cowards! That's what my grandmother says. They're a disgraced family – no one cares whether she gets baptised or not!' Moshi had always willingly offered information he'd received from his grandmother, who'd seemed to know a lot about which families had been disgraced as a result of which actions of their ancestors. For Moshi and Amantle, she'd also been a great source of information about who'd bewitched who, and when.

'*My* grandmother says no one should have been forced to fight for the English! "It was never our business," is what she says. And why does Apollo get to keep his name?' Amantle's own grandmother hadn't been short of opinions about the English and the Boers, and hadn't quite made up her mind as to which of the two tribes was the worse: she'd thought they both loved wars and that both of them would fight you at the least provocation. Many times they'd heard her say, 'A Boer will kick you as he looks you in the eye, but an English man will smile at you and then kick your backside when you're not watching.'

'But Apollo's an English name; it's an American name,' Moshi had responded, clearly proud to be clarifying matters for his friend.

'Really?' Amantle had been sceptical: to her, Apollo had sounded like a Setswana name.

'What are you two whispering about?' Mrs Seme had finally demanded.

'Nothing, mistress!' they'd chorused, curtseying to show respect.

32

'All right, now,' the teacher had continued; 'rule number one: no whispering in class. Do you understand?'

'Yes, mistress,' the class members had answered in unison.

'Rule number two: no crying,' had come the next imperative.

'Yes, mistress,' had come the response.

'Rule number three: you don't leave the class without permission.' She'd been working her way methodically down the list.

'Yes, mistress,' had come the reply in unison.

'Rule number four: all toilet business must be done in the toilets – no going in the bush.' Toilet business had obviously been an issue in the school.

'Yes, mistress,' had come the predictable response.

'Rule number five: this stick is hungry after close to two months of not touching any bottom,' had been the last, scary, rule. 'Form a line, and no running; no pushing; no talking. Our class is the middle one in this block to our left. Move – and quietly!'

On this, their first day of school, the forty-two children had naturally run, pushed and whispered as they jostled to form a line: forty-two newly shaven heads glinting in the sun. Although most of the children had been excited to be starting school, the eyes of a few of them had glistened with tears because those children were away from both their mother and their familiar surroundings.

By the time morning playtime had eventuated, Amantle had become tired and hungry. She hadn't slept very much, having been excited at the prospect of starting school the next day. She'd now wanted to run home to get something to eat – but the rules had been made very clear: no one was to leave the school compound without first getting permission. And permission had never been granted; in fact, if you'd asked for permission, you could have gotten a beating. Mrs Seme had made that prospect very clear.

Seven-year-old Amantle had therefore sat, her stomach growling, wondering why she'd wanted to come to school in the first place. She'd heard about the beatings even before she'd seen Mrs Seme's stick. Around evening fires, older cousins had described the beatings in such graphic detail it had been a wonder anyone in his or her right mind wanted to go to school. Nevertheless, the village had been full of children who wanted to go to school, and Amantle had been the first sibling in her family to do so. She'd still been unable to believe that her father had changed his view about sending his children, especially a girl child, to school: he'd always said they'd all have a secure future by working hard in the fields and at the cattle post. 'The lazy will eat the faeces of their age mates,' he'd told all seven children many times. He'd firmly believed in rising early, and been fond of saying that cattle, 'the wet-nosed gods, without which a man knew no sleep and with which a man knew no sleep', equalled wealth.

Then, one evening, Amantle's new future, which the family had never before discussed – or at least hadn't seriously discussed – had been carved out for her. Half a year ago, her mother had declared, 'The child must go to school.' She'd had frown lines on her forehead, her eyes had been unblinking and her chin had been set tight. She'd always set her face that way whenever she was expecting the children's father to contradict her. The sun had just been setting, but because it had been the middle of June, they'd been already huddled together in the *setlaagana,* the brush enclosure in which all the cooking was done. Amantle had been playing *khupe* with her brother Moratiwa, but had paused to listen.

'Which hand?' Moratiwa had demanded, annoyed that a break in the rhythm of their playing had been made.

'The eating hand,' she'd responded, not caring whether she'd won or not. 'And I'm not playing any more.'

Disgusted, Moratiwa had thrown the piece of charcoal into the fire. 'Amantle, that's not fair! I was winning!'

Amantle had ignored her brother's outburst; he was only two years older, so she'd treated him more as an age mate than as an older sibling. She hadn't even prefaced his name by using the honorific 'Abuti', which she'd used when she'd been talking about her other brothers. That night, she'd ignored her brother, and when she'd examined her hands, she'd noted the soot from the piece of charcoal they'd been playing with. She'd wiped her hands on her blanket, and waited. Her father hadn't responded; he'd been staring at her mother. However, a smile had been playing on his lips, and the flames from the fire had leapt in front of his face and lit up the smile. The western horizon had been crimson-red from the flames of the setting sun. The porridge had been bubbling in front of Amantle. She'd closed her eyes, willing that 'the child' be her – she'd wanted to be 'the child' so badly she'd thought her heart would stop.

'Of course she must go to school. I, too, agree,' her father had finally answered. Her mother's eyes had flown to her father's face, searching: she'd obviously expected to have to defend her proposal, and in the face of having her husband agree, she'd been lost for words.

Amantle's father had continued on quietly, as if speaking to himself. 'She must be prepared for a new tomorrow, for greater things. Yes: I agree the child must go to school. Yes: we must help her meet the new wind.'

Amantle had then opened her eyes. The firelight had now been licking at a broad grin on her father's face. The sun had by now disappeared, and had left no evidence it had ever been there. One moment, there'd been a hovering disk; next moment, it'd been gone. Her mother's face had softened, and she'd nodded with satisfaction. 'Which child?' Amantle had wanted to scream. Clearly, her brothers Lesaka and Molemoge had been too old – as had been her sisters Naniso and Mmadira. However, she'd realised that her brother Moratiwa was only two years older than she, so it might just have been the case that he was 'the child' her parents were discussing. She'd wanted the answer to be 'Amantle, of course,' but she'd been the last born of seven, and none of her older siblings had been to school. Her older brother who was closest in age to her had been nine years old, so it might well have been the case that 'this child' was him. Oh, how she'd wanted to be 'the child'.

'Amantle, would you like to go to school next year? You're seven years old now – you're old enough to start school next year.'

A hush had descended around the fire. History had been in the making: the last born and seventh child of the Motsei and Meleko had been about to embark on an unprecedented journey. Even Moratiwa's face had lost its anger and softened in wonder.

'Yes, mma! But why next year? I have to wait for next year? Why can't I start when schools start?' Her gratitude had quickly been followed by a desire to have it all now.

'Of course you have to wait for next year. You have to wait for the beginning of the new year: you can't just join a class midway through the school year.' Her mother had been smiling at her across the fire. A gust a wind had redirected the airflow, and Amantle had coughed and spluttered. She'd now gained an excuse to move to the other side of the fire in order to be close to her mother without making it obvious she'd wanted to. She couldn't have behaved like a baby craving for her mother's lap when her parents had been discussing her going to school.

Then, six months later, there she'd been, sitting through her first playtime, hungry, and wondering why she'd wanted to start school so badly: she could have been at home, helping her mother do one or another domestic chore. Although her mother had been known to take a grass broom to the children occasionally, the air at home hadn't been polluted with the constant threat of violence. For one thing, her mother hadn't held the broom in her hand every minute of the day as a constant reminder of what could happen to Amantle if she made a mistake; also, Amantle had been able outrun her mother. Mrs Seme hadn't used her stick yet, but Amantle had been in no doubt she'd use it soon.

Playtime had finished, and Mrs Seme had stood at the class-room doorway, calling out her students' names to make sure no one had run off home. 'Norma Molefe!' she'd shouted. Norma had scampered past the teacher, into the classroom. He'd been a stout little boy whose eyes were rather large. His khaki shorts had been too large for him, and had been held together at the waist by means of a home-made belt. His shirt had been too small for him, and his little belly, which had been marked with a toadstool of a belly button, had been constantly revealed.

Mrs Seme's face had assumed a puzzled look. 'Norma is a girl's name,' she'd explained. 'You can't be called Norma – what is your home name?'

'Tshiamo, mistress,' the boy had replied.

'Well, then,' the mistress had begun, 'you'll have to go back to your home name. Norma is definitely a girl's name. You're now Tshiamo Molefe – understand?'

Norma had nodded mutely as Mrs Seme had taken a pen, crossed out the name Norma and replaced it with 'Tshiamo'. Amantle had perceived an opening, so she'd asked, 'What about Eileen: isn't it a boy's name? I could go back to my home name.'

'No; Eileen is a girl's name – so you don't have to worry about changing back to your home name.' Mrs Seme had then gone on with calling out the names of her new charges.

Amantle had remained Eileen within the school compound, and Norma, whose mother had actually told the principal his name was Normal, a translation of 'Tshiamo', had lost his English name – except, of course, when the other kids had been mean, in which case they'd called him 'Norma the girl' or 'Norma girl'. They'd chanted, 'Norma; look at Norma: Norma girl; Norma girl; look at Norma!' However, whoever had said the words had to remain a few metres away, because 'Norma the girl' had a terrible temper, and had been able to punch and kick for a long time before a teacher had come along to intervene. But then perhaps his father had actually named the boy Norman, after the local tractor dealer, the father's employer.

By the time Amantle's first day at school had come to an end, she'd experienced quite a few firsts. She'd felt the cool smooth - ness of a windowpane. She'd done her toilet business in a walled-in structure. Her school, Lady Sarah Benchford Primary School, had contained pit-latrine facilities. However, the window and the pit latrine had been among the many new things to which she'd been introduced as a result of going to school. Yet another first had been the phenomenon of the key: to her fascination, she'd found out that each door in the school had a key, and that at the end of each day, someone used the key to lock it. None of the doors at either her house or her neighbours' house had been lockable; some houses hadn't even had proper doors. Until then, the only key she'd ever touched had been a small, brown key her grandmother had permanently secured on a string around her neck.

On the evening of her first day at school, Amantle's belly had been full with porridge and a bean stew, and in her heart she'd been happy to be going to school. She'd lain on her back, next to her mother. When her father had asked her about her first day, she'd told her family about all the new things she'd encountered. Her father had begun the conversation in response. 'I do have to say that the faeces houses are a very good idea indeed: you can't put so many people together – especially children – in a fenced-in area and expect the bushes to be enough. There are people who thought that money should have been used to build more classrooms – you were one of them, Mma-Lesaka, weren't you?'

'No, Rra-Lesaka,' Amantle's mother had responded, 'I wasn't against the faeces houses; I was against having them inside the classrooms, like at Mr Walters'. I just can't imagine going to do toilet business inside a house you sleep in and keep your food in! That's pure madness.'

Amantle's father had taken up the gauntlet. 'No: there I agree with you, my wife. Mr Walters has many good ideas when it comes to agriculture, but I have to say that when I learnt about the new house he's building and his plans to build a faeces room inside the house, I was shocked. Now, some people aren't even too sure about some of his ideas on cattle rearing. How can you trust a man who shits inside a house? I hear that's the new craze in Johannesburg, and that it's even spread to Gaborone – but I can't imagine it!'

'But Rra-Lesaka,' Naniso had countered, 'I hear these faeces houses are really clean. They use water to wash away the faeces, so you can't even smell anything.' She'd offered the comment as she was mixing the sorghum to make *ting* for the following day's sour porridge.

'Ao, Naniso, my child,' Amantle's father had retorted in mock horror; 'how can you even think that people – adults – could go into a house to relieve themselves in that way? And you know how these white people are: when they're at home, they literally stay indoors – they cook in there, eat in there, sleep in there and pass the day in there. Now they don't even want to leave the house to shit! That's amazing!'

Amantle had been half listening as she continued to look at the sky. She'd noted that at least three kings had died somewhere in the world: three shooting stars had brilliantly marked the monarchs' demise. She'd allowed herself to speculate about the families they'd left behind, and she'd silently wished the kings well. She'd hoped none of them had young children who'd just started school. She'd made a wish to the moon for her own parents to live a long life.

Within weeks, Amantle and her classmates had been learning their 'ABC' and '1, 2, 3'. Amantle had proven to be a quick learner, and had found everything she was learning to be interesting. Her only problem had been that she was unable to share any of her new information with anyone at home: there, no one had seemed to care about her 'ABC' or '1, 2, 3'. Soon, she'd been able to add up the numbers she'd learnt in order to make even bigger numbers, and she'd been able to mix up the letters in order to make words. To her fascination, she'd discovered that by mixing up the letters, she was able to write both her home name and her school name, though she still hadn't liked the latter. Standard 1, which had been what her first year at school was called, had turned out to be a great year, even if she'd had to go through it answering to a strange name.

Also, to her great relief, it had turned out that Mrs Seme wasn't all that bad. She'd hit her charges no more than had Amantle's own mother. She'd used her stick to give painless taps. And she'd been kind and laughed a lot. During the cold months of May, June and July, she'd allowed each of her pupils to bring a blanket to school to use as a coat.

Sometimes Principal Modiega had objected to the wearing of blankets: 'Mrs Seme, we can't have children wearing smelly blankets in school! What if the inspectors were to come and find pupils wearing blankets over their school uniform? Really, I can't allow that.' Her yellow dress had fluttered in the wind, and her long, yellow earrings had swayed to the rhythm of her exasperation.

However, whenever this scenario had occurred, Mrs Seme had stood up to her superior without budging. Mrs Seme had been younger than Mrs Modiega and should therefore have been more respectful, let alone known that the older woman was both a principal and a chief's daughter. Standing firm, she'd said, 'Well, if the inspectors have a problem, they can provide the children with suitable warm clothes; better still, they can have the schools closed during the winter months. I don't see why we should let these poor children suffer just because some inspector sitting in Gaborone thinks that doing things his way is necessarily the right way! Let them come and remove the blankets from these cold children!'

'Does everything have to be a political statement with you?' Mrs Modiega had shot back. Amantle had heard that Mrs Seme was from South Africa, and that her husband had sustained a gunshot wound in some political march and later died in prison.

The younger teacher had had a trace of contempt for the older principal, and had replied, 'Everything is political, missus principal. May I go back to my class now?' And without waiting for an answer, she'd turned and walked back to her class.

And with that comment, discussion about the subject had been concluded, at least for the season. The children had continued to wear their smelly blanket to school, and Mrs Modiega's only reaction had been to wrinkle her nose.

The school children's blankets had been smelly because the children used them at night as well as during the day, the children's mothers washed the blankets only infrequently, and the children had to share their blankets with younger siblings who remained untrained to wake up at night when they needed to do their toilet business. Sometimes the younger children had wet their mat and blanket simply because they'd been trying to hold on in order to avoid having to go outside into the cold air. Also, although a standard rondaval had a diameter of five metres, on average, seven children had slept in it. During winter nights, the rondaval had been a crowded place. On summer nights, though, its smells had been more pleasant, because the family members had preferred to sleep in the *lapa*, and all they'd otherwise needed to protect them from the elements had been the *lapa*'s hard floor and half walls.

During Amantle's primary-school years, Mrs Seme and Mrs Modiega had continued to have spats about all sorts of things. By 1986, when Amantle had been nine, southern Africa had become

40

more political, and people had begun to be more open about questioning the way things were being run.

Amantle had worked hard in both primary and secondary school, and as evidence, her high-school certificate had been dominated by a string of A's. At the end of her schooling, at age twenty-one, she'd been confident she'd be awarded the scholarship through which she'd be able to travel to Britain in search of more education. She'd needed the post-secondary education in order to transform herself, a village girl from Molope – a village of no more than 3000 people – into a doctor. She'd made the decision to become a doctor during her first year of high school, 1991, at age fourteen. She'd spent the rest of her school years in Kanye, a big village to which every school child in Molope hoped to move after he or she had completed primary school. In fact, the rest of her family had moved to Kanye during the drought year, when she'd had to drop out of school.

Now, in 1999, she was a 22-year-old Tirelo Sechaba Participant. As she walked towards the health clinic located in the village of Gaphala, she pondered the fact that for as long as she could remember, she'd known she wanted to be a doctor. She remembered the words her prospective host had spoken when Amantle and her fellow TSPs were presented to the villagers the day after they'd arrived: 'I'll take the one in the long, brown skirt: number two from the right – yes, that one. Yes: the one with the neat hair – she looks well mannered.'

Lined up like that at the *kgotla*, the village meeting place, and seeing the villagers being urged to choose a TSP to host, Amantle had thought the government could have devised a better and more dignified selection system. She felt as if she and the other TSPs were being auctioned off. And it didn't help to see that the *kgotla* kraal next to where the TSP selection was taking place was full of cattle waiting to be auctioned off! Later, she was to find out that her host had two grandchildren who were younger than ten; an elderly, deaf mother; and limited agility because she had two painful knees. Amantle was also to find out, clearly and on her first night with her host family, that she was expected to help care for the whole family. She'd been expecting as much, so she wasn't especially alarmed at the prospect: she was a girl, and taking care other people was what she'd been trained to do from an early age.

Aspiring TSP Daniel Modise, his shirt billowing, his jeans mutilated, his ear pierced with several silver earrings and his dreadlocked hair unruly, had had to be pushed on to a reluctant couple. Nineteen and belligerent, Daniel hadn't wanted to be in this village, far away from his home. He hadn't cared whether he got picked or not; he'd planned to get back to Ramotswa, his hometown, one way or another. He hadn't planned to spend a year in this Godforsaken place, away from TV, a phone, his girlfriend and the opportunity to steal his parents' car.

'These TSPs can be a problem. Let me not start with one who's obviously bad mannered – and we wanted a girl, not a boy.' These were the words Head Man Baareng's wife had uttered as the TSP official was indicating to them that they had to take Daniel.

'Please, head man: if you don't take him, who will? Your home is the best one for a young man like him,' the TSP officer had implored.

The head man and his wife hadn't been at all happy to take Daniel in; nevertheless, the requirement had been that Daniel be placed in a family. Also, the head man had had to lead by example: the government was asking everyone to make sacrifices in order to ensure the success of the scheme, the intention of which was to give young people an opportunity to serve the nation before they embarked on their long-term career or work path. So, yes: Mr and Mrs Baareng had had to take the sloppy, belligerent and angry Daniel – dreadlocks and all! 'Take off those earrings right now! Take them off! Are you a woman or a man? And tuck in your shirt. You have no manners, young man! If you're going to live in my household, you're going to have to learn my rules very fast. I have ways of taming wild young men – ask anyone in this village.' Head Man Baareng had been antagonistic towards Daniel from the start.

Bad move, the TS officer had thought to herself. She'd wanted to be done with this whole matching process so she could head back to Maun; after that, she'd intended to visit the village each month to check on how the TSPs were faring.

Daniel had looked at the head man belligerently, but had complied: he'd taken the earrings off slowly, placed them in his mouth, and made a major show of tucking in his shirt by deliberately doing a bad job of it. He'd have loved to be ordered to leave the village immediately; he'd have hopped and skipped out of there gleefully. His matching had been a week ago.

Now, here was Amantle, on this beautiful morning, going to work at the village health clinic, for the first time. The village was really a cluster of small villages, each of which had a head man. Most of the homesteads comprised a cluster of mud huts, but some of them also contained a few four-cornered, tin-roofed structures. The government's structures were located amid the four-cornered buildings.

The villages shared a clinic, a primary school, a wildlife office and a bore hole. Once a month, a big government truck rolled into the villages, and the drivers distributed food to pregnant women and children younger than five. Sometimes the bore hole broke down, in which case men brought in water in huge containers. Except for one or two rickety old trucks, the only vehicles that entered the village were government ones, called 'BX'es because of their registration plates. The villagers relied on the 'BX'es to take them in and out of the village. The clinic ambulance, which was actually a Toyota Hilux van in which the government had thrown in a canopy and a mattress for a bit of comfort, was the mode of transport the villagers used most.

Amantle was the only TSP in her small village. Daniel and six other TSPs were being billeted in neighbouring villages, in the schools and wildlife office as well as through the drought-relief project. Amantle wasn't expecting to see them except, perhaps, on weekends. After she'd spent her first few nights with her host family, she'd been sure she was lucky to have been picked up by Mma-Nono, a retired bank clerk whose home was among the village's most modern. It comprised four well-built huts, a nice pit latrine and a water tap in the yard. And Mma-Nono was certainly a kind woman. Amantle didn't mind preparing breakfast for the family before she set off for work. She was already fond of Sewagodimo, Mma-Nono's ten-year-old daughter. Clearly, the girl had been named Sewagodimo: 'one who fell from heaven', or 'falling star', because Mma-Nono had had her when by then she should have been long into the menopause. The little girl had a sunny personality, and was indeed like something special that had fallen from the sky. Amantle had taken to her almost immediately.

Once Amantle was inside the clinic yard, as she was walking towards the clinic building, she realised the building wasn't yet open. She looked at her watch and noted that the time was 7.25: five minutes before opening time. About fifteen patients were already waiting to be attended to. They were mainly pregnant women and women with young children, but a few men were there as well. 'Good morning, my older people,' Amantle said respectfully. 'The clinic will be open soon: another five minutes and you'll be able to see a nurse.' She believed that even on her first day she must be businesslike and professional. She sat down on one of the low cement walls designed for sitting.

The group included two men wearing dirty, makeshift bandages – one man's was around his head, the other's on his foot. Amantle was later to find out that both men could point to drink as the source of their injury. One of them had tripped and fallen, hitting his head on a log while he was staggering home drunk; the other had stepped on a snake and been bitten while he, too, was staggering home drunk. For some reason, the snake-injury man received sympathy whereas the log-injury man didn't. Amantle didn't think it was fair, because the patients agreed that had the snake-injury man not been drunk, he wouldn't have stepped on the snake; however, perhaps they were basing their assessment on additional information she didn't have. She asked them, 'Are there many snakes in the area? Does the clinic have enough medicines? The nurses must be part of the community now.' She wanted to make friends, to be part of the group.

The waiting patients were curious about her, but said nothing in reply: the mothers continued cooing to their children, and the two men looked away. To lighten the mood, Amantle decided to introduce herself, and to explain that she came from another part of the country and had never seen foliage that was so lush. When no one responded, she realised she'd gone on too long in an effort to allay the patients' discomfort.

One of the men eventually asked, 'How many clinics do you have in your village?'

'Oh, I don't know; let me see – about seven; maybe ten. And we have a hospital as well. It's a much bigger village than this one. Why do you ask?' She was happy to be involved in some conversation at last.

'We only have this one clinic and these two nurses, and it's for all the five villages in this area: Gaphala, Moruti, Seretseng. Serube and Mphaleng! All of us, we rely on this one clinic and its two nurses! And the nurses won't be here at 7.30 as you say – they'll come when they feel like it. They hardly ever feel like com - ing on time. And when they do come today, they'll abuse us with their sharp tongues.'

Implied in the information was the fact that Amantle was expected to be no different. She kept quiet, and decided the best approach was to wait and see. She didn't want to stumble across a landmine on her first day at work. Instead, she started to silently play eye games with a little girl who'd been watching her: she winked, and the little girl winked back; she winked twice, and the little girl did likewise. When they were into giving five winks per eye, the little girl's face finally dissolved into a broad smile. The little girl then took the lead and started silently playing a new game: twitching her thumbs. Amantle twitched her right thumb in response. When the little girl started to flare her nostrils, Amantle couldn't help but laugh out loud. By then, a friendship had been established, and the little girl moved over to Amantle, much to her mother's amazement.

'M'phefo is shy – she doesn't take to strangers! I can't believe she's letting you touch her,' the mother commented.

Amantle replied, 'Oh, M'phefo and I have been talking up a storm in our own private language, haven't we, little one?' She gave her attention to the little girl. 'My name is Amantle. I gather yours is M'phefo: is that short for Mmaphefo?' She smiled at the little girl. M'phefo had now placed her tiny hands on Amantle's lap. She nodded in response as her mother watched with interest.

Amantle went on: 'So, you're the little girl of the wind, are you now? I bet you're as fast as the wind, like your name.'

M'phefo smiled in response.

'And how old are you?' Amantle was now holding M'phefo's little fists in her hands.

In response, M'phefo let out a giggle and disentangled her hands from Amantle's. She held out her right hand, fingers straight, and then with her left hand carefully bent back her thumb. Amantle observed that the little girl had suffered a rather severe burn at some point and that as a result her right thumb had become stiff.

'Oh, you're four years old? You're such a big girl! Can you be my friend? I'm new in this village: I need a friend.'

M'phefo responded by stepping up on to the wall and perching her little bottom on Amantle's lap.

By now it was 7.45 but neither of the nurses had yet arrived. The houses they lived in were located in the same compound the clinic was located in. The waiting patients could see the blue front door of both nurses' houses. Neither door had opened yet.

'Should I go and find out what's holding them up?' Amantle offered. 'M'phefo, do you want to go with me?' Amantle had already stood up and gently slid her new friend off her lap. The waiting was getting to her, and she believed it was her duty to do something about it.

'You seem like a nice enough young girl: I'd suggest you not do that – they'll be angry with you, and even angrier with us. Let's all just wait; we're used to it.'

A woman with a profusely sweating infant responded by de - claring he'd boil over from the fever if the nurse didn't show up soon.

'Put him under the tap and run cold water over him: that'll cool him down.' Amantle made the suggestion having failed to keep her mouth shut as she'd promised herself.

'You want those women to shout at me? Especially the short one – she'll shriek at me for wasting water,' was the woman's answer in response.

'Let me do it, then,' Amantle insisted. 'The child is burning up and has to be cooled down.' With that, she lifted the boy from the woman's lap and walked to the tap. Once they were there, the woman had to come over and help. She and Amantle looked at each other. The child was a bridge between them, and they liked what they saw in each other's eyes.

At eight o'clock, one of the blue doors swung open, and a woman with a towel wrapped around her body walked out carrying a plastic bowl of water. She tossed the water out, threw a glance in the direction of the group of waiting patients and walked back into the house, closing the blue door behind her. About fifteen minutes later, she emerged again, this time dressed in her nurses' uniform. She carried a bowl in one hand and a bunch of keys in the other. She walked towards the group, walked straight past it and un-locked the clinic's main door. She didn't even utter a simple 'Good morning'.

Amantle stood up, confused: she wanted to present herself to the nurse, but was at a loss how to begin because the uniformed woman's approach had been very brisk, she'd failed to greet the group and she had a closed face. Instead, Amantle winked at M'phefo. The little girl smiled and winked back, and Amantle silently followed the nurse into the clinic.

The nurse looked back at Amantle, apparently noticing her for the first time. 'You must be the new TSP. Why didn't you come for the keys? You're not like the last TSP, are you? She was always late and did nothing; just wasted our time.' After uttering these presumptive words, the nurse strode on and didn't bother waiting for Amantle to respond. 'Tell them to come in to take their number cards. Tell them I want order: they mustn't rush in like a herd of cattle.' She pointed her head at 'them' to indicate that 'they' were the patients.

The nurse, who Amantle was soon to learn was called Mrs Malala or Nurse Malala, then entered an office and proceeded to eat her breakfast. Next, she angrily pushed a brown envelope aside: it had been opened, and it was clear that she already knew its contents. 'Every government letter that comes in I hope is a transfer letter – but it never is. I don't know when they're going to get me out of this sorry place. Just look at that bunch of dirty people: why should I be the one to work here? There are people who've never, ever left the Gaborone area – *never*! But me, I've been here now more than three years. Before that, I was in Verda. I should have been transferred out last year – but no! You're lucky you're just a TSP: you'll be out of here in twelve months. What are you doing standing there?'

Twenty minutes later, Nurse Malala declared she was ready to see the first patient. From the patients, Amantle was to learn that Mr Malala, a driver for the Wildlife Department, based in Maun, came very infrequently to see his wife. She was to learn that when he did come, he spent time in the village in the company of a woman. The door to the woman's hut then remained closed for hour upon hour. What Mr Malala and the woman did inside was anyone's guess. The speculations constituted much needed fodder for gossip in the village, in which not much ever happened. Whenever Mr Malala departed, Nurse Malala's mood became especially foul. Today, Amantle had the misfortune of starting work soon after the latest of Mr Malala's visits.

It quickly became apparent to Amantle that she was to be the 'gofer' during the nurses' consultations. Nurse Malala's role was to send her here, there and everywhere: 'Go and get a mop next door and clean up this mess,' she ordered when a child threw up; 'Go and call the GDA from out back.' Amantle had no idea who or what a GDA was until Nurse Malala explained it was the blue-uniformed woman giving out food rations in the back section of the clinic. 'A GDA is a General Duty Assistant – don't you know anything?' was Nurse Malala's explanation and rhetorical question. 'And go and tell those women to get those kids to shut up – do they have to make so much noise? Do they have to let these dirty children run wild like that?' She threw it in for good measure.

At the end of her first day, Amantle was tired from trying to absorb too much at once. She still wasn't sure what her formal duties were to be. During the afternoon, the other nurse, Nurse Palaki, had popped in to find out whether Nurse Malala needed any help. The second nurse had then decided that Amantle was to be given the job of cleaning out the clinic's storeroom. She'd addressed Nurse Malala: 'That storeroom can be used as an additional office. It's been a mess for years. This TSP could go through the stuff in there and throw away useless things; there's nothing but old bits and pieces in there anyway. That'll also give this TSP something to do.' As she'd spoken, she'd hardly looked at Amantle.

The two nurses had settled the matter and failed to invite Amantle to comment. The young TSP had hoped to have the chance to learn more about diseases and how they were cured. She'd wanted to help dispense prescriptions to patients so the patients could return later to tell her how much better they felt. She didn't want to clean up any storeroom. However, she had no say in the matter: she'd been assigned storeroom duty, and that was that.

CHAPTER 6

The following morning, the first of the two nurses to arrive at the clinic, Nurse Palaki, didn't show up until 8.30. The waiting patients gained some consolation in the fact that at least she'd eaten her breakfast at home. Nurse Malala arrived an hour later. It was the nurses' policy not to see patients in the afternoon so they could devote themselves to completing their paperwork during those hours. However, the only paperwork Amantle saw them involved in was fashion and love-story magazines; she was also witness to some napping.

By the time Nurse Palaki arrived, Amantle was at an advanced stage of her storeroom-cleaning task. The room was dusty, and papers were piled up everywhere. After Amantle had made a few trips back and forth to ask Nurse Palaki about what to throw away and what to keep, the task had become easy enough, if boring. By noon she'd made part of the cement floor visible, and her sneezing, caused by inhaling the dust, had subsided. By late afternoon, the shelves contained only boxes and files, and Amantle had cleared away all the loose papers. She'd decided to leave dealing with the boxes and files until the next day. Also, she'd collected miscel - laneous pills, tablets and capsules in a box, and planned to leave it till the next day to figure out how to dispose of them: she wasn't about to be responsible for poisoning some curious child.

By the time she'd left the clinic to go home, she was proud of the progress she'd made – cleaning a storeroom mightn't have been why she'd chosen to work in a clinic, but having attacked the trash pit it was, she'd begun to be filled with a sense of purpose. She'd developed a plan to re-file the documents, re-label the boxes and create an inventory of what was left in the storeroom. She figured she'd require another ten days or so to finish the job. She thought that if she could prove herself capable of doing this job, the nurses might give her a more glamorous task. She intended to suggest she be given the jobs of opening the clinic at 7.30, and writing down the patients' names and complaints. She'd even offer to read their clinic cards to see whether or not they were presenting with a new complaint. She'd make notes about whether the previous treatment had worked: she'd already observed that many patients were going away grumbling that the nurses weren't reading the patients' cards, and that the nurses kept giving them the same medication even if it hadn't worked before.

As it turned out, Amantle was never allocated the glamorous assignment; she never even got to finish the first one. On the fourth day of the storeroom-cleaning assignment, things took a different turn. Among the many boxes in the storeroom, she came across one bearing the label 'Neo Kakang: CRB 45/94'. She instantly recalled that during her first day at the clinic, one of the patients had been a woman whose surname was Kakang. The two nurses expressed the view that the box should be thrown away. 'That storeroom's been like that for more than three years – whatever's in the box can't possibly be useful,' was Nurse Malala's summation.

'But what if it is?' Amantle offered. 'The least we can do is get the family to look and let them decide.'

'All right: do whatever you want to do, TSP girl. It's just an old box – I don't know why you have to make such a big fuss over it.' With that, Nurse Malala went back to leafing through the latest issue of her favourite clothes catalogue.

Amantle resented the fact that Nurse Malala never called her by her name; she always called her 'Mma-TSP', or 'the TSP girl', or even 'the storeroom girl'. However, her policy was to bite her tongue: she had a whole year to spend with these two incom - petents, and had promised herself she wouldn't do anything to make the year any more miserable than it had to be.

She decided to ask a patient to send the Kakang family the message that she'd found a box bearing their name. Within an hour of the despatch, the woman who'd been at the clinic on the first day arrived. It was the woman Amantle had helped try to reduce the temperature of an infant, who, it turned out, was the woman's grandson.

Amantle began: 'I've no idea whether there's anything valuable in the box – I haven't opened it – but I thought you should have a look. It might be nothing, but I didn't think it was for me to just throw it away.' She was already worried she'd hauled the poor woman from her home to examine a box that contained nothing of value.

'Thank you, my child. My name is Motlatsi Kakang. We met on your first day here, remember? You did the right thing. If it contains nothing for us, I'll still know you meant well. You have good manners, my child. There are some who wouldn't have cared.' Kakang looked meaningfully in the direction of the nurses' consulting rooms, and winked conspiratorially. 'May you grow old and have white hairs,' she offered, by way of a blessing. With a smile, she added, 'And the little girl M'phefo sends her greetings – yes, she's a neighbour's daughter, and she asks about you all the time.'

Feeling better about the whole thing, Amantle went into the storeroom to retrieve the box. It was light, and except for the fact it was sealed with masking tape, might have been empty. 'The label here says "Neo Kakang". Do you know anyone by that name? Is she a member of your family? I though she might be; that's why I wanted you to have a look.'

In response, Kakang looked up sharply. Another woman who'd been breastfeeding her baby yanked the infant off her breast and stood up. In protest, the baby gave a howl. The mother smacked the infant and told him to shut up, whereupon he quietened in - stantly.

'What did you say?' Kakang asked in a whisper.

Amantle was alarmed by the response her words had elicited. 'Have I said something wrong? Please tell me: what have I said wrong?' She looked from one woman to the other, hoping for some reassurance that all was well. She found no signs of reassurance on either face.

'Please open the box, my child,' Kakang asked in a gentle voice. Weariness was evident in her voice. Her shoulders were slumped, and her eyes were brimming with fear.

Amantle ripped the masking tape off the box and opened the flaps. She looked inside and saw a bundle of clothes: a very small bundle, resting at the bottom of a rather oversized box. She reached inside and lifted the bundle out. It was held together by more masking tape. From that first glance, she was sure the items had belonged to a girl about twelve: a skirt, a top and a pair of panties.

Before Amantle could absorb what she was seeing, Kakang let out a wail: a piercing, heart-rending, painful wail: '*Ijooo*! What am I seeing? My child! My child! Neo, my child! *Ijooo*! I'm seeing things! Surely I'm going mad! What is this child showing me? Neooooo! Neooooo!' She'd placed her hands over her head, and was pressing and squeezing them, as if she were trying to keep her brains in lest they spill out and she were rendered completely mad.

The patients and nurses spilled out of the clinic. More people came into the yard in response to Kakang's wailing. The woman who'd been breastfeeding her son had joined in the wailing, and the infant had had no choice but to join her. Whispers of 'Neo' began to be heard among the patients. It was clear that on hearing the name, they'd all had a memory return to them. Even Amantle thought she should be remembering something. However, that something wouldn't come into focus; Amantle was preoccupied with the fact she was the centre of this upheaval. All eyes were on her and the box at her feet. She felt responsible for the chaos unfolding in front of her.

'What's going on, Amantle?' It was Nurse Malala asking the question: being placed under pressure, and having no time to think of ridiculing Amantle, she'd called her by her name. Also in the question was assignment of blame.

'I have no idea,' Amantle answered. 'The box contained these clothes here – look.' She held out the clothes for Nurse Malala to see. It was then she realised the clothes were stiff from being caked with a thick, brown substance. The skirt had a blue corner, but the original colours of the three items of clothing were otherwise not obvious. The word 'blood' flew into her mind and lodged there.

And almost simultaneously, the words 'ritual murder' exploded in her head.

'Oh, my God!' It was Nurse Palaki now. 'Wasn't a child called Neo reported missing in this village about four or five years ago? Why are her clothes here at the clinic?' She wasn't asking anyone in particular but was floundering as she tried to make sense of the senselessness in front of her.

Motlatsi Kakang grabbed the clothes from Amantle and hugged them to her chest, sobbing. They were so stiff Amantle was expecting to hear them break as the wailing woman was crushing them against her chest. The crowd began chattering and whispering, and Nurse Malala despatched the ambulance driver to call the police. Amantle gently pried the musty-smelling clothes from the distraught woman and held her in a hug. She sent some of the patients off to call other members of the Kakang family.

When two men and a woman from the Kakang family arrived, the group's mood began to change from shock to anger. People were muttering about what to do to the police officers when they arrived. 'We shouldn't let them into the village: there was a cover-up five years ago and there'll be a cover-up today!' a stout man at the back of the group shouted.

'And this TSP – where did she get the box? How come the box comes when she gets here? She must answer,' was the group's instant response.

Amantle looked up, alarmed. She was still searching for a response when a man came to her rescue: 'No. She isn't to blame. God sent her to find the hidden box: she's the one we must thank.' This was from Rra-Naso, a man who Amantle would come to like, even though she'd been in the village for only a short time. He had gentle eyes and a tendency to ever so lightly touch whoever he was speaking to; it seemed he gave these gentle brushes with his hands in order to constantly seek human contact. He was a dear old man who never failed to say a kind word to people. At least twice when Motlatsi Kakang had brought her grandson to the clinic, Rra-Naso had stopped by for a chat and to check on the infant.

'What about these two nurses?' someone asked. 'They've never treated us with respect. They look down on us. How do we know they didn't hide the clothes?' Being government employees, the group was targeting the nurses for that and no other reason; had the setting been a school instead of a clinic, teachers would have been the immediate targets. It didn't help, naturally, that the two nurses had never even tried to be part of the village – they considered themselves to be superior and resented the fact they'd been posted a long way from their homes.

'I only came here two years ago – please, you know that; you all know that; surely you all know that! Please!' There was fear in Nurse Palaki's voice as she offered the justification for her behaviour. Her usual arrogant tone had dissolved into a trembling, pleading one. If things hadn't been as serious as they were today, her pleadings would have been funny: during the two years of her posting at the clinic, she'd never found it necessary to use the word 'please' when she was talking to the villagers.

'I was posted here three years ago. I know nothing about that box. You must believe me: I know nothing about any of this.' Nurse Malala was equally afraid.

The group members had moved closer to the nurses, and were now closing them in and glaring at them. 'Baying for blood' was an expression that came into Amantle's head. 'But you've never treated us as human beings! You treat us with contempt! You come late to work! You shout at us as if we were little children. Is that not so?' The accusations were coming from a pregnant woman who the nurses had turned away the previous day for coming in a day earlier than the appointed time. The fact she'd walked from a homestead fifteen kilometres away had been immaterial in her attempt to persuade either nurse to see her. Her pleas that she couldn't read and that her son had misread the '6th' as the '5th' had also fallen on deaf ears. When she'd stated that her baby wasn't moving, Nurse Malala had threatened to postpone her next appointment until the following month. As a result, the woman had spent the night at a relative's house and caused her own family anxiety by failing to return home. This morning, her husband had walked the fifteen kilometres to find out what had happened. Because he was also absent from home, the couple's two children, both of whom were younger than six, were without an adult. No wonder the woman was angry.

The two nurses kept quiet. They glanced around surreptitiously to figure out an exit.

'You're not going anywhere. We're not going to let you go and cook up a story with the police, like what happened in 1994. And the police aren't taking those clothes away again. I'm for binding your hands and legs, and putting you in the storeroom.' These strong thoughts were mouthed by one of Motlatsi Kakang's relatives.

When Nurse Malala looked around the crowd, searching for sympathy, her eyes met those of Palai, a police officer who was home on leave. However, the hope that had sprung into her heart died as she realised that today the man was merely a villager, not a police officer. His loyalty was to his people, not to the people who paid him his monthly salary.

CHAPTER 7

As the group waited for the police to arrive, the villagers chattered, and aggression and anguish started brewing among them. Amantle finally pieced the story together, from what she was remembering she'd heard in radio bulletins and read in newspaper reports. Ever since she was very young, she'd been avidly reading the papers and eagerly listening to radio broadcasts.

Amantle had been seventeen when young Neo Kakang had disappeared, and although the adults present thought of 1994 as being only a few years ago, for her it seemed like eons. At the time, she hadn't known what to believe about the reported story of the girl's disappearance. All kinds of bizarre stories were always being reported on the radio and in the papers. 'Young girl vomits snakes'; 'Dead boy seen driving family cattle'; 'Man turns into python and kills grandmother': people were confronted with newspaper stories such as these on a reasonably regular basis, and the radio equivalents were no different. When, therefore, Amantle had heard about the alleged ritual killing of a child in Gaphala village, she hadn't known to what extent she could believe the story. She'd hoped the story was just that: a story. As a child, she'd been warned repeatedly to look out for all kinds of dangers, especially when she'd been in primary school and had to spend a lot of time away from her parents.

On most Fridays during her primary-school years, except from June to September, Amantle had walked the ten-kilometre distance between Molope village and Rasitsi Lands. It had been in the Rasitsi Lands that her mother and sisters had ploughed and then tended the family's crops most of the months between October and

June. Sometimes her father and brothers had also worked there, but most of the time they'd worked even further away, at the Kgomokgwana Cattle Post, taking care of the family's herd. During the time her mother and sisters had been at the lands, she'd slept at Moshi's house, under the care of Moshi's older sister, Mmina. Mmina had had a crippled leg, and it had been for that reason she'd been assigned the task of caring for 'the school children', which was the collective name of her four charges: Moshi, Amantle and two of Moshi's cousins. About once a month, either Amantle's mother or one of Amantle's sisters had come to the village to sweep out the yard, clean the rondavals and generally check on things; otherwise, it had been the weekends that Amantle had seen her family at the lands.

To get to the lands, Amantle had walked with some of her older cousins and neighbours, who'd done the trip countless times. Amantle's school had broken up in the middle of the afternoon, and she'd then had to hurry to meet her walking companions to begin the journey to the lands. They'd finally left at about 4 p.m., and always had to walk fast so they wouldn't have to walk at night; otherwise, they might have met ghosts and ended up either lost or dead. 'Ghosts are cunning and full of tricks,' countless people had told Amantle countless times. However, most of the tricks the ghosts play are actually harmless. One trick they favour is to lie across the path of unsuspecting walkers and turn into a pillow. The walkers, thinking they've found themselves a valuable item, pick the pillow up. Because the best way to carry a pillow is to strap it to your back, the walkers strap it on. Then, after they've walked about five kilometres, lo and behold: the pillow has suddenly sprouted a head and limbs. Having revealed itself, the ghost de - mands to be returned to where the walker found him or her. Unless you want to have a ghost attached to your back for the rest of your life, you'll naturally have to walk back to the spot at which you found the pillow, because only then will he or she let go. This ghost trick is so well known that Amantle wondered who'd be stupid enough to pick up a pillow on the road at night – and a meaner ghost could lead you to a pit and make you plummet to your death.

The ten-kilometre walk between Molope and Rasitsi Lands is also undertaken by big, black men from the north, heading for

South Africa's goldmines. They carry suitcases surrounded by swarms of flies. They grab young girls out walking alone, rape them and cut them in two, across the waist. They stuff the bottom half of the corpse into their suitcase and carry the suitcase for days, so they can re-use the half-corpse until either they've found another young girl or the half-corpse has broken up from rotting. The big, black men from the north have a prominent forehead; flaring nostrils; large, white teeth; and black gums. They speak a strange language, too.

And if the ghosts or the men from the north don't get you, you still have to worry about encountering the men out looking for 'hairless lambs'. Those men speak Setswana and can therefore trick a child into stopping and listening to them while they're pretending to be kind or to be simply looking for directions. They prefer to capture darkish children because they find they can use them to make the best *dipheko*, which means 'traditional strengthening medicines'. Those men can *lobela* you *dintsi*, that is, kill you so effectively, efficiently and secretly that not even flies will find out you've died. Those men are after body parts, especially young breasts, anuses and brains. They're known by many frightening names, including *Bo-Rakoko*: 'The Brain Men'. Because their powers are so strong, it's impossible for them to get caught.

While Amantle had been walking the ten kilometres, she'd darted her eyes this way and that, and looked out for a pillow, a suitcase-carrying man or just a kind-looking man. She'd wondered what happened to the cloud of flies following the men from the north when it was night time: as far as she knew, flies slept at night, so would they leave the suitcase and cling to trees until the sun came up? If so, would they hurry after the men the next morning, or find another rotting carcase to feed on? After she'd learnt that a house fly lives for a few days before it dies of old age, she'd wondered how many generations of flies the men from the north carried with them during their long journey to Johannesburg – Gauteng, 'the place of gold'.

As Amantle had grown older, she'd started to doubt these accounts; nevertheless, a school child did occasionally disappear, so it seemed that ritual murders mightn't belong to the realm of myths after all.

Today, Amantle started to recall the newspaper and radio reports
that one afternoon, twelve-year-old Neo Kakang had gone missing
after she'd been sent out to bring the family donkeys home from
the fields. The villagers had embarked on an all-night search of the
village and its surrounding fields. The search had continued for
five continuos days, aided by police officers, buy no trace of Neo
had been found. Finally, the villagers had come to accept that Neo
was gone forever.

There'd been a theory, which the police had favoured, that wild
animals had attacked, killed and eaten her. However, the villagers
hadn't subscribed to that view: they'd argued that if wild animals
had been responsible for the death, the searchers would have found
Neo's bones. Wild animals don't eat clothes, and they leave bones
around. Vultures would have led the villagers to the little girl's
remains: when anything died, the vultures always informed the
entire village of the occurrence. Naturally, some people had
thought it possible that a crocodile had dragged Neo into the river,
in which case no vultures would have even known she'd died.
However, that possibility was remote: Neo had known she wasn't
to go near the river by herself, and had had no reason to go so far
away that afternoon. Someone had spotted the family's donkeys
very close to the homestead before Neo had gone off after them.
The villagers had believed that someone either enticed the child
away or simply grabbed her and took her away.

Shosho had called at Motlatsi Kakang's home in order to tell
her and her relatives he'd just been to the police station and
delivered to the officers a skirt, a top and a pair of underpants
caked in dried blood: items that could only have belonged to Neo.
He'd been on his way to his cattle post when he'd made the
gruesome discovery. The police had driven him back to the place
at which he'd found the clothes, so they could have another look.
As a result, Shosho had spent the whole day with the police and
never reached his cattle post. When he'd told the officers where
he'd found the items, they hadn't understood: if the clothes had
been there all the time, the villagers and police officers would have

recovered them during the search. People had had to conclude that someone had placed them there after the search. The family members had agreed to go to the police station the following day.

Because the police station was a good thirty kilometres away, the family members had set out by donkey cart first thing in the morning. By the time they'd arrived, they'd been weary and hungry. And having lost a child in painful circumstances, they'd expected to be attended to immediately. However, a gruff police officer had barked at them, 'Do you see this line? Join it. Everyone has a sad story to tell – just wait your turn.' He'd hardly looked up as he stapled some papers together and, with an exaggerated flourish, stamped some documents.

Shosho had thought that if he could make himself heard, things would change, because he'd been at the station only the previous day – and the family's tale was an especially sad one. He'd ventured, 'I was here yesterday, chief. These are the –'

However, he'd been unable to finish the explanation. 'Didn't I just make myself clear? Sit down and wait your turn. What's wrong with you – are you deaf or drunk?' The police officer had looked around and used his eyes to invite the other officers to affirm his point of view.

After the family members had listened to a woman reporting having been raped, a man reporting having lost a cow, a man reporting having had his field destroyed by his neighbour's cattle, a man reporting having lost his driver's licence and a woman reporting that an entry in her child's birth certificate was erron - eous, it had finally been their turn to say their piece. An uncle told the police officer, 'We've come to find out about the clothes Shosho has found: we want to see if they're Neo's.'

The officer had responded, 'Do you want to make a statement?' He'd asked all previous complainants the same question. Clearly, whatever training he'd received, he'd most clearly understood and best mastered the part about taking statements from members of the public. He'd ended every complainant's statement with a signature that was a work of art: all loops and dashes and dots. His masterpiece had seemed to amaze even him, and he'd been given to staring at it every time he'd executed it.

61

Mma-Neo had interjected. 'Statement about what? I don't understand: we made statements describing how Neo was dressed the day she disappeared.' The previous taking of statements had been laborious: each person had had to tell his or her story in Setswana, one sentence at a time, after which the police officer had muttered the translation into English in order to rehearse it and then written the sentence down on his form. At least ten forms had ended up as crumpled balls in the office bin. Mma-Neo hadn't been in the mood for a repeat performance.

'Oh, I see,' began the officer. 'You come from that village where the child disappeared. Why didn't you say so? Why can't you be clear about what you want? Let me call the police officer handling your case. Constable, tell Detective Sergeant Bosilo he has witnesses here to see him.'

Detective Sergeant Bosilo had come, and had immediately recognised the Kakang family. He'd addressed Shosho: 'You were here yesterday. You brought the clothes. Constable, go and get the clothes from the exhibits locker. Neo Kakang: that's the name of the deceased. And bring the docket from Office 3.' The detective sergeant had then turned to the small, sad group and said, 'All we want at this point is for you to look at the items to tell us if they're the ones Neo had on when she disappeared. And, may I warn you, they're not a pretty sight: steel your hearts.' He'd said the last bit sympathetically.

A few minutes later, the constable had returned holding the identifying docket but nothing else. He'd reported that the exhibits locker contained no exhibits bearing that description in question. Detective Sergeant Bosilo had looked through the docket, cross-checked its information in a book, given the constable a series of numbers, and ordered him to go back into Office 3 and bring the items. He'd looked at the group of anxious people and shrugged, as if to say, 'This incompetence is what I have to deal with all the time.' His sympathies had been with them: they'd been allies.

Again, the constable had returned, still without any clothes. The detective sergeant had then gone to do the search himself, but when he'd returned, he too had been empty-handed. Whereas he'd walked away with a look of determination on his face, he'd walked back slowly, his face clouded with confusion and perhaps a touch of fear. The two police officers had then retreated to a corner, and when they'd approached the small, anxious group, the more senior one had announced that they were unable to produce the items at that time. 'That's not really a problem,' he'd declared, trying to project confidence he hadn't felt. 'You've already given statements describing the items, and there's no urgency for you to see them today. I'm sure this man here – what's your name: Shosho? – yes, Shosho here must've told you what he found.'

'But we want to see for ourselves. That was my daughter. I have to see what was found; I can't just hear it from others. Please,' Motlatsi Kakang, Neo's mother, had pleaded of the officers.

'Listen: we'll get the clothes, and then we'll bring them to your village – is that better?' The detective sergeant had hoped to use his authoritative voice to make the mother retreat.

'Why can't we see them today? We've come this far.' Neo's mother had been insistent.

'You can't see them today, because the exhibits locker is locked, and one of the police officers has left with the key,' the detective sergeant had announced. The constable had looked at his superior sharply: that he was lying had been plain obvious.

'Then we'll wait,' Motlatsi Kakang had stated, stubbornly.

'No – you will *not* wait. This is an order. You must not interfere with police investigations, or you could be in serious trouble. You understand, woman?' Even in his firm voice there'd been a trace of fear; it had almost been as if he were begging her, not ordering her, to go.

'We'll wait outside the police station; that way, we won't be interfering with investigations.' Motlatsi Kakang had spoken again.

The constable cleared his throat in order to attract his superior's attention. 'Sir, why don't we just tell these people the truth?' When he'd asked it, he'd looked his boss in the eye, as if to say, 'Trust me.'

'What "truth"? You shut up, constable! Did I say you should speak?' The detective sergeant's voice had been almost a whine. His strong voice had been disintegrating under the weight of a fear that had been evident for all to see. That he was hiding something had been clear to Motlatsi and her relatives. Just what he was hiding hadn't been clear. Theories had started to form in each person's head.

'Sir, the truth is that the items were sent off to the laboratory in Gaborone for analysis of the blood.' The constable had charged ahead. 'Usually, we wait until we've arrested a suspect, but there was a lot of blood on the clothing, so it was thought best to act fast. You see, maybe those clever people at the laboratory in Gaborone can help us with the investigations. That's why the clothes aren't here: they've been sent to Gaborone.' The constable had then turned to his superior and looked hard at him: they'd both known it was a lie, but they'd silently agreed it was a better lie than the 'locked locker' one; at least they'd been able to use it to buy more time.

'Why didn't you say so at first?' Neo's mother had challenged the constable. She hadn't been fooled by either of the officers: a dead daughter gives people strength. She'd never have thought she could challenge a man of the law.

'Because police investigations have to be kept secret. You mustn't tell anyone in your village about any of this. If someone killed the child, that person can learn how far we are in our invest-igations and can thwart our attempts to get him. You understand, don't you? We have to be careful.' The detective sergeant's voice had come across as a bit more confident than before.

The Kakang family hadn't believed the officers, but hadn't known what they could possibly do about the situation. They'd asked the two when they could expect to see the clothes, and the constable had replied 'One month,' whereas the senior officer had replied 'One week.' The two of them had replied at the same time. The senior officer, perhaps confident it was a matter of looking harder and asking other police officers about the circumstances, had promised to bring the family the clothes in a week's time.

'What do you mean "if" someone killed her – do you think she died of old age? What is this nonsense about "if" someone killed her?' Motlatsi Kakang had begun to fear that her child's death would go unsolved, just as many similar cases in other villages had remained unsolved. This had been almost every one of the vil-lagers' first concern when it had first become clear to them that they were being faced with a murder the purpose of which was harvesting of human parts, that is, a ritual murder. Motlatsi had become filled with anguish at the very thought of the pain and fear her daughter would certainly have experienced before she died. Motlatsi had imagined the knives, and wondered about their shape, size and colour – even how sharp they were. She'd tried to block out the images of knives slicing up her small, defenceless daughter. She hadn't been able to either sleep or eat well since her daughter had disappeared. The stress and lack of energy she'd been enduring had been evident in her hollow eyes and dry, sallow face.

'We're due to come to your village to pick up witnesses in the head man's cattle case next week anyway. We'll bring the clothes then.' The detective sergeant had been making a promise he wasn't sure he could fulfil. He'd had no clue what had happened to the box of clothes, which he'd personally labelled and placed in the exhibits locker. He'd needed time to think.

The tired, anguished family had then stood up to leave. As they'd reached the door, Motlatsi Kakang had looked back and used her deep, sad eyes to arrest the detective sergeant's attention. In a soft voice, she'd said, 'Man of government, as you go about your job, just remember: I haven't lost a goat, and my cow hasn't been hit by a car. My daughter was killed – by people who expected you'd do nothing about it. Are you going to let them get away with it, as has been the case every time they've killed?'

A hush had descended over the office as Motlatsi had turned, tears streaming down her face, to follow her defeated relatives.

The Kakang family had then returned to their village in order to wait for the police. During that time, the villagers had told and retold the story of how Shosho had found the clothes and delivered them to the police, and how the police couldn't produce them.

CHAPTER 8

Two weeks after the villagers had returned home, a police van had shown up at Motlatsi Kakang's home. 'Are you Motlatsi Kakang, the mother of the deceased, Neo Kakang?' an officer had asked Motlatsi.

'Yes, I am,' Motlatsi had replied. Then she'd asked her own question. 'Do you have the clothes you promised to bring to show us? It's been two weeks now – we were about to go over to the police station.' By this time, she was close to half her original size: she'd lost her appetite as a result of the overwhelming grief and anxiety she'd been experiencing. How can a person possibly feed her body when her soul is withering away?

'I'm the investigator in this case. My name is Detective Sergeant Senai. I've taken over from Detective Sergeant Bosilo. I've come to give you an update on the investigations.' The detective sergeant had had a pleasant voice and manner.

Motlatsi had addressed one of her daughters. 'Salome, go and call your uncles and aunts, quickly. Tell them the police are here to give us a report. Call Rra-Naso as well – he's been my "walking stick" these past weeks. He'll want to know what the police have to tell us.' She'd then explained to the detective sergeant, 'It isn't wise to receive an important report alone: many ears are always better than two.'

Detective Sergeant Senai had tried to dissuade Motlatsi from calling other people, but Motlatsi had insisted. When everyone had finally been seated, he'd reported to the family members that it was the police's conclusion that the child had been killed by wild animals. They'd suspected that the animals had been lions. 'You all know there are lions in these parts. Occasionally, old lions can't hunt fast game any more, and will instead attack a human being. You all know that. The case is therefore closed. This is what I've come to tell you. I know I bring sad news – but it's better to know than not to know.' The detective sergeant had been told he'd be offering the family an act of great courtesy by going to them to tell them the police's conclusions instead of waiting for them to come to the police station. He'd been immediately posted to Maun Police Station having completed a year-long crime-detection course in England. Although he'd been unhappy about being transferred from Maun to Gaphala police station, he'd understood that transfers were part and parcel of being a civil servant. About the local villagers interested in the Neo Kakang case, the station commander at Gaphala Police Station had told him, 'These are simple village people, but we still must be courteous: go over and give them a verbal report. We're closing the case.' Today, however, on hearing the villagers' response to his report, he'd started to think that things were quickly developing in a direction he hadn't anticipated.

'But that's not what we were told last time. And what about the clothes? Can we see the clothes, please? That's what we're expect - ing today: to be shown the clothes so we can confirm they were indeed Neo's.' Motlatsi's voice had been calm, but had belied the rage beneath the surface. She'd been expecting some kind of strange story, but not the suggestion that Neo had been killed by wild animals: the police couldn't possibly have hoped to sell that story to anyone in the village.

'I have no idea what you're talking about.' The detective sergeant had seemed genuinely surprised – or perhaps he'd simply been a good actor. 'What clothes? The clothes were never found. It's our conclusion that the lions – or whatever animals they were – dragged the body away from around here. Or perhaps another animal buried them – but no clothes were ever recovered. Surely you know that! You were involved in the search. What clothes are you talking about?' Lying and telling the truth in one breath had been proving difficult: he hadn't believed the lion story himself, but he'd wanted the villagers to believe him about the clothes.

'Salome, go and call your Uncle Shosho, please,' Motlatsi had repeated to her daughter. She'd then addressed the detective sergeant again. 'Mister detective, why did the other police officers not come today – the ones who took the statements? The ones who told me – us – that the clothes had been sent to Gaborone? Why are you here and telling us a new story?'

'You must understand, ma'am, that no one owns a case. A case can be taken over by another officer at any time; government doesn't belong to any one person – so I'm now investigating this case.' Although Detective Sergeant Senai had appreciated that Motlatsi Kakang was grief stricken, he'd been angry because she was showing lack of respect towards him. As a police officer, he'd thought he had a right to be respected.

Motlatsi, however, had decided to tell it like it was. 'Let me tell you what happened to my niece, mister detective: she was killed for *muti*; *dipheko*; *ditlhare*: traditional medicine. You know it; I know it; we all know it; any fool can see it. The question is "Why are you running away from the truth?" Who are you protecting? You come here, telling us stories about lions. That's nonsense, and you know it. Shosho saw the clothes. They weren't torn, except, perhaps, for the panties. Did the lions take off the clothes? Is that what you're expecting us to believe? You think we were born yesterday?'

By then, the detective sergeant had risen to his feet. He'd started shouting back at Motlatsi, and the family's neighbours had begun to take an interest in what was going on. Some of them had started filing through the gate in order to hear. This hadn't been a private matter; it had been a village matter, and the neighbours had believed they didn't need an invitation to attend.

Motlatsi's cousin Sello had then picked up on his mother's point. 'Everybody knows it's big people who commit ritual murders, not small men with little influence. And we're always hearing stories of the police covering up these murders. We never thought we'd see that happen right here, in our village. The case is closed, you tell us. This case, mister detective, is *not* closed. It won't be closed until you give us the clothes, and then we'll work on the case in our own way, and the killers will know that they're not the only ones who know powerful traditional doctors: we'll go deep into the Kgalagadi Desert and find the best of the best. We trust you brought the clothes.' He'd extended his hand to make it clear he was ready to receive the clothes.

Detective Sergeant Senai had begun to sweat. He hadn't thought it a good idea to stand up, because the villagers might have misinterpreted his rising as being an act of aggression. However, he'd felt vulnerable sitting down, having an angry man towering over him and seeing more people filling the yard. People are usually afraid of the police, but these ones hadn't seemed cowed at seeing his fancy van and the two accompanying constables wearing police uniform. He'd glanced at the van but not been able to spot the two constables who'd accompanied him. 'I've reviewed all the notes about this case. No clothes were recovered. Everything that happens in a case is recorded. If there'd been any clothes, there'd be mention of it in the docket. You must be mistaken.' The detective sergeant had been trying to inject some authority into his voice. He'd also been seething that he hadn't been told everything before he'd been sent to talk to the villagers.

The assembled relatives had then looked at the detective sergeant: was he lying, or hadn't he been told everything? Shosho had now arrived and had begun repeating to the Kakang family what he'd found, observed and done.

Detective Sergeant Senai had been puzzled, but had tried to hide his confusion. *This man, Shosho, isn't making up a story,* he'd thought to himself. *And neither are the mother and her cousin.* He'd wondered what was going on. 'All I can tell you at this point is what I've already told you. I can't tell you more.' He'd stood up as if to leave – but someone had blocked his way.

Motlatsi had ordered him: 'You're not leaving until you give us the clothes. You're hiding something. You're protecting someone. Salome, go and call the neighbours.'

It had hardly been necessary to call the neighbours: the yard had already been filled with neighbours, some of whom were carrying sticks. An angry mood had begun to develop. Some of the villagers had hustled the two constables over to join their senior; the two had been hiding in the police van.

The detective sergeant had pleaded, 'Please listen to me: maybe I didn't understand the docket – why don't you let me go back and read it again?' He'd needed a way to get out of the atmosphere of aggression that was building up around him.

A man had grabbed the detective sergeant. 'You have the docket in your hands: read it now and tell us if it tells you anything new. You really think we're idiots. You think because we can't read we're stupid? We'll show you who's the stupid one.' He'd then pushed the detective sergeant against a tree. There'd been a thud as the detective sergeant's head bounced against the tree trunk.

The detective sergeant had become unravelled and now pleaded in a loud voice, 'Please believe me when I say I was given this docket as it is. There was no mention of any clothes. If you harm us now, it won't help you. What you want are the clothes. And if you say they were delivered to the station by this man here, they must be there. Perhaps someone forgot to mention that fact in the docket. If you let us go, I promise to come back tomorrow to bring the clothes. You see, the other police officer was transferred to another village, and I based my conclusions on what he wrote in the file. Just give me another day – I won't disappoint you.'

The group had then finally let the three police officers go; the idea of detaining them had been born out of utter frustration. It had already been three weeks since Neo had disappeared, and to the family and villagers, the police had been acting very strangely indeed.

On the way back to the police station, Detective Sergeant Senai had tried to query the two constables about whether they had any knowledge of the clothes.

Constable Moruti had responded as best he could. 'All I know, sir, is that Detective Sergeant Bosilo was a frightened man before he left. I think that man, Shosho, did bring the clothes. I wasn't on duty then, but that was clear enough from the talk at the station. Bosilo put them in a box, labelled the box and asked that it be put in the exhibits locker. Perhaps he put them there himself; I can't remember. But the following day, when he asked that it be brought out, the box was gone – it had vanished. At first he thought it had just been misplaced, but it was gone; just gone – no trace! The exhibits book showed that the box had been given a number and all. The procedure for exhibits had been followed.'

On hearing this account, Detective Sergeant Senai had become angry: the humiliation he'd just suffered in front of his juniors, at the hand of local villagers, wasn't something he was likely to forget in a hurry. 'Why wasn't I told this? Why isn't there any mention of all this in the docket? I've looked at the investigation diary, and there's no mention of any clothes or any box.'

Constable Monaana had then chipped in. 'It seems to me that Detective Sergeant Bosilo has fixed the record, sir. Forgive me for saying something like that about a superior officer, sir. I think he made another diary, sir. That's what I think, sir. I'm worried about it, because those people at the village know about the clothes. One of them saw them. The others spoke to Bosilo, and he confirmed that the clothes existed. I don't think they're going to accept that that man Shosho was drunk.'

Senai had been driving rather fast for the sandy road. His agitation had been increasing with every minute that passed. 'What are you talking about? Who said anything about Shosho being drunk?'

In responding, Constable Monaana had almost started whining. He'd been doing his best to hold back tears. 'I was involved in the initial investigation, sir. Detective Sergeant Bosilo instructed me to say that Shosho never brought any clothes. I was to say, if I were ever asked, that he was drunk, and only talked about clothes. I was instructed to make a statement saying all this. Surely you read my statement. But he did bring them – I saw them with my own eyes: a skirt, a blouse and a pair of panties, all caked in blood. None of them torn, expect for the underwear. How can I just say I didn't see these things? I asked for a transfer as well, but was told I'd be working with you to make sure things stayed under control. Sir, I'm afraid too. I don't want to be involved in ritual-murder cases. Why does Bosilo get to be transferred and I'm left here? It's not fair. He was the senior officer: he should've been the one to stay.'

Senai asked in reply, 'Does the station commander know all this? Did you ever meet him to discuss all this?'

By now, Monaana hadn't been able to hide his own fear. 'Not as the whole team, sir. He called me after Detective Sergeant Bosilo left and just ordered me to do as the sergeant had advised. I made my statement and gave it to him. That's all. He, too, seemed frightened, if I may say so, sir – and I've made so many statements in this case I don't know what I've said exactly any more!'

Senai's level of anger had increased dramatically. 'So you two are telling me you lost important exhibits, that you've cooked up a cover-up story, and then you let me walk into that yard to say all that nonsense, and you didn't think I ought to be told – is that it?' The increase in his anger had had a direct bearing on the speed at which he was driving. He'd now pressed down on the accelerator. The two officers had clung on to their seats. The road had been sandy and narrow, so that only one motorist at a time had been able to negotiate it – and the van had now been going through cattle posts. Having survived the villagers, the two younger officers had been keen to survive the trip back. Neither of them had chosen to respond to the detective sergeant's question for quite a while. Finally, Constable Moruti had resumed the conversation, in a low, hoarse voice in which his utter desperation had been evident. 'But what are we going to do, sir? Maybe, if we just don't go back to the village, they'll just forget about the whole thing.'

Senai had been unable to control himself. 'You think that woman's going to forget she had a child named Neo? You think she's going to forget that one day the child disappeared? You think she's going to forget that the police lost the only evidence they had and that they came, in a brand-new Toyota Hilux with nice big letters saying "POLICE", to say the child was killed by lions that were skilled at undressing their victims? Is that what you think's going to happen?' As if to emphasise the question, he'd slammed on the brakes, thereby almost making the van capsize. 'Jesus, you're an idiot! You're all idiots! That fat ass of a station com - mander's an idiot!' He'd then gotten out of the car and gone to lean against a tree.

The two officers hadn't known what to say or do. Their superior had parked the vehicle immediately before a curve, and if another vehicle had come by just then, it would have slammed right into theirs. They'd finally decided that rather than take their chances at surviving a head-on collision, they'd take their chances at surviving an attack by their superior. They'd gotten out of the vehicle.

Senai had barked rather than shouted his next, obvious, question. 'What do you think happened to the clothes? And all I wanted was a nice, quiet two years before my retirement! What do you think happened to the clothes?!'

Constable Monaana had begun in a weak voice, 'Maybe, sir, like Detective Sergeant –'

'I'm asking for *your* view, not what that idiot said. What do *you* think happened? *You! You! You!* Can't you use your own head just for *once? Jesus!*' Senai had reached the end of his tether.

'I think the killers took the clothes away,' Monaana had offered.

'How?' Senai's anger had only just given way to curiosity.

'You know how they have powers: maybe they made me think I put them in the locker but I didn't; maybe they opened the locker with their powers, at night, when no one was looking. But they must've taken them – because they just disappeared.' Monaana had started whimpering with fright. Ever since the box of clothes had disappeared, he'd been having frightful nightmares. The child, Neo, had been coming to him at night, standing by his bed but saying nothing. He'd been experiencing her face as a blank, ovular shape, featureless except for big, round, frightened eyes. She'd been just standing there, looking at him, blood dripping from her armpits, chest and private parts. He'd already made three visits to his traditional doctor, but things hadn't improved at all. It hadn't been as if he'd taken part in the girl's murder. He hadn't been able to understand why she was coming to him: was it for help, or was it to blame him for giving her clothes to her killers? The traditional doctor had told him he was in a way responsible for the clothes' going back to the killers, because he'd neglected to strengthen himself before becoming involved in a case such as this.

The detective sergeant had then brought the constable back to the present by challenging him with yet another question. 'Why did they throw the clothes away in the first place if they wanted to keep them? Why throw them away, only to get them back again?'

'Sir, can you move the vehicle from the road? I'm sorry, sir, but I'm afraid someone's going to drive into it soon. I'm sorry, sir, to mention it, sir – really sorry, sir.' Monaana had tried to keep his counsel about the car's precarious position, but had failed: he'd had no desire to walk in that part of the bush – what with ritual murderers and lions prowling the plains.

Senai had responded by walking to the vehicle and, as he was getting in, slamming the door.

The constables had then scrambled in through the passenger

door: they hadn't been about to allow themselves to be left behind in the bush.

'You haven't answered my question, though.' The detective sergeant's aggressive tone had hardly lessened while the trio was settling into the van. He'd floored the accelerator, and the constables had once again found themselves clinging to their seats and hoping for the best.

Monaana had given breath to his next thought out of desperation. 'Maybe the clothes had been worked on so all of us would be confused. You see? It's worked. Detective Sergeant Bosilo became confused, and now the case is closed. The child was eaten by lions. Why can't you just accept that, sir, and close the case?'

Senai had all but ignored the junior constable's plea. Instead, he'd turned to Moruti. 'Constable Moruti, you've been quiet – what do you think?'

'Sir,' Monaana's partner had responded, 'I just want to be transferred to another station. These people are powerful: I don't want to end up dead or mad. I can't sleep at night; I can't eat. I just want to leave this village, sir!'

'I see,' had come the short reply.

On reaching the station, Senai had immediately sought out the station commander, who'd casually asked, 'How did it go?'

'Sir,' the detective sergeant had begun tentatively, 'I have to say I wish I'd been told about the clothes and their disappearance. I knew this was a ritual-murder case, which everyone preferred to close for lack of evidence. Now, I find there was more to it than what I'd been told. And the villagers are angry. I thought Detective Sergeant Bosilo was transferred down south for medical reasons.' It had been a caged challenge: it was a superior officer he was talking to.

The station commander had then looked at Senai for a while without saying anything. When he'd finally opened his mouth, his voice had been firm, his manner of speaking one of a man in control. His whole presentation had invited no contradictions. Both men had been in the police force long enough to know what happens to junior officers who dare to challenge their superiors. The station commander had clearly been in command. 'Detective Sergeant Senai, listen to me, and listen to me carefully. I'm going to say this only once: the child was killed by wild animals – *full stop*! The claim that there were any clothes was made by a drunkard who can't be trusted – *full stop*! Your mission today was simply to tell that to the Kakang family. If I want you to go out to detect anything, detective sergeant, I'll tell you! Have you done your job, Detective Sergeant Senai?'

'Yes, sir, I have,' Senai had replied. 'But they don't believe that story. I didn't know about the clothes, so I told them I'd look into the matter and report back to them tomorrow.'

'Since when have the police been reporting to ignorant villagers about their investigations? You've told them the conclusion reached by this station, and that's that. You're not going back there again: *am I clear?* That's an order, detective sergeant: *am I clear?*'

'Yes, sir,' had been all that Senai could muster.

'Stand up straight, and salute like a real officer!' The commander in command had decided to pull rank.

'Yes, sir!' Senai had complied, but it had been impossible for the station commander to miss the expression of contempt on his junior's face.

The station commander had then merely grunted, and the detective sergeant had dutifully left the office. Once outside, he'd muttered to himself and cursed the station commander as well as the station commander's mother, grandmother and great-grandmother. His mood of fury had reached its peak. His family traditional doctor had been more than 300 kilometres away, and as a result of the most recent developments, he'd known he needed to consult him desperately. When he'd been preparing to come on this assignment, he'd consulted the diviner in order to find out whether the road was clear. The diviner hadn't seen any major obstacle in the detective sergeant's path: using the bones, he'd only uncovered the usual petty jealousies. Perhaps both men had taken the divination to be routine and mistakenly failed to seek out hidden obstacles. Now, however, it had become clear to the detective sergeant that a problematic situation such as this should have stared the diviner in the face. Perhaps, the detective sergeant, had thought, it was time to look for a new diviner. *You can't be too careful with diviners these days,* he'd thought. *It isn't like the old days, when no one dared play games with a profession such as divination.* These days, by contrast, all kinds of charlatans had started to litter the scene. Not that Senai's diviner might have been a charlatan, though: he'd inherited his powers from his grandfather, who'd in turn inherited his from his father . . . But still, why hadn't the diviner seen that if Senai were transferred to this village, he'd be pitted against the killers of Neo Kakang?

Two days after Detective Sergeant Senai had visited the village, some of the villagers had stoned and then torched a police vehicle that had come to collect witnesses in a petty-theft case. However, the villagers hadn't harmed the two officers; instead, they'd told them to pass on the message to Senai that things would get worse unless he brought the clothes. The next day, the villagers had torched another government vehicle and given the driver the same message. When they'd torched a third vehicle, the state had responded by displaying a show of force.

When young paramilitary-police officers had descended on the village bearing weapons for quelling riots and driving tank-like vehicles, the villagers had ignored them and gone about their business as if nothing were wrong. Frustrated and spoiling for a fight, the officers had taunted the villagers, but the villagers had kept their cool: they'd refused to be drawn into what might have ended up as a blood bath. Although the younger, more belligerent villagers had wanted to respond, the elders had been stern in issuing orders that no one confront or in any way give the police a reason to attack the villagers. The villagers had then returned to their fields, visited the health clinic and gone to the shops as if the police weren't camped in their village.

However, the villagers had been holding secret meetings right under the police's nose. Groups of them had been meeting at the Kakang home and planning strategies for their next move. Finally, they'd agreed that the head man would call a *kgotla* meeting before which the station commander, in the presence of the area's member of parliament, would have been instructed to make a formal report to the villagers.

No meeting had ever taken place, though, and after the villagers had endured weeks of a show of force from the authorities and accompanying frustrations, the stand-off had fizzled out. The villagers had resumed their life, and the authorities had resumed theirs.

Over the next year, although spats had occasionally broken out between the villagers and the authorities, what the authorities had expected to happen had happened: the anger among the villagers had ebbed – that is, until Amantle's storeroom cleaning resulted in something totally different from cleanness.

CHAPTER 9

Motlatsi, Neo's mother, couldn't believe that the wound she'd been nursing in the hope it would one day close had been ruptured in so bizarre a way. The TSP girl's discovery of the box containing Neo's blood-caked clothes was so bizarre that Motlatsi was unable to think of any theories to explain it. Her neighbours and friends were coming up with all kinds of theories, none of which quite made sense. Was it the work of the family's ancestors, ready, after all these years, to reveal the truth? Was it the work of the devil, intent on stirring up old hurts? Was it the work of God, answering Motlatsi's many prayers for justice?

During the five years since Neo's death, Motlatsi had developed a rhythm to help her cope with the loss. Her eldest daughter, Tebogo, had since had a child, Maemo, and Motlatsi was occupying herself by raising him. The pains of the womb are always eased when the woman has a new baby to attend to. Also, Motlatsi had formed a very close friendship with her neighbour Rra-Naso. Over the past five years, he'd shown her nothing but kindness. He had a furrowed brow, twitching fingers and a gentle manner, and had been a constant source of strength and comfort. From the deep sorrow he felt, a person would have thought he'd lost his own child. He had, in fact, lost his wife, and so was possibly better equipped than any neighbour to understand Motlatsi's loss. 'Mma-Tebogo, you have to let peace enter your heart. You have to be strong for the older children.' As he spoke these words, he'd look into his friend's eyes, but quickly look away when he saw the hurt, which always seemed to be raw.

'I try, Rra-Naso,' she'd say; 'I try. But she was such a small thing. Such a tough little child, too; always obedient, though, and willing to do as adults asked. But so small for her age – the smallest in her class; the smallest among her age mates. But always the toughstest.' Motlatsi would pause, thinking of her daughter: she'd been a little springbok, always running and playing. 'Why couldn't they have mercy on one so small? How could they have been so cruel, so inhuman? What kind of person kills a small little girl?'

Rra-Naso wouldn't answer; he'd only listen kindly. He'd heard these questions many times before.

Mma-Neo would continue in a quiet voice, almost to herself. 'But perhaps she was born marked for something like this.'

'What do you mean "marked"? Rra-Naso would chide. 'Don't blame the child for such a horrible thing – or the ancestors either; her killers are the ones to blame, no matter who they are, and no matter what anyone might think of them. That kind of brutality can't be excused – ever!' So much vehemence would be evident in his voice; so much pain. The outburst would inevitably be followed by involuntary rubbing of a scar on one of his fingers, as if he were seeking comfort in remembering an injury that was much smaller than the one on both their minds.

Mma-Neo would then revisit the circumstances of Neo's conception. 'I could never talk about how she was conceived: that's always been too painful. Everyone knows there was a scandal involved. But now I think, *Perhaps she was always marked, always meant to leave me. Perhaps she was never my child, really: perhaps I merely carried her for others. Perhaps, in a twisted way, it's the will of God.*' She'd then stare off into the distance.

'I have no idea what made you leave Mahalapye for this place, but whatever it was, Neo was killed by cruel men seeking power – or perhaps out of cowardice. But whatever their motivations, they're to blame. They chose her like you'd choose a chicken for a Sunday lunch and killed her like you'd kill a goat. That, Mma-Tebogo, can't be the will of God: God would never will something like that.' Since Neo's death, Rra-Naso had never called his friend Mma-Neo; to him, she'd always been Mma-Tebogo, after her eldest daughter. She'd appreciated that; he'd been such a con - siderate man. He'd understood that saying the name Neo was like tweaking a wound that refused to heal. Tears would roll down his face, and Mma-Tebogo would cry as well. They'd become two people aged before their time, linked by loss and despair; two people whose healing was now being ruptured as a result of the accidental opening of a dusty box. 'Please, let's talk about some - thing else. Let's try to get our minds off this subject, or we'll both end up insane – assuming we haven't gone mad yet.'

However, for five years, Mma-Tebogo – Motlatsi – hadn't been able to get her mind off that fateful day, many years ago, when she'd gone out seeking to improve her life, only to come back changed forever. Her life had certainly changed, but she hadn't been sure the change could be called an improvement. But still, the change had brought Neo, so in one way there'd been an improvement: a child, whatever his or her source, was always an improvement in a person's life.

Motlatsi had gone to a man called Samesu, who lived in a small village just outside Mahalapye village. The man, she'd been told, specialised in female conditions. He could help a barren woman become pregnant, just as he could cure sexually transmitted diseases. He could find a husband for a woman who was seeking one, just as much as he could help a woman win a promotion at work. People had reported he was especially good at correcting conditions relating to wombs: tilted wombs; painful wombs; barren wombs; bleeding wombs; unattractive wombs – you name it: he was the expert. Female pilgrims would attend from afar to seek him out for his renowned expertise.

Motlatsi's 'female condition' had been that her partner of eight years, who'd made her pregnant eight times and with whom she had five children, was showing no inclination towards marrying her. He'd seemed to be comfortable with the arrangement, where - by he slept and ate at Motlatsi's parents' house but had no demands placed on him to help within that home. Occasionally, he'd spent nights at his other girlfriend's house. At first, that aspect hadn't been a major problem, because he'd been discreet – and anyway, everyone knows a man can't be with just one woman. No, according to Motlatsi, the problem had assumed serious proportions when he'd become less discreet and started to show less and less sexual interest in her. It had been then she'd decided to consult Samesu. Her hope had been that he'd move things along so she'd soon be saying 'I do,' in front of a marriage officer.

She'd secretly taken a bus to Samesu's village and ensured she'd arrive there early in the evening: a person doesn't seek the cures dispensed by the likes of Samesu in broad daylight. An enterprising man had discovered that desperate women had a need for 'sunset transport'. He'd asked no questions, as long as the women paid his exorbitant fares without question. When Motlatsi had arrived at Samesu's compound, she'd found seven other female patients waiting there. All of them had been quiet and restrained, and because it isn't the thing to do, she hadn't asked any of them what was ailing them.

The queue had moved rather fast, and it had soon been her turn. Once inside the hut, she'd been confronted by a naked man, his body glinting in the dim light. His body had been almost pitch black, and had been oiled, so had a velvety, magical look. She hadn't expected the diviner to be naked, and because he'd just stood there as if nothing were wrong, she'd taken it that this was his usual state during his divinations. She'd heard that some diviners and priests worked in the nude, although she'd never encountered one before this.

'Come in, mma; come in. I see you come from afar. You're weary: sit down.' His voice had been musical. In it had been suggested a calmness that was both welcoming and frightening: a voice a person might use in order to coax a reluctant animal, only to bag it when it approached.

Motlatsi had hesitated.

'Come in. If you want your man to come closer to you, you can't go back now.' Again, the soothing and kind voice.

However, he'd made this prompt diagnosis even before she'd sat down, and she'd been won over by him. She'd moved towards this naked, beautiful man – and he *had* been beautiful.

'Sit down; sit down here.' The diviner had pointed to a mat on the floor. He'd then sat next to Motlatsi.

His nakedness had loomed large before his patient's eyes. She'd tried to look at his face only, but her eyes had kept on flying to the area between his legs.

'To reach nature, we have to be natural: you'll have to take off your clothes.' By this time, Samesu had become busy preparing his instruments of divination, and Motlatsi had begun to feel she had

81

no option but to comply. She'd been naked many times in front of doctors and nurses at both the clinic and the main hospital. Tonight, she'd convinced herself that this setting was no different; she had, after all, alighted on a doctor of the best kind.

When she'd completely disrobed, the diviner had started speaking to her in the same gentle, reassuring voice. 'You have problems of a female nature, don't you?'

'Yes, I do.' She'd tried to keep her legs together, but the diviner had started rubbing some ointment on her ankles, then on her legs, and then up her legs towards her private parts.

He'd then gently pushed her legs apart, working in a slow, gentle rhythm. 'Your man is the issue – is that not so? Please open your legs. Don't resist, please. The medicine must cover your entire body, otherwise I'll give a wrong diagnosis.'

'Yes, it is.' She hadn't been sure whether she was saying yes to the question or the request to open her legs. She'd therefore opened her legs and said yes again, just to cover both questions: she'd wanted to have both the correct diagnosis and the correct treatment. She'd borne five children to raise, and wanted to ensure their father came back to help her raise them. She wouldn't obtain that result if she let modesty get in the way.

'Tell me about it. Before that, drink this.'

Motlatsi had drunk from the offered cup. She'd started being confused about what she was feeling: she'd felt both ensnared and calmed. She'd felt like a baby bird: helpless but not fearful – just blissfully powerless. 'We have five children, but he won't marry me.'

'That's not all – what else?' The rubbing had continued. He'd now started using circular movements to rub her belly. He'd moved on to gently pushing her back on to the mat.

'Now he has another girlfriend.' Motlatsi had been trying to keep her mind clear: something had started happening to her, and she was losing control.

'All men have girlfriends – that's not the problem, is it? Here: drink this.' Again he'd offered the cup. He'd pulled her up to a sitting position so she could have a drink. When he'd pushed her back again, he'd encountered little resistance from her. He'd gone back to the inner part of her legs. 'What's the real problem?' he'd asked in his gentle, soothing voice.

Fumes had started filling the room, and Motlatsi hadn't remembered seeing him light anything. 'He – he – he doesn't sleep with me any more.' She'd blurted it out.

'Your mother doesn't sleep with you any more – so that's not the problem; you have to say the problem if you want me to help you.' His hands had stopped moving, but had just begun hovering over her exposed vagina. She'd found herself arching her body towards his hands – but he'd moved them away. He'd then put more of the ointment on them and begun rubbing it into his own inner thighs. That he was ready for a sexual encounter couldn't possibly have been doubted.

'He won't have sex with me – not as often as before. I'm afraid he doesn't want me any more.' Motlatsi had sat up now, to come closer to the soothing voice.

'Your woman-ness has lost its power – it happens sometimes. I'm going to put this medicine inside. You just lie back and relax.' With that, he'd pushed her back gently. He'd spread her legs and started stuffing some smooth, warm, lotion-like cream into her. 'Now I'm going to push it in. Just lie back and feel yourself come back to life. Yes: just lie back; lie back. I'm pushing it in so it'll work.'

By that time, he'd gotten on top of her and she'd begun responding to him. Her woman-ness *had* come to life, as he'd promised it would. Before she'd known what was happening, she realised she was having the best sex she'd had in a long time – perhaps ever.

She'd then faded into sleep. She'd been vaguely aware that Samesu was continuing with the rubbing and oiling, and many sessions of sex. She, however, had been too far away to be a part of it. She'd wanted to object, but the objections had formed in her head only and gone no further. Her lips had refused to obey her, as had every other part of her body.

It hadn't been until hours later that she was able to sit up. She'd looked around and seen that Samesu had dressed and was now busily preparing packets of medications, as if nothing momentous had just taken place between them.

'Sit up and take these. This is for drinking, and –'

'Why did you do that?' she'd demanded.

'Do what?' he'd asked in reply.

She hadn't responded: she'd been too confused to clearly articulate what she wanted to say. She'd also felt ashamed.

The diviner had looked at her for a while before continuing preparing his packets. He'd shaken his head, as if Motlatsi were some ungrateful child who wasn't worth chastising. 'Listen to me, if you want to be cured. I've only started the treatment, but it's up to you to continue and complete it. Think about it carefully before you throw away everything we've gained today.' He'd then proceeded to explain how she was to use his medications. Over the coming months, it would be necessary for her to have additional sexual encounters of the sort that had just taken place; naturally, he hadn't called them that: 'treatment sessions' had been what he'd called them. He'd then named his price: P250.00, and Motlatsi had paid in silence.

As she'd walked to the bus stop, she'd cried. Silent tears had rolled down her face. She'd felt stupid for having allowed herself to be raped by Samesu. However, she'd known she wouldn't tell anyone about her experience. She'd known she could be pregnant, or, worse still, that she could have contracted some sexually transmitted disease. HIV infections had been on the rise, so it could well be the case that she'd just signed her death warrant. She'd been sure she'd been raped, but she hadn't expected anyone to share that view of the sexual encounter – after all, she hadn't resisted. And if the truth be known, she'd enjoyed it – the first part, anyway. But even so, she'd been raped. She: a 35-year-old, literate teacher, the head of a neighbourhood committee for preventing crime, had walked into a hut, encountered a naked stranger, taken off her clothes and had sexual intercourse with him – who'd possibly call it rape? Still, she'd called it rape. And she'd also known it was a rape she'd never report – not to anyone.

Nine months later, she'd given birth to a baby girl, and called her Neo, which means 'gift'. By that time, the cause of her eight pregnancies and father of her five children had left her for the other woman. Disgraced and humiliated, she'd moved to the village of Diphala in order to hide from her shameful past. She'd taken her six children with her, knowing her former partner would give her no support. It had never even occurred to her to approach

Samesu to seek child support from him for Neo. Occasionally – and very occasionally – she'd returned to her former village to see her family. Her younger sisters hadn't looked her in the eye. She'd had no way of knowing what people had told them about her and Neo, but whatever it had been, they'd been filled with shame as a result of it.

Even in deciding to flee, though, she'd chosen a village that, even though remote, some of her relatives lived in. She'd believed that no one could live without having some blood relatives around. She'd thought her ancestors mightn't know where to find her if she called for them to help. Whereas, in her previous situation, people had blamed the father of her children for not marrying her, in her new situation, people had blamed her for cheating on him. And now Neo had been killed; conceived under the spell of a diviner, she'd perished at the hands of men who wield the powers of diviners. Had it been her fate to perish in that way? Had the sole purpose of her existence been to perish in that way? Had she been planted just for that type of harvesting? Had the men who killed her really had any choice in the matter? Perhaps Neo had never belonged to Motlatsi – the mother had been only the nurturer. But Motlatsi had loved her so!

Mma-Neo had been brought back to the present on hearing Rra-Naso deliver one of his heart-breaking coughs. 'Here,' she told him, 'have another cup of warm water: it'll help calm your chest.' She'd looked at her friend with concern.

'Thank you, Mma-Tebogo; thank you.' The old man had proceeded to sip from the offered cup in silence.

CHAPTER 10

Five years had slowly elapsed, and now, in 1999, the sergeant on duty at Maun Police Station had had to respond to a report written by an ambulance driver. The villagers in Gaphala had claimed that a box containing evidence from an old murder case had been discovered in a storeroom. The sergeant had responded by sending two clumsy constables to Gaphala to investigate the claim. The constables hadn't appreciated the nature of the find until they'd driven into the village and been met by an angry mob. The villagers had then refused to hand over the box containing the evidence, which Amantle had given them for safekeeping.

Finally, the villagers had offered the constables TSP Amantle. A self-declared leader had stepped forward and announced, 'She's a government employee: you can take her – but you're not taking anyone or anything else. We demand answers.'

A voice had risen from the back of the crowd. 'Yes – and *she* found the box! Maybe *you* sent her to pretend to find it! How can we trust *you*?'

Now, an hour later, Amantle was in Maun Police Station's charge office. She watched as people shouted at a desk constable to make themselves heard over sounds constantly hissing from two-way radios. The people had to shout at the constable across an impersonal counter that was both too high and too broad. Amantle was waiting to be seen by the sergeant who'd sent the two constables to Gaphala.

One of the charge office's many wall posters bore a photo of a handsome man who had a dashing smile and a cocky posture. As Amantle looked at the arrogantly smiling face from across the room, she couldn't possibly have known she'd one day use the same photo to try to track the man down. Under the photo, in bold, confident handwriting, was the caption 'Silas Molemi. Race: African. Hair colour: black. Eyes: white.' To pass the time, Amantle looked at and read the captions under the other posters. Bashi Moreti's eyes were described as being red, and he did indeed have bloodshot eyes. Agang Bonosi's eyes were also described as being red, but his mug shot was black and white rather than colour, so Amantle couldn't tell whether he did indeed have red eyes.

As she waited, she looked through the low windows and noticed two goats fighting but without much passion for the bout. Behind them was a pit latrine, and just behind it a river. She wondered how wise it was to instal a pit latrine on the bank of a river the water of which was used for all kinds of purposes, including drinking. She then saw a swirl of blue, arms flailing and legs stomping, charge out of the pit latrine, whereupon the fighting goats disengaged and took off. When the arm flailing and leg stomping stopped, a woman stood where the goats had been, wearing only her underwear. A small, curious crowd gathered around her, and the nature of her complaint became obvious when her swelling hand came into view: a scorpion had stung her as she'd been reaching for newspapers serving as toilet paper. Wanting to help, a man picked up her blue dress from next to the pit latrine, but dropped it when a member of the crowd told him the source of the woman's pain. The woman now stood exposed in her not very flattering underwear.

Back inside the charge office, a woman carrying a mop pointed it at Amantle and asked, 'Are you Amantle? They're calling you in Office 2 – down the corridor, that way.' The mop carrier didn't pause; nor did she say where 'that way' was. Amantle assumed 'that way' was in the direction from which the mop carrier had just come. She pulled herself away from the scorpion drama and found that Office 2 was indeed only two offices down from where she'd been waiting.

She knocked on the door and entered the room. Across a brown, scratched desk, sitting on a brown, torn swivel chair was a man in his thirties wearing a pin-striped suit. The charge-office constables had been wearing police uniform: a blue shirt and blue trousers. The police-uniform shirt was really a cross between a shirt and a jacket, and required a belt to give it some shape. For fat officers, it wasn't a good look at all to have their belt riding over a protruding belly. Worn on officers who forgot to wear a belt, the shirt–jacket resembled a maternity dress; worn with a belt, as it should be, on trim, beautifully shaped, young officers, it resembled a nice, short dress.

The officer sitting in Office 2 didn't have to suffer the indignity of wearing a top that couldn't make up its mind about its true identity: he worked for the Criminal Investigation Division, so didn't have to wear a uniform. 'Sit down. You *are* Amantle Bokaa, aren't you? You're the TSP at the clinic.' He addressed Amantle as he rearranged some forms, a rubber stamp and an ink pad. A pen protruding from the corner of his mouth bobbed up and down as he spoke.

'Yes, sir,' came the reply.

'Tell us what you know.' There was authority in his voice.

'About what, sir?' Amantle asked.

'Don't play games, young woman: you know why you're here.' There was a suggestion of tiredness in his voice and manner: feigned tiredness from a man who was sure who was boss.

'No, actually I don't know why I'm here. I was ordered to get into a police vehicle; I was told I'd be told why when I got here,' came the honest response.

'Listen, if it wasn't for you, we wouldn't be having two nurses held captive by villagers right now – so don't play ignorant. I'm waiting to take your statement, so start talking.' He held a pen, poised ready to start writing.

'Once upon a time, there was a frog and –'

'Why are you doing this to me? Why are you refusing to co-operate with the police?' He looked at Amantle, perhaps hoping to frighten her into co-operating.

'First, tell me why I was ordered, like a criminal, to come here: am I under arrest?' she enquired.

'No, you're not under arrest – but you might end up being

under arrest if you obstruct us in our investigations.' He was snappy.

'Oh, I'd be happy to leave now so you're not obstructed in your investigations – and what investigations might they be?' She was cocky and assertive.

'Listen, young lady,' the police officer warned her, 'I have no time to waste: I need your statement.'

'Shouldn't you guide me about what you're interested in? I could start telling you my life story, but how would I know it's what you're interested in?' It was a good point.

'Okay. There's a near-riot in that village: we want to know what set things off and who's now leading the disturbances.' It was a vague enough lead-in.

'Why is there a near-riot in the village?' Amantle glared back at him.

'It's because of the box of clothes you allegedly found in a storeroom! That box disappeared from this very station five years ago! Now, how did you suddenly find it in that storeroom? Those can't be the clothes – how did they get there? Do you understand what this means?' His voice was shrill with fear and desperation. His feigned authority evaporated during his passionate delivery.

'How did it disappear from the station five years ago? Does your file say how it happened?' It was a reasonable enough question.

'Who's asking questions here? You're here to answer questions, not ask them.' He was trying to re-assert his authority.

'Well, the only answer I have you already know: I found the box in the storeroom. You already know that, because you've just told me. You already know the box disappeared from this station: that'll be interesting information for the villagers, because they were told a completely different story five years ago. They'll be happy to know they were right all along – not that they ever doubted it for a minute. Well, thank you. Can you have someone drive me back now, please? I'll pass on the information to everyone that you now agree with the villagers that you had the clothes and they disappeared from here. Now, when should I tell them the disappearance happened?' She was relentlessly articulate.

The police officer had become agitated: he'd said too much, and he didn't know how to take the information back.

To increase his discomfort, Amantle said, smiling, 'A pointed finger you can pull back; words you can't take back, officer. Give me the paper: I'll write my own statement.'

'Just talk and I'll write,' he commanded.

'No; you give me the paper, and I write the statement. I don't want any arguments later as to whether I said this or that. The form, please, officer – I'm literate, you know.' She glared back at him.

'How old are you?' he asked. 'Aren't you a TSP?' He was trying to figure out how a girl her age had the guts to question a man wearing police uniform – he was used to dealing efficiently with obedient villagers, regardless of their age.

'What relevance is my age? I'll put it down on the form. Do you want this statement or not?' She was standing firm.

The officer reluctantly handed over the form to her so she could write her statement on it. When she'd finished writing, he read her words and told her he wasn't happy with the result. She took the statement back and looked at it. 'Do you want me to add to the statement that Sergeant Monaana didn't like the information I gave him? That *is* your name, isn't it? You aren't very big on introductions here, are you? I've been passed from man to man, and none of you has ever bothered to introduce himself. Bad manners, you have. Should I make an additional statement about how you want me to change my statement so I put down what you want, not what I know? Is that it?' She was deliberately trying to rile the officer in the hope he'd make more indiscretions as a result of his anger.

Former constable Monaana didn't want any more grief from this obnoxious young woman; he wanted the statement.

However, Amantle insisted she obtain a photocopy of it before she left. 'Where's the copier? I want to make a copy myself,' she stated.

'What do you mean you want to make a copy? We don't make copies of statements to witnesses – and we certainly don't allow witnesses to touch police property!' he thundered back.

'I don't know what I supposedly witnessed. And I'm not giving you this statement until after I have a copy in my hand – so you can arrest me if you want.' She sounded as if she'd welcome being placed under arrest. Inwardly, though, she was scared this inept officer might just be crazy enough to arrest her after all.

Perplexed, the sergeant went off to report to the station commander about the demand the pesky young woman had made. A few minutes later, he returned and told her the station commander wanted to see her. He immediately led her to his superior's office, located further down the corridor.

The station commander's office was large but cramped with all sorts of furniture and broken gadgets. At least three broken fans lay unused in one corner. *The guy must be some kind of hoarding freak,* Amantle thought. *Tasteless decorator as well.* The walls were painted a sickish-looking green. The ceiling, originally white, had big, round, brown stains on it, the result of a leaking roof. The floor had been a common enough cement grey until someone had been given blue paint, and the result was now painful to look at. Amantle figured the disaster must have been recent, because behind the door she could see fresh clumps of blue paint. That the station commander's last meal had included egg or custard was obvious from the blob of yellow on his tie; custard was usually a wedding or Christmas dessert – Amantle thought it was most probably egg.

'Sit down and tell me why you're obstructing police investigations.' This man had a booming voice; it wasn't kind though – it was a voice that was used to giving orders.

'All I want is a copy of my statement – that's all,' she replied simply.

'Why is that important to you?' he bellowed.

'The detective sergeant here has already told me how things tend to disappear from this office. He tells me one of these disappearances involved clothes of a murder victim – sorry, sir, a lion victim. I just don't want my statement to disappear. I know that termites eat papers, and there are plenty of papers around in these offices. I know that disappearances lead to reconstructions – and reconstructions aren't always the truth, are they, now?' She stared back at the station commander, determined she wouldn't be the first to blink.

'You don't believe that story circulated by the villagers that the clothes disappeared from this station, do you now?' The station commander was frowning in feigned puzzlement.

'The sergeant believes it too,' Amantle explained. 'He's the one who told me about it: ask him.' The ghost of a smile appeared on her face as she shot back the instruction.

Sergeant Monaana hung his head. The station commander grunted, then shouted, 'You blubbering idiot! You didn't say that to this girl, now, did you? You're an idiot! How you ever got promoted to sergeant I'll never know!' He was so angry his eyes threatened to leap out of their sockets. He had his hands pressed to the sides of his head, as if he were physically trying to contain the anger.

Amantle decided to rub salt into the wound. 'Some people believe he was promoted precisely *because* he was an idiot, sir: only an idiot would've done such a bad job of covering up for the mysterious disappearance of the clothes, sir. What did you do with the clothes, though, sir? He didn't tell me that.' She repeated the 'sirs' to rile the station commander.

'You can't call a police officer an idiot,' he shot back. 'I'll lock you up for that.' His shoulders leapt forward, and with them his eyes.

Amantle, however, didn't flinch. 'I don't think so, sir. You see, you'd have to arrest yourself first, because you called him an idiot before I did – I only agreed with you. I'll be – what's your terminology again? – Accused Number Two? And you'll be Accused Number One – or do you plan to turn state witness? That'd be so terribly unfair, sir.'

'Just shut up!' the station commander shouted.

'What will be the charge, sir?' Amantle continued on as if the station commander hadn't interrupted her. 'It'll have to read "The accused, Amantle Bokaa, did, on the second day of June 1999, call a brilliant sergeant, promoted for losing, hiding or surrendering to persons unknown, certain exhibits in a ritual-murder case –'

'I said shut up, young girl! If you continue, you'll end up in the lock-up! You think this is a game? And you go around saying this is a ritual-murder case and you'll end up in trouble – I'm warning you!' The station commander was sweating from the effort involved in expressing his anger.

'Nah – you're not going to lock me up. You're all in a pickle, and locking me up will just get you deeper into it. Please show me the copier, station commander. I'm tired, and I want to get back to Gaphala village before sunset. And, sir, I'm sorry to keep on saying this was a ritual murder: of course this was a lion case – or was it hyenas that killed the poor child? I keep on forgetting. What animal was it again, sir?' Amantle pushed the point home. 'Show her the copier and get her out of here. I don't want to ever set eyes on her again. What happened to good-mannered girls? Isn't she just a TSP?' The station commander grunted, and Sergeant Monaana interpreted the sound to mean 'Get out!' He did get out, and in getting out, led Amantle out of the gaudy office filled with salvaged trash.

Amantle made two extra copies of the statement and gave the original to Sergeant Monaana. Soon, she was on her way back to Gaphala, driven in a police van by a young constable. Her attempts to pump him for information, however, proved futile: he sang all the way in order to avoid having a conversation.

As soon as Amantle and the sergeant were out the door, the station commander rang his secretary, Constable Nnono, who worked in an adjacent office. When Constable Nnono, a young man who'd seen Amantle go into his boss's office and who'd eavesdropped on the conversation, took the call, he didn't wait for his boss to tell him what he'd called about. Instead, he took the opportunity to say what was uppermost in his mind. 'Sir, that girl who was here, Amantle Bokaa: wasn't she the one who caused all that trouble at National Stadium last year – I mean when there was that students' march against the army?' The younger police officer's voice was so full of apology he was hardly making sense: he was petrified of his boss, and would have been happier out in the streets, fighting what crime was out there, instead of sitting there, typing away like some little girl and fielding the station commander's calls. He could never understand why the police force didn't hire secretaries as all other government offices did: *Pretty girls wearing short skirts would be good for morale,* was his view.

'*What are you blubbering about?*' the station commander barked; 'get me Mrs Molapo on the phone – *now!* Who's Mrs Molapo – is *that* what you asked me? Why do I have a secretary if I have to figure out simple things like that? "Who's Molapo?" You ask *me*? *Me*?! Do I look like a receptionist to you? Do I look like a constable? Constable, how can you possibly hope to succeed in investigating anything if you can't even remember even the most basic information? God of the Israelites, what I have to deal with! Mrs Molapo is the director of Tirelo Sechaba, okay? Now, get her on the line, now! *ASAP!*'

Constable Nnono wished his boss had listened to him when he'd given him what he was sure was valuable information: that the TSP girl was more trouble than she looked. Also, he was afraid he might be blamed later for not having warned the station commander about her.

However, the station commander was now grunting and shouting, and not listening to anyone.

'Mrs Molapo on the line, sir.' Constable Nnono had now found the phone-call recipient, and now remained on the line in order to listen in. He was afraid of his boss, but viewed eavesdropping as being part of his job: it was one way through which he could figure out who was important and who wasn't – information he needed in order to do his difficult work. Today, when he listened in and found out his boss's plan to get the TSP girl out of the area, he sighed with relief: he, too, agreed she had to be re-assigned as a matter of urgency. However, he decided to remain on the line until the conversation ended.

'Mrs Molapo, this is the station commander at Maun Police Station. I need a favour from you. There's a young girl, by the name of Amantle Bokaa, stationed at the Gaphala Clinic, and we have reason to believe she might be in danger. I can't say too much at present, but I'd suggest you write her an urgent letter re-assigning her to another village – preferably in another district – ASAP!' *The civilian ought to be impressed by the police lingo,* he thought to himself.

'What kind of danger are you talking about?' Mrs Molapo asked. Her first thought was *Another girl being done a favour by a powerful man.* She wasn't going to allow any corrupt practices to flourish in her department: she'd built a reputation for having no favouritism in placements, re-assignments and early terminations, and she wasn't about to jeopardise it at the ring of a phone.

'Like I said,' the station commander began, 'I can't say too much at present: it's a sensitive police matter.' There was firmness in his voice – he believed in being firm when he was dealing with civilians.

'Then may I suggest you put your urgent request in writing, sir?' Mrs Molapo was being equally firm. The current crop of TSPs had been in the field for fewer than two months, and she'd already had about thirty transfer requests from among them, for all kinds of reasons. Although most of the TSPs had cited health reasons, most of their requests had to do with the fact that the young people were reluctant to go to the country's remote outposts. The TSPs from the Gaborone area were the worst of the lot, and Mrs Molapo wasn't about to be tricked into organising a transfer just because some station commander thought the police ruled the world.

Today, she wasn't helped by the fact that that morning, when she'd been driving to work, she'd been held up in the traffic because of what she considered to be an unnecessary police road-block. The whole city seemed to be under construction at present, and the police weren't helping things by installing numerous road-blocks. The drink-drivers were continuing to mow down innocent road users, and the police were setting up annoying roadblocks through which traffic was being held up even more and the police were failing to stem the tide of road accidents. Also, Mrs Molapo hated witnessing the arrogant way in which the police officers spoke to motorists.

'We have very little time, Mrs Molapo,' the station commander advised; 'you need to act now. If you fax me the letter of transfer, we can have the clinic ambulance pick her up and we can have her out within hours.'

'If it's so urgent, why don't you just offer to move her to a safe place for a couple of days – or until the danger's gone? I imagine she, too, wants to be out of the danger. Why do you need a transfer letter from me? And are other government officers being moved from the village? What about the other TSPs in the nearby villages – are you planning to have them moved as well? I have the list here in front of me, and let me see: there are five other TSPs in that cluster of villages. How is it that she's the only one in danger?' Mrs Molapo asked the questions in earnest.

'Mrs Molapo,' the station commander began, 'clearly you don't appreciate the seriousness of this matter. Don't say I haven't warned you if that girl ends up in trouble. I was hoping you could help before we have an innocent girl end up involved in problems she knows little about. Good day, Mrs Molapo.'

'Wait, Mr –'

But the line was dead.

When Constable Nnono heard the click on the line, he again became concerned. He decided he had to go in and inform his boss about the girl, Amantle. For the moment, though, he remained in his office. He walked up to the door and leant against it to make sure he'd know if anyone was opening it; it wouldn't do to lock it. He lit a cigarette, and puffed hungrily and rapidly. He then stubbed out the small remaining portion, walked over to the window and tossed out the butt. He then took out two pieces of gum and chewed them quickly. He swallowed repeatedly, trying to kill the tobacco smell on his breath. For an added oral-hygiene precaution, he pulled out the bottom drawer of his desk, and retrieved and opened a jar of mayonnaise. He scooped a spoonful of the mayonnaise into his mouth, swirled it around in there and swallowed it. He firmly believed that mayonnaise killed tobacco breath. He now felt as ready as he'd ever be to see his boss.

At his superior's door, he paused to straighten his shirt and make sure his belt was in place. He cupped his hands, breathed into them and deeply inhaled the trapped breath. Satisfied, he knocked tentatively. A grunt emanated from the other side; he took it to mean 'Come in,' and he did. His boss always grunted to mean 'Come in,' 'Go away,' 'Stay,' 'Sit,' 'Shut up,' 'Stand up,' and so on: it was for a junior officer to interpret a grunt, and it wasn't uncommon for him to misinterpret one. The consequences of misinterpretation varied from being made to march up and down the yard, like a tin man, to being made to work extra hours. The other officers told a story about how one constable had failed to correctly interpret one of the grunts and been punished by having an overnight stay in one of the station's cells.

As Constable Nnono walked in, the station commander slammed one of his desk drawers shut. There was a secret in that drawer, and the constable planned to find it out one day – *Probably some 'naughty' magazines,* he thought, *or perhaps his traditional medicines*. The station commander was so cunning he'd probably know if anyone ever touched the drawer. The constable hadn't mastered the courage to find out what lay in the drawer that the station commander was always slamming shut whenever he walked into the office. It seemed to him that the more anxious his boss got, the more often he turned to whatever was in the drawer. The constable's curiosity was tamed by the possibility that the drawer contained traditional medicines: he wasn't about to get himself blind or crippled just because he was curious. But still, if magazines of naked women were in there, he thought it'd be great to get a peak once in a while . . .

'What do you want, constable?' the superior officer barked. 'And stand up straight! Are you a police officer, or what? Don't stand there, drooping like mucus from a filthy child!'

'Yes, thank you, sir. Sir, I wanted to tell you that that girl, Amantle Bokaa, caused trouble at National Stadium two years ago, sir. She was the leader of the students who organised the march on National Army Day – the ones who called themselves the Children for Peace, sir. There were riots, sir, and an army officer was fired, sir.' The constable paused: he didn't want the station commander to understand him to be saying that he, the station commander, could be fired. He bit the inside of his lip, and waited.

'Continue,' was the only response.

'I don't know much more, sir – but maybe head office has a report on her, sir. There was a commission of inquiry, because she complained she'd been unlawfully arrested, sir. Then some soldier was fired, and I think two police officers were suspended from duty. There were pictures of her in the papers for weeks. I just thought you should know, sir.' He was trying to read his boss's face: he knew a grunt was coming, and wanted to interpret it correctly. However, when it did come, it was accompanied by two clearly articulated demands: for him to produce all the papers relating to the commission of inquiry and for him to call Detective Sergeant Maladu at headquarters.

Later, while listening in on the phone conversation between his boss and Maladu, Constable Nnono found out that Maladu had been one of the six commissioners appointed to the commission of inquiry. He wasn't happy as a result of hearing the conversation.

He lit another cigarette: as long as his boss remained on the phone, he didn't have to stand by the door to smoke. However, when he finished the cigarette, he decided to chew more gum and down more mayonnaise. It bothered him that by the time he died of cancer caused by smoking, he'd have a mouth full of rotten teeth from the sugar in the chewing gum, and his butt would be spilling over his chair as a result of all the mayonnaise he'd ingested. He thought that if only he could be assigned to real policing, he'd get the chance to walk and exercise, and smoke less. He was already sporting a gut that would be more at home on a man who took home a much bigger pay cheque. His colleagues were teasing him by commenting that he was a constable who had a station commander's figure. He silently blamed his boss for the fact he had a thickening waist, increasingly browning teeth and a hacking morning cough.

CHAPTER 11

Mrs Molapo's curiosity was aroused: something about the call from Maun didn't make sense. She called Amantle at the Gaphala Clinic. 'Is that the Gaphala Clinic? Can I speak to Amantle Bokaa, please?'

Amantle picked up the phone. 'This is Amantle speaking. Who am I speaking to?'

'This is Mrs Molapo from the Tirelo Sechaba office in Gaborone,' came the reply.

'Yes, Mrs Molapo?' Amantle asked.

'Are you in any kind of trouble?' Mrs Molapo enquired.

Amantle decided to be cautious. 'Why do you ask?'

'Because I've just received a very strange call from the station commander in your area: he says you're in some kind of danger, and he wanted you to be transferred out of the village immediately – not just out of the village, in fact, but out of the district. What was it all about?' Mrs Molapo had to know.

Amantle thought fast: she knew she had to come up with a quick and believable story. 'Ah, the station commander exag - gerates – even though I'm sure he means well. It's just that I was asked to clean up an old storeroom, and some people thought it was an unfair task for a TSP. I don't mind at all; I didn't complain. Someone else complained on my behalf without asking me. Yes, I think it's just the storeroom cleaning that caused the problem.' *A bit of truth is better than no truth at all,* she thought to herself.

'Who complained, then?' Mrs Molapo persisted. 'How did the station commander get involved?' She was sure something fishy was going on. She'd expected the girl to jump at the opportunity to be moved to a village closer to shops and other conveniences; it didn't make sense that she didn't even want to be re-assigned.

Amantle had to think quickly again. 'I think it was a police officer. Maybe he thought he was doing me a favour: he kept on saying I shouldn't be cleaning a storeroom – said I should be in a nice village, next to nice things. But Mrs Molapo, I'm fine here. Please don't transfer me: I'm okay – really! I live with a nice family, as well.' She was trying to sound happy and enthusiastic.

Mrs Molapo, however, perceived a flaw in the argument. 'Why was the police officer interested in your work?'

'I really don't know,' Amantle replied. 'I think he'll be transferring to another district himself, and he was feeling sorry leaving me here. I don't even know him that well. He said the station commander liked him and would do him favours; I had no idea he was planning my transfer. I'm sorry you've been troubled over this – there really was no need.' *Let me give her a bit of what she already suspects,* she thought.

'I'm happy to hear that,' Mrs Molapo responded. 'I guess that's the end of the matter, then. I'm happy you've settled in. I guess I was right, then.' She made the final comment more to herself.

'Right about what, Mrs Molapo?' Amantle was being pushy, and knew it.

'Never mind,' Mrs Molapo decided to end the conversation. ''Bye.' She hung up. Still, something persisted in bothering her . . . Then the penny dropped, and she knew what it was: the Bokaa girl had been in the papers about two years ago – something to do with a riot and unlawful arrest. Mrs Molapo suspected the station commander didn't want someone who had her reputation to encroach on his turf. 'Well, tough luck, officer,' she muttered to herself, 'because she's staying right there!' She was happy to contribute to inflicting a bit of pain on a police officer – any police officer. The police weren't her favourite people.

Amantle wondered about the phone call, and hoped Mrs Molapo would maintain her attitude of expressing contradiction towards the police. As she considered her position, she came to the conclusion – not for the first time – that amazing things tended to happen to her. Most probably, the reality was that when amazing things happened, she didn't run away, as most people would: she became intrigued and involved.

There'd been the time, for example, when she was twelve and had told her friends that the school principal wanted to talk to them in her office. When they'd gotten there, she'd told the principal that notwithstanding their parents' orders to the contrary, they were continuing to swim in the river. It was no secret that the river was dangerous: filthy, infested with bilharzia, deep in places, and able to flow swiftly and aggressively without giving much notice of its intention to do so. As a result of her revelation to the principal, her friends had been lashed for indulging their suicidal tendencies and had later lashed Amantle for being disloyal. They'd then ostracised her, by refusing to play with her and putting the word out that she was a 'big mouth' and the principal's favourite. However, they'd stopped swimming in the river. A month later, two girls from their school had drowned while swimming in the same river. Amantle's friends had decided to forgive her, and had encouraged everyone else to do the same.

There'd also been the time she was woken at night from a sweet dream, the details of which she was never to recall, in order to help one of her cousins, who was having a baby. She and the cousin had been at the lands, and their nearest neighbours had been about two kilometres away. Amantle had been thirteen, and had never seriously considered how the baby growing in her cousin's tummy would make its way into the world. Her cousin had already borne three children, and tonight had urgently and sternly instructed Amantle to fetch sand to create a bed to soak away the blood, to sharpen and boil a knife, and later to dispose of the placenta. Amantle had completed all these tasks aided by only the light of the moon. The baby had chosen to arrive two weeks early, on the one night that no adult, other than her mother, was at home to help deliver her.

CHAPTER 12

Things were happening fast, and Amantle was finding herself at the centre of the action. She'd been hoping to spend some quiet time in Gaphala, but she'd quickly begun to realise that her hopes weren't to be fulfilled.

She wondered whether she was headed for another confrontation with the authorities, as had happened during the 'peace march', as the newspapers had dubbed the 1997 students' brave protest march against the army. Amantle had been in Form 4, her second-last year of high school. She'd known she'd been held out as being the leader of the march, but she herself hadn't seen things that way. There'd been Simon Motlotle, who'd called the first meeting and then suggested the students march. Then there'd been Rita Leselo, who'd broken into the school's art room and stolen the paints the students used to make the banners.

Amantle herself had decided to join the march only after she'd been assured it wouldn't involve violence. One of her cousins had been expelled during school riots that had resulted in burning down of the school, injuring of two teachers and arrest of fifteen students. Amantle had had no intention of being expelled, although she'd believed it was necessary to mount some kind of action. She'd then gone about recruiting other students to urge them to join the march. On the day of the march, she'd held the main banner at the head of the line – but despite having taken that prominent position, she'd never described herself as being the leader, as the authorities and newspaper journalists had decided to call her. However, once she'd been labelled in that way, she'd had more urgent matters to deal with than trying to straighten the record.

Today, then, she decided to phone one of her friends: the lawyer Boitumelo Kukama. 'Is that Kukama, Badisa and Co.?' she enquired. 'This is Amantle Bokaa. May I speak to Ms Kukama, please?'

'Hi, Amantle. This is Boitumelo. We were beginning to wonder whether you'd forgotten all about us – "out of sight; out of mind"? We all enjoyed your time here with us. Many clients ask about you. How are you doing?'

'Listen! Listen!' Amantle was impatient. 'The clinic phone is the only phone in the whole village, and I couldn't possibly call before. Now I'm in charge of the clinic, because the nurses are kind of "indisposed", shall we say? The circumstances are bizarre, but I can't elaborate now; I'll call again when I have more time to talk. I just wanted to let you know you might soon be hearing interesting stories about this village and a five-year-old case involving the disappearance of a twelve-year-old girl. Her name was Neo Kakang. Can you look up whatever you can about the case? Everything! Pull out old newspaper reports about the case. Call your friends in the Attorney-General's Chambers and pump them for information. Do you have any friends in the police? Call them and ask them as well. Do it fast, before they get cold feet. As long as they think the case is old and buried, they'll be willing to talk. Tomorrow will be too late: no one will talk to you then. "The brown stuff will be hitting the fan soon,", as you'd say. Remember these names: Detective Sergeant Senai, Detective Sergeant Bosilo, Constable Moruti, and Constable Monaana; I'll give you more names as I learn more. And remember that the ranks are five years old: we're talking "April 1994". And one more thing – and then I must hang up: if I need you, will you come up? I might need a lawyer before long here. I've already been threatened with arrest, but I think that was just to scare me. I know it's a lot to ask, but think about it – don't give me an answer now.'

'Amantle, what are you involved in up there?' Boitumelo enquired. 'I thought TSP was a tame enough assignment. And isn't that village in the middle of nowhere? What could possibly happen out there?' She was both alarmed and excited: she'd been working on a lease agreement and she was bored stiff. What Amantle was talking about had great potential for excitement.

'Two words: "ritual murder"!' Amantle replied. 'I won't say any more at this point – but I'll call later, tonight. And one more thing: can you go and talk to my parents and tell them that whatever they hear over the radio, I'm okay? You know how my father is: worries over nothing. Thank you.' Before she hung up, she promised she'd call again.

She'd become very close to Boitumelo earlier that year, when she was doing a five-month stint with Kukama, Badisa and Co. She'd learnt a lot and enjoyed helping with the firm's legal work. Having the job had been a great way for her to keep busy after completing an especially taxing final two years of high school. It had been during her second-last year as a student that she'd helped lead the group of students – albeit a small group – to mount the protest against the army.

The government had set up a commission of inquiry to investigate the people and circumstances involved in the protest. At the commission's conclusion, an army officer had been fired and two police officers suspended from duty. When Amantle had sued for unlawful arrest, Boitumelo Kukama had become her lawyer. However, the process hadn't unfolded easily, and now, almost two years later, the participants had hardly had time to put the case behind them. It hadn't been helpful for Amantle and the group members that by the time the commissioners started taking evidence from them, in 1998, the group members had become busy preparing to sit for their Form 5 end-of-year exams.

Amantle had had times in which she wasn't sure who the group's friends were. Even some of the students who'd been expected to give evidence had gotten cold feet. Parents had come to the school to tell the principal that their children would rather concentrate on their studies than give evidence. It'd been hard work trying to keep the group intact and getting other students to give the commissioners information about what they knew. The group members had experienced intimidation from all quarters. Kukama and a journalist friend of hers had become Amantle's strongest allies, and had guided and supported her through the ordeal.

In the end, the students had triumphed, but Amantle viewed the triumph as being in many ways limited. For one, the commissioners' final report, which they'd submitted to the Office of the President, had never been made public; Amantle had come to learn rather quickly that a public report wasn't necessarily – in fact was hardly ever – the result of a public inquiry. What little information she'd garnered about the report was in bits and pieces she'd managed to get by way of her pure ingenuity and Boitumelo's persistence. In the report, the commissioners had made various conclusions and recommendations. However, people hadn't complied with all of them, and Boitumelo was even now continuing to push for people to fully comply with them.

After Amantle phoned her, Boitumelo tentatively phoned some friends and acquaintances to find out whether any of them knew about a ritual-murder case that had occurred five years ago in Gaphala. From her enquiries, she drew only blanks, but didn't conclude that anyone was keeping anything from her. However, she realised that five years ago, no one she'd asked would have been a lawyer or police officer. She decided to enlist Nancy Madison, a British law student, to go on a 'fishing expedition': to read newspaper reports about the case, write a report about what she found and make a list of all the names mentioned in the reports.

Within hours, Boitumelo had read enough reports to be convinced that Neo Kakang's disappearance had, in fact, been due to yet another ritual killing for *dipheko*. The circumstances surrounding Neo's disappearance, the fruitless search for her, the community anger, the official position taken were all too familiar. Only two years ago, Boitumelo had been contacted by a social worker from Morule to help a thirteen-year-old girl who'd be - lieved her father had sold her to ritual killers. After the frightened girl had twice fled from the same three men, she'd decided to get help from other people. Boitumelo had interviewed her and gone away convinced the girl had reason to suspect her father of being complicit.

With the help of the social worker and a sympathetic government official, the girl had been transferred to a boarding school located far from her village. The real reason for the quick and surreptitious transfer hadn't been stated in any official document. Boitumelo had kept in contact with the girl over the two years since the incident and had encouraged her to stay at school. All the girl's aides had banked on the reasoning that in two or three years' time, she'd have been too old for the men to view her as being good *dipheko*. Boitumelo had many times wondered which poor, unsuspecting girl had taken her client's place. She'd reasoned it was unlikely that the killers had stopped making plans merely because one girl had been rendered unavailable: they'd had an elected position to win, a business to expand or a promotion to gain – they'd have had to find another girl. Perhaps they'd have to look for her in another village in order to minimise their chances of being detected. Ever since the incident, Boitumelo had been unable to read about a child killed in a crocodile attack, a train accident or a fire without wondering whether the authorities had been covering up a more sinister cause of death.

Today, Boitumelo was wondering what it could be that Amantle had stumbled across whereby the Kakang case had been brought back to life, when her phone rang. It was her secretary, announcing that the next client in the reception area's never ending queue was there to see her.

CHAPTER 13

'Can I speak to the station commander, please? This is Amantle Bokaa at the Gaphala Clinic.' Amantle breathed deeply, to calm herself. She had a vague idea about where she was going with all these developments. *I'll probably end up in gaol at this rate*, she thought to herself: aiding and abetting a kidnapping were serious crimes.

The station commander came on the phone.

'This is Ms Bokaa on the phone – not "TSP"; not "little girl"; not "young lady": do you understand that?' If she was going to rot in gaol for being a kidnapper, she might as well be rude to a station commander: the judge wouldn't increase her sentence because she'd been rude to a senior police officer.

'Who the hell do you think you are to talk to me like that?!' The voice on the other end of the line was, predictably, a bellow.

'You're not listening – if you were, you wouldn't be asking me that question. You will address me as "Ms Bokaa", and I will not call you "old man" or "station commander", or any of those silly names: I will address you as "Mr Badidi" – is that a deal? Good. Now listen. I'm only a messenger here. The villagers want you to know they don't want any SSGs in their village. I'm to remind you that the nurses are still their guests and that the villagers have the clothes. These are the two things you're interested in, aren't they? You're not to circulate any nasty rumours that the nurses are hostages: the villagers want you to know they're not holding any hostages.'

Mr Badidi had choked on his saliva when Amantle referred to SSGs: members of the Special Support Group, a paramilitary-police unit the government called in to quell riots. And when she'd mentioned the word 'hostages', she'd rubbed salt into the wound.

'Young girl –'

Amantle hung up, whereupon the phone immediately rang again. She and the group of villagers around her ignored it. *Let him stew for a while,* they decided. After a while, she called Mr Badidi again. 'If you insist on insulting me, I won't be your go-between. I'm doing you a favour, you know; I don't have to do this.' She didn't believe a word she was saying: she was scared, and wondering where the whole thing would end.

'Yes, Ms Bokaa,' came the meek reply.

'Good: that's a major improvement in your attitude. Now listen. You can either attack this village with your SSGs and arrest everyone or you can listen to what the villagers want: the choice is entirely yours – but the villagers would like you to consider the consequences very carefully. If you chose the first route, you won't find either the nurses or the clothes. You don't have a big enough prison to hold the entire village – and there are children to think of: of course, you might decide to arrest them as well. If you choose to listen to the villagers, you'll have to be patient: they're still consulting among themselves. What will it be, then, Mr Badidi?'

'Can you give me the names of the villagers who are involved?' He was attempting to put the power back where it belonged.

'You'll have to call the Omang Office or the Citizenship Office or the Census Office for that information: the whole village is involved.' Amantle enjoyed delivering that line.

'How about the people in the office with you right now?' he asked, still trying.

'What about them?' Amantle was feigning incomprehension.

'Can you give me their names?' He had to spell out his request.

'Just a minute – let me ask them their names.' She paused before answering. 'Sorry: they refuse to give me their names.'

'You think I'm stupid enough to believe that?' The station commander couldn't quell the tide for one more second: there was a flash of anger in his voice.

'The extent of your stupidity isn't the uppermost concern in my mind right now – so get on to more relevant matters, please.'

'I can't just sit here and let you run things over there – I have to report to headquarters, and they'll decide whether to send in SSGs or not. The minister will expect to be told.' His frustration was seeping down the line, even as he was trying to sound strong.

Amantle continued to call the shots. 'Don't phone yet – give the villagers three hours.'

'*Three hours!*' he shouted. 'Three hours is too long! Some upstart of a constable might call a friend, who'll call a friend, and then the whole thing will take a different turn.' He was on his feet.

'Okay: two hours, then,' she replied, calmly.

'What do you need with the time, anyway?' He simply had to know.

'The villagers want to draw up a petition and have everyone sign it – that will take time. Then they'll invite you in, and you can have the clothes back, and the nurses can go back to their duties. The villagers want you to know they're just as anxious as you to have the nurses back doing their usual job. You see, the villagers are already tired of feeding the nurses and emptying their chamber pots.' *A bit of humour never went astray,* she thought.

'Can I speak to the nurses?' He tried the question on for size. 'How do I know you haven't harmed them?'

'Wait a minute,' Amantle commanded him, and then paused. 'Are you still there?' she went on. 'Here: talk to Staff Nurse Palaki.

Nurse Palaki came to the phone, and Amantle let her begin speaking into the receiver. 'Are you doing –'

However, Amantle considered three words to be enough, so cut the nurse off mid-sentence. 'Are you satisfied now? I'll call you every thirty minutes – and the villagers want you to know that if they so much as smell a helicopter, the deal's off. They'll disappear into the bush – clothes, nurses and all; you can arrest and kill whoever you want then. Remember what happened to the station commander in Sasawe after he was ordered to send in SSGs? You don't want to be the scapegoat, now, do you?' It was an effective question tag through which to finish describing his worst-case scenario.

He, however, remained intransigent. 'I'm not convinced this is the way to handle this, Ms Bokaa: can't we think of another way? What about –'

It was left to Amantle to interrupt him one more time. 'I'll call again in thirty minutes.' She finally hung up, also unconvinced she was handling the matter the right way.

CHAPTER 14

'Can I speak to Ms Kukama, please? . . . Boitumelo, this is Amantle. Listen: things have escalated dramatically. Just listen: I need you up here, or close to here. When was the last time you went camping? Pack the truck as if you're going on a camping trip: yes – tents and all; extra tyres, too. And bring two mobile phones and their chargers: yes – one Vista, the other Mascom; you never know about reception out here. And bring a phone directory. And bring the office cameras – still and video. Yes, the whole "nine yards"; water and petrol as well. Don't forget the mobile phones. Don't let anyone know where you're going. Come with Milly – she deserves this scoop. Send a fax to the Francistown High Court and ask for a judge. Find out who's on duty for urgent cases; then head for Gantsi – no, you're not going to Francistown: "Francistown" is to throw anyone off who might be remembering you'd been asking about the Kakang case. When can you be in Gantsi? I think seven hours; then three more hours should bring you here. And if you can, get a map of the district from Surveys and Lands. No – forget about that: we don't have time for it. I'll call you every hour to give you progress. I have to go: I'm due to call the station commander now. And one more thing: bring your laptop – and paper, of course. Just bring everything necessary for you to prepare legal documents in the bush.'

During the tirade, Boitumelo tried to argue against implementing the plan, but Amantle ploughed ahead. At the end, she explained she didn't have much time, and affirmed she'd phone her friend again later in the day, when she'd listen to her express her reservations. She emphasised, however, that the next few hours would be precious, and that they would in fact be critical.

'What was all that about? You seem pretty agitated – was it your friend again?' It was Nancy Madison, who'd been sitting in Boitumelo's office when Amantle's call came through. She was new in Botswana, and was sure she'd come to the right place. Ever since Amantle's first call, she'd been looking through old newspaper reports about Neo Kakang's mysterious disappearance. She'd also done her own reading about similar disappearances. From what she could find out in the limited time she'd had, it seemed to her that the disappearances always resulted in civil disturbances the government had to quell by sending in paramilitary police. Not much evidence existed that the few arrests the paramilitary police made ever resulted in an actual court conviction. However, so far, she hadn't had much time at all to conduct research into the matter – and her village's small library wasn't about to yield the kind of information she'd need in order to draw that kind of conclusion.

'Yes,' Boitumelo replied, 'that was Amantle. She's on to something big, by the sound of things. She wants Milly and I to go up to meet her.'

'Where's "up"? Nancy asked. 'Can I come?'

Boitumelo replied, 'She's in a village at the edge of the delta – apparently a very beautiful place. I've never been there myself.'

'Really?' Nancy queried. 'The Okavango Delta? That's sup - posed to be one of the last wildernesses on earth, if you can believe all the ads. I'd love to go with you and Milly, if that's okay with you.'

'I don't see why you can't come,' Boitumelo answered. 'But you have to realise it's going to be a long drive – and the roads aren't tarred all the way. What do you have from your research?'

The two women then talked for a while about the information they'd been able to piece together. They worked themselves into a state of excitement at the prospect of trekking across the Kgalagadi Desert. Before Nancy had left England, she'd read a lot about Botswana, and had been hoping that during her six months' stay in the country she'd be able to squeeze in a trip to one of the country's famous game reserves. She'd never thought it would be possible to combine work and pleasure, as she was now destined to do. 'When are we leaving?' she asked Boitumelo.

'First thing tomorrow morning,' Boitumelo replied; 'it's a long drive. If all goes according to plan, we should reach Gaphala around sunset tomorrow. We'll take the Gantsi road – it's shorter in terms of distance, but isn't tarred all the way. That means we'll be slowed down quite a bit during the last three-quarters or so. Are you still into the idea?'

Nancy could barely contain herself. 'Am I? Of course I am! What do you want me to do?'

Boitumelo's tone changed to conspiratorial. 'Keep your voice down – that's the first thing: Amantle doesn't want anyone else to know about our trip. We have someone working within the A-G's Chambers, and if word gets out we're heading to Gaphala, a few doors might be slammed in her face. As it is, she's not sure she'll give us any information, but I think she will. As you can imagine, she's feeling conflict about whether she should be talking to me – so we can't tell anyone just yet where we're going, or why. Brief Milly when she comes in – I'm off to Gaborone to meet Naledi; that's the friend who might or might not talk to me.'

'When will you be back?' Nancy asked. 'Shouldn't we pack tonight if we're leaving tomorrow morning? Exactly what time are we leaving tomorrow? What should I take? And for how long will we be away?' She was a planner, and wanted lists, times and measurements.

'Don't "go British" on me now, okay?' Boitumelo smiled as she said it. The two women had been over this one before the time Nancy had failed the 'faucet test', a test that all Boitumelo's American and British interns had failed. She'd told Nancy, who was staying with her at the time, that the house had hot water. Very few of the village's houses had hot water, so having it had been something worthy of reporting to a new house guest. Next morning, during breakfast, Nancy had reported she'd had a cold shower because there'd been no hot water. Boitumelo had responded, 'I had a hot shower, and you could have, too, if you'd turned on the hot-water faucet.'

'Well, I did,' Nancy had replied, 'and I got cold water.'

However, she'd hastened to add, 'I'm not complaining; really, I'm not – the water wasn't that cold.'

Concentrating on buttering her toast, Boitumelo had responded, 'I guess you've just failed the faucet test.' She'd then reached for the jam jar and wondered why the British, in their exactness, buttered their bread but did not 'jam' it. *Unreliable lot, these British – with language, anyway,* she'd decided. *Just when you think you've figured them out, they slip away.*

'What do you mean?' Nancy had asked, bemused.

'You had two faucets to work with,' Boitumelo had explained. 'You turned on the one with the red dot, expecting it to yield hot water. When it didn't, you concluded there was no hot water. It never occurred to you to try the other one: the one with the blue dot! That's the faucet test. You've just failed it.' She'd smiled as she looked at Nancy. 'I guess your explorer spirit, made famous by all those crude, British brutes who roamed Africa before our time, died a long time ago.'

'Am I missing something? There's a lesson here, is there not?' Nancy had been puzzled: why was her new host being so rude to her?

'Yes, there is a lesson,' Boitumelo had responded; 'a few lessons, really. Forget about your ancestor explorers: they're not part of this lesson – my mind wanders sometimes. Over the next six months, it'll help you to remember this: we're not very big on measurements and timing here. A client tells you she'll be here at 10 a.m.; what she really means is she'll try to be here before lunchtime –'

'And what time is lunchtime?' Nancy had interjected.

'Depends,' Boitumelo had explained. 'Lunchtime is before the afternoon; around 1 p.m. is lunchtime. The lesson here is you don't set aside everything at 10 a.m. waiting for the client: you plan for both her coming and her not coming. You plan things so that if she shows up later, or if she doesn't show up at all, your day isn't shot to pieces. You always have a replacement plan – an "in case" plan.'

'But how can you work with such uncertainty?' Nancy had asked. 'I mean, how can you run an office with such unreliable clients?'

Boitumelo had responded by asking her own question. 'Who said they were unreliable? That red-dot faucet in there is reliable.

It'll yield cold water every time you turn it on – almost always, anyway. Occasionally, someone building a house will dig up a water pipe because no one can remember where the pipes are – but that's a different story. Just like my clients are reliable. They won't always turn up when they've said they will. I rely on that uncertainty, and plan for it. I don't go into a tizz because they're late; I plan for the possibility.'

Nancy had frowned. 'I'm not sure that makes sense at all.'

'And you ask any one of them, "How far is your village from here?" and they'll answer "Not far," or "Very far." If you really want that information, get it from some place else: we don't go around carrying that kind of information in our heads. You ask my clients how old they are, and they'll give you their year of birth. We see no reason to keep working out our age on a yearly basis, when we can keep just one date in our heads. That's just the way we figure things. It's different, perhaps, because we have different priorities. What I'm saying is if something doesn't make sense to you, stop and wonder whether it isn't *you* who doesn't have the right frame of mind to figure it out. All I ask of interns is that they approach everything with an open mind. This isn't Manchester; this isn't Britain: be prepared for the unfamiliar.' Boitumelo had admirably bridged the cultural gap by applying and explaining the faucet test.

'Well, thanks,' Nancy had responded. 'No doubt I have a lot to learn; I never thought otherwise. But I'm curious: did you switch the faucets deliberately?'

'No,' Boitumelo had replied, 'I didn't. But of course I could have warned you about them. You'll find many faucets like that in many houses. You might come across two red dots or two blue dots. Perhaps there's a prankster of a plumber on the loose in this country – but then perhaps it's just another demonstration of our motto: "There's no hurry in Botswana." Knowing which faucet is the right one would no doubt save all of us, collectively, a few thousand seconds every morning. I guess we've decided that losing a second here, a minute there, and an hour – and sometimes a day – there is okay.'

Nancy had required more convincing. 'You have no problems with all this? I can't imagine how anything can be accomplished in a climate like that.'

114

Boitumelo had started packing her briefcase in preparation for going to work. 'Some people say we're lazy and unproductive. Perhaps they're right – of course there's some truth in it. But don't let anyone catch you saying it. You watch today: we'll get to the office, and at least one worker won't be there. There'll be a note – if I'm lucky, there'll be a note – saying a relative's ill, dead or dying. Most relatives are ill, dead or dying on Mondays – especially Mondays after pay days. Someone ought to do a study into how the relatives of all workers suffer health hazards brought about by "Monday after pay day" – it's a particularly unhealthy day, I tell you: sometimes the workers are afflicted themselves!'

Nancy had smiled. 'I gather you're not too happy after all about the red-dotted faucet that yields cold water.'

Boitumelo had smiled back. 'Come on! Let's go to the office. You'll love the work; chaos and lack of certainty will only add to the excitement.'

The faucet-test discussion had taken place a month before the call from Amantle came through. Having been reminded of it, Nancy now smiled, and raised her hands in mock surrender. 'All right! All right! No timing; no measurements.'

'On a more serious note,' Boitumelo began, here's a list of stuff we need to pack. Just feel free to look through the house; there's stuff in the storeroom as well. Tell everyone you and Milly will be working at home today – an "urgent application". And don't forget to have my secretary call Francistown about a judge – that's just to add credibility to our story about an urgent application. I'll be back before six this evening; call me if anything comes up.' She was already out the door and hurrying away. However, she turned back to add, 'I was kidding: please, do "go British" on me on this – we can't afford to forget anything. Make up a list of what you think we'll need if we end up on a dirt road, away from petrol stations, mechanics, food stores and phones. There won't be an alternative faucet to try – unless we bring it! Thanks! See you this evening.'

CHAPTER 15

As soon as Amantle finished her phone conversation with Boitumelo, she addressed the group of villagers around her. 'Let's start by agreeing on what we want, what you want.' She was undoubtedly the leader: through finding the box, she'd become the central person in the affair. Also, because she was standing up to the police, she'd earnt the villagers' respect. By now, the clinic had evolved into being the nerve centre of the events taking shape.

Mma-Neo was the first to respond. 'I want the truth from the police. I want to know who killed my daughter. I want to know why they're protecting the killers; why they lied to me, to all of us. I want her body so I can give her a proper burial – even if it's just bones.'

An old man whose cheeks had collapsed piped up. 'We want to keep the clothes. We want a divination to find out the truth; to find the killers.' His teeth had long vacated his old mouth. His eyes were white with cataracts, and his hair was sparse and coarse; it hadn't come into contact with a comb for quite a while.

The next person to speak was a woman who tended to clap her hands to emphasise a point. Because of her thin frame and her fondness for the hand and shoulder gesture, she had the look of a praying mantis. 'Yes: a divination is important. We want to find out who sent the clothes here, and why. We want to see the killers by means of the bones.'

Rra-Naso was next, and his tone was one of earnestness. 'I think we must be careful here. A child was killed brutally five years ago. My heart goes out to you, Mma-Tebogo, but what are we planning for the two nurses? We must not spill blood to revenge the spilling of blood.' He frowned, and squeezed his eyes; he seemed to be going through pain. He rubbed his small finger, which was deformed from the past injury.

'The nurses are our insurance against an attack: we can't let them go.' This was a firm and uncompromising statement from the praying mantis.

Rra-Naso qualified his statement. 'I'm not saying we must let them go. But can we agree, right now, that no harm is to come to them? I'm an old, tired man; my heart can't take the spilling of any more blood.' The old man begged with his eyes, with his frail body. His body then went into spasm as he became gripped by a coughing fit. You wouldn't have had to be a nurse to see he was suffering from some chronic chest infection.

Another voice rose above the crowd. 'They were never nice to us anyway. They insulted us and called us dirty. They resented being here and made us know it every single day. They lived in their nice little houses and never thought we were important enough to deserve a visit from them. Why should we care what happens to them?'

Rra-Naso now couldn't help spitting over some of the villagers as he simultaneously coughed and spoke. 'You must care, because your conscience will never let you forget. You must let them live – not just for them but for yourselves.' It was hard to ignore the pleading expression in his eyes. Out of politeness, no one acknowledged the raining spittle.

A middle-aged woman now had a turn at speaking. 'We all know, Rra-Naso, that you've been affected by the death of Neo very much. I'm sure Mma-Neo appreciates the many times you've gone over to her house to offer her comfort. We all know your son's been almost like a son to Mma-Neo: hauling wood; bringing in the goats and the donkeys. But you can't go soft just because you've been so saddened.'

Rra-Naso considered the words, and then responded. 'Listen, please: I'm not long for this world: this TB will kill me soon, if my heart doesn't just stop. Please hear me; listen to me. Don't spill blood: you'll never be able to wash it off. Make a promise not to spill blood – ever; otherwise, I'm out this door, and I'll be your Judas: I'll give you to the police – unless, of course, you want to spill mine as well: I'm not long for this world anyway, so killing me won't be a major loss.'

Silence ensued: it was clear that Rra-Naso was serious about his threat and challenge.

It was Mma-Neo who finally broke the silence. 'I agree with Rra-Naso: you can't wash away blood with more blood. The nurses aren't to be harmed – but we don't have to tell the police that, do we?'

It fell to an older man to state the conclusion. 'The mother has spoken: the nurses will not be harmed.' There was general agreement among the villagers, and sighs of relief ensued all round. Rra-Naso exhaled, and was immediately seized by another bout of coughing.

Some of the villagers murmured about how Rra-Naso had been affected by Neo's death: 'Neo would be the same age as Naso – seventeen, she'd be.' 'A man with a white heart, Rra-Naso; this has aged him before his time.' 'Such a sweet man; so much love. He's supported Mma-Neo through her ordeal – a good man.'

In response to the compliments and expressions of sympathy, Rra-Naso reached for and squeezed Mma-Neo's hand. He then closed his eyes and furrowed his brow, as if in pain. It was obvious he was embarrassed by the villagers' sympathetic looks and comments. 'It's Mma-Tebogo who needs your sympathies, not me. I'm just a weak old man: don't mind me.'

Amantle decided to interrupt the meeting by placing another call to the Maun police-station commander. 'This is Ms Bokaa. Is that Mr Badidi? I see you're answering your own phone now – that's good: cut out the middleman; waste of time.'

Badidi wasn't in the mood for sarcasm. 'Can you please cut out the drama? This is serious.'

Amantle wasn't in the mood for beating around the bush either. 'What's serious, Mr Badidi – that you lied to the villagers, or the reason you lied? The child was the subject of a ritual murder, wasn't she?'

His response was weak. 'I'm not ready to answer that question at present.'

'Well,' Amantle commented in reply, 'at least you've moved on from your lion story: that's a development. I have a message for you from the villagers – and don't ask me their names, because they refuse to tell me them. First, no government vehicle is to come into the village.'

Badidi felt deflated, first up. 'How can I control that?'

Amantle pushed on. 'Find a way; I can't think of everything, Mr Badidi: I'm only a TSP, remember? Who's due to come, anyway? Only the Old Age Pension people. Tell them something – the road isn't passable; or better still, hide their petrol: you're good at hiding things, if that's what happened to the clothes. All government vehicles have to be refuelled at your station. Lose the key to the pump: put it in a box, label it, and put it in the exhibits locker – it'll show up here in five years' time.'

'Okay; okay,' he conceded, 'you've made your point. Then what? I can't keep a lid on this thing forever.'

Amantle felt it was time to put the next question to him. 'What's the source of your anxiety?'

'The nurses, of course,' came the reply.

'The nurses are fine,' Amantle assured him. 'They've chosen to remain here, though. They're free to go, but they've chosen to remain; that goes for me as well – no more calls to the TSP office to try to get me transferred.'

'Let me speak to the nurses,' he beseeched.

'Not now,' Amantle replied; 'they're seeing patients.'

'I don't believe you,' he stated, point blank.

Amantle had the next line ready to go. 'Neither did the villagers when you said Neo was killed by lions.'

'I wasn't even here then,' came the true response.

'Yes,' Amantle concurred. 'And just keep in mind why your predecessor was retired early, on a lean pension: he covered up for other people. Or perhaps he was in partnership with the killers – and I'm not talking about the phantom lions.'

He got the picture. 'What are your plans?'

'To continue as the messenger between you and the villagers,' came the curt reply.

119

Accordingly, he changed the possessive pronoun from second to third person. 'I mean what are *their* plans?'

'They want the following,' Amantle began. 'Listen carefully. First, they want the Minister of Labour and Home Affairs, or whoever's the minister in charge of children's affairs. Is there such a minister? Well, find out. If there isn't, create one; there should be one. Second, they want the head guy – real top guy – in the police. That'd be the Minister for Safety and Security. And the Chief of Police, of course. And the following officers: Constable Moruti; Constable Monaana; Detective Sergeant Senai; Detective Sergeant Bosilo; and that guy who was your predecessor. And find out the name of the head of that laboratory in Gaborone who analyses blood in murder cases – would that be the forensic laboratory? Just get the name. That's all. Your next job is to locate all these people; find out where they are. Your predecessor's probably scratching his bum somewhere at a cattle post; find out where. The villagers are working on a petition to present to all these people – and they don't plan to go to Gaborone to present it; Gaborone's coming to them. You'll be told when the petition's ready. They're not very literate, so it's kind of a painful process – writing, that is, and getting signatures and thumb prints; tedious process, that.'

He went back to one of his earlier questions. 'Can I talk to the nurses?'

'No,' Amantle insisted; 'you can't; they're busy, as I've already told you. I'll call you again in thirty minutes.'

Badidi decided to appeal to her on a personal level. 'I'm under pressure to do something here: the other officers are looking to me to make the next move.'

Amantle had her direction at the ready. 'Tell them you're talking to Gaborone; stall them; use your brains. I'll call you in thirty minutes; then we'll be ready to roll. Get all your vehicles ready: there's going to be a party. Just remember it's in your interests to wait, for one simple reason: if you act prematurely, there might be violence, and if there's violence, you'll be blamed – that you can be sure of; I don't have to tell you.'

Before Mr Badidi could respond, the line went dead.

120

CHAPTER 16

Naledi Binang looked much younger than the twenty-five years she'd clocked up; she could, in fact, have passed for eighteen. She was therefore accustomed to receiving plenty of compliments from her friends and colleagues. However, she was also accustomed to having people dismiss her as being a little girl; they often forgot she was a professional

Today, she found herself trying to sit up straighter, hoping to seem older and more mature. The task was made all the more difficult because directly in front of her was sitting a rather large colleague whose broad shoulders were almost entirely obscuring her view of Mr Pako. She and her colleagues had been lawyers for fewer than forty-eight hours, and were being blessed with the presence of the legendary man, who now declared, 'There are good lawyers and there are bad lawyers; there are more bad lawyers than there are good ones. It's up to you what type you choose to be. None of you are dumb, otherwise you wouldn't be here. But being a good lawyer means being more than just "not dumb" – it's about passion; it's about commitment; it's about pride in your work. Any questions?'

This year, as head of the Prosecution Division of the Attorney-General's Chambers, Mr Pako was walking ten law graduates through their first briefing session. His short temper was legend - ary, and people said he'd once marched out of his office, across the expanse of lawn in front of it, through the main mall, past the university, and all the way to the Magistrate's Court buildings, wearing full court robes – on a swelteringly hot day! People also said that hopping behind him, also wearing full court robes, had been a new lawyer who'd been arrogant enough to contradict Mr Pako although the young man had been a lawyer for fewer than forty-eight hours. People said the conversation had gone something like this: 'Young man, you graduated only this past Saturday, right?'

'Yes sir,' the young lawyer had replied.

'Go and robe for court: you and I are going to court!' Mr Pako had bellowed.

People said that the young man had hesitated: he'd thought that either he was in the presence of a mad man or it was meant to be a joke; he'd no doubt been hoping for the latter explanation.

Mr Pako had then bellowed again: 'Young man, I said go and get your robes! And as for the rest of you, you sit right where you are: no one move!'

People said that the formally attired odd couple had collected all kinds of spectators as they made their way to court: the fat, sweating man and the small, embarrassed one; the determined, marching man followed by the mortified, hobbling one. People said that at the Magistrate's Court, Mr Pako had interrupted a trial and announced that the most brilliant lawyer the country had ever known would be taking over the proceedings. People said that Mr Pako had then sat down and commanded the young man to take over the trial.

The sitting magistrate, however, had decided to challenge Mr Pako: 'Mr Deputy Attorney-General, with respect, there's a trial in progress: you can't just barge in and take it over. And why are you robed? This is the Magistrate's Court, not the High Court.'

People said the magistrate hadn't challenged Mr Pako without feeling trepidation, because Mr Pako didn't reserve his temper outbursts for new lawyers. Similar to the young lawyer accom - panying Mr Pako, the magistrate had been new to his position and been much younger than Mr Pako.

Mr Pako had then let rip. 'I'm the head of the Prosecution Division of the Attorney-General's Chambers of the Republic of Botswana, and I'm charged with all prosecutions in this republic. I can and *will* come in any time, anywhere, anyhow!'

Perhaps people had made up parts of the story; perhaps there'd been only a threat; perhaps the odd couple had gone only as far as the main mall; perhaps they'd driven, not walked. However, people never doubted that Mr Pako was liable to erupt when annoyed by the slightest irritant. People didn't call him Mount Vesuvius – 'Mount V' for short – simply because of his mountainous proportions; it was also because of his tendency to erupt like a volcano.

Thus it was that Naledi and the other new lawyers nodded their heads in agreement with him and tried to look intelligent without saying anything. They were elated to at last be where they were. The government was training only about twenty lawyers a year, and Naledi and her colleagues were among this year's chosen few. Today, nevertheless, they were petrified of Mount V. Naledi craned her neck in order to see him better, but withdrew her head at the first sign Mount V was looking her way.

Naledi hadn't wanted to be posted to the Prosecution Division; she'd been hoping for the Drafting Division, or even better, the Lands Division. Working in the Prosecution Division, she'd no doubt come into contact with thieves, thugs and other undesirables. And among the members of the list headed 'Undesirables', she counted criminal lawyers: she was convinced it was impossible for lawyers who practised criminal law to remain untainted by the accused with whom they came into contact. She wasn't too keen to become a component of the sleaze she associated with a prosecutor's work. She knew two lawyers working in the Drafting Division, and both of them were civilised and ladylike. They each drove a nice car and lived in a nice neighbourhood. She knew only one prosecutor, and he was always either hitching a ride from a friend or coaxing his old venture van to make one more trip to the office. Whenever she encountered the lurching van, with its sick sound and smoke, she thought it quite clear that the van would rather not have been bothered to make the effort. She was aware that her group's male lawyers believed prosecution to be the most glamorous of the three divisions, but couldn't imagine how anyone could possibly consider it glamorous to have criminals in close proximity. Had it been up to her to choose her division, she wouldn't be sitting on this chair today, craning her neck and withdrawing her head to the tune of Mount V's sharp looks delivered in sideways sweeps.

Naledi had long known that within government circles, people were usually discouraged from making choices. Employees were likely to be assigned jobs they'd rather not do, and equally, if employees showed enthusiasm for a job, it was usually a prerequisite for not getting to do it. Naledi was convinced that this culture whereby the powerful thwarted the desires of the less powerful wasn't limited to her profession: a police officer who said he was fond of traffic work was more likely to be assigned desk work, and a student who declared she was interested in computer science was more likely to be forced to go into nursing. When Naledi had indicated she wanted to work in the Lands Division, her new boss had announced that she wasn't hired to be hidden away, and without even enquiring about the reasons for her preference, had informed her she was to be assigned to the Prosecution Division. Perhaps, had she kept quiet, she'd have been assigned to the Lands Division after all.

Mount V spouted forth. 'Now, all of you: I want you to go back to your offices and start reading the Penal Code and the "CP and E". Understand? Because each one of you will be in court before this month is over. Understand?' Even his voice rumbled like an erupting volcano. His eyes blazed across each graduate, and his double chin wobbled threateningly.

Back in the graduates' offices, Naledi once again started to think of ways to get out of the Prosecution Division. The division was also known as Pompeii – the Ancient Roman city that was buried when Mount Vesuvius erupted, in the year 79 – because the division was a veritable pressure-cooker. And it didn't help that its employees had to work under constant threat of volcanic eruption. 'I need to find a way to get out of Pompeii – what about you?' Naledi was asking Linky Motlhatlodi, her office mate. To share an office with him was yet another choice she'd never have made.

'Just forget it, okay?' Linky responded. 'Mount V's not going to let you. And with your grades, he wants you here. He might let me go, just to get rid of me: he's already told me he doesn't like my attitude – as if I like his! But you? Forget it: just enjoy being buried.' He was smiling; he'd always been an irritatingly happy-go-lucky person. He was always 'just making it', and saw no reason to put in any more effort than was required. At law school, he'd done just enough to pass and waited till the last minute to hand in his assignments.

'The guy frightens me – he's demented, if you ask me.' Naledi was paging through a copy of the Penal Code. 'And it's crazy he can expect us to just read this thing – I mean, I can't believe that's how a new lawyer's supposed to spend her first days at work. Do you think he'll give us a quiz or something?'

'"Or something"!' Linky replied. 'Now, no one's ever been able to accurately predict what Mount V's likely to do – so, like I said, just relax and enjoy the lava. You'll live: he hasn't killed anyone – yet.' He was shuffling his deck of cards; for as long as Amantle had known him, he'd had a deck of cards in his hands.

'You're enjoying this, aren't you? You're as demented as he is.' Naledi shook her head: over the five years she'd been with Linky in the same class, she'd never quite gotten used to his carefree, almost irresponsible attitude.

'No,' Linky replied. 'I'm not enjoying this. But to tell you the truth, I don't care, either: I'm not going to let some fat, crazy man get on my goat. This is a government office; there was work here long before we were ever hired; there'll be work long after we've died – so I plan to work at my own pace and no one else's. Do you know it's almost impossible to get fired from a government job? And you get promoted every two years, whether you work or not: great deal, I say!' He then invited Naledi to join him in a game of casino. She declined, whereupon he started up a round of solitaire.

Naledi couldn't keep quiet. 'I don't think that's the right attitude – and I don't think you should be playing a game of cards during working hours.' Secretly, though, she was hoping Linky's poor attitude would engender Mount V's fury and that the man-mountain would thereby ignore her a bit more. She found herself thinking about Mary, the graduate in the next office, who was an obsessive nail polisher and make-up repairer: how was she going to survive there, in Pompeii? People said that Mount V didn't hold women in very high esteem: he considered they lacked the stamina he believed was required in order to practise law. He'd already shouted at Mary that a mirror wasn't one of a lawyer's tools of trade. Naledi, however, had thought that he himself needed a mirror: his reluctant beard, and his hairy nostrils and ears, were desperately in need of attention. His face reminded her of a patch of desert on which clumps of dry but determined vegetation had settled. Naturally, though, she wasn't about to suggest he use Mary's mirror: it was Naledi's plan that with reference to Mount V, she'd do no suggesting whatsoever.

Six months after her 'baptism by fire', Naledi was still trying to find an interesting way in which to read the Penal Code, which Mount V was repeatedly telling the twenty employees they had to know by heart. Then, one day, the phone rang and she was summoned to Mount V's office. So far, the employees' assignments had been to read very simple dockets, draft charge sheets, deal with inquest dockets and accompany more-experienced counsel to court. Outside the offices, or 'chambers', as Mount V insisted the premises be called, all the employees pretended to be knowledgeable. Inside, however, all of them dreaded the day Mount V would give them a docket and tell them they must obtain a 'Guilty' verdict. His attitude was that it was unacceptable to have a lower than 80 per cent conviction rate – after all, he said, the police weren't in the habit of going around arresting innocent people. Stories abounded about how, on the day of a trial, he'd 'sprung' an unprepared young counsel by re-assigning the senior counsel and instructing the poor, petrified young one to take over the trial. Therefore, whenever an employee's phone rang and it was Mount V, not his secretary, on the line, the standard joke was to cover the phone and whisper to everyone, 'Mission Burial!', in reference to the fact that a volcanic eruption was imminent.

Today, then, it was Naledi's turn to whisper, 'Mission Burial!'

'Enjoy the heat,' Linky responded, grinning.

'I'll be over right away, sir,' Naledi said into the phone.

Once she'd entered her boss's office, she was met with a pair of appraising eyes – almost as if he were reconsidering his decision to call her into the office.

After giving her a lengthy stare, whereby she was caused great discomfort, he pushed a file towards her. 'Ms Binang, I want you to read this and tell me what you make of it. Give me a written opinion.'

'When do you want the opinion, sir?' Naledi asked. She had no idea how a lawyer went about formulating an opinion.

'I want it before the end of today, Ms Binang,' he replied promptly; 'typed and signed, by 4.30 p.m.'

Naledi blurted out, 'The file –'

On hearing the two words, Mount V had no option but to correct his junior. 'We don't have *files* in these chambers: this isn't just any other government office! We have *dockets*. Understand? *Dockets*. Do you think you can remember that?'

'Yes, sir,' Naledi quickly answered. 'I think I can remember "docket" – no problem.' She added the last two words with a tinge of defiance.

Mount V looked at her, the young lawyer, but decided to let the moment pass. His mood was one of calm; it seemed that no eruption was in sight – but then his legendary eruptions weren't always preceded by rumbling. 'What did you want to ask?'

'Nothing, sir,' Naledi replied. She'd decided that whatever questions she had in her mind she'd ask one of the division's older lawyers: she knew at least two who'd help if she asked.

'And you're not to consult anyone about this matter: this is a confidential matter – no discussions with anyone about any aspect of this case! Now, go and get cracking.' He continued to look at her as if he weren't sure she was the right person for the assignment.

When Naledi got back to her office, she examined the cover of the docket before she read the documents enclosed. On the front of the docket was the title 'Neo Kakang: CRB 45/94'. The docket was five years old and comprised statements from various people, some of whom were police officers. Its contents told a story about a child who'd disappeared and never been found. Although the docket wasn't very thick, Naledi thought Mount V was asking too much to give her only one afternoon to read and formulate an opinion about its contents. She resolved to deal with the matter then and there rather than have to offer apologies about her handling of it later. She phoned Mount V to tell him it was her opinion that she'd need more than one afternoon in order to complete the assignment.

On hearing the summation, unable to believe that the young woman could be so audacious, the man-mountain choked on a scone he'd been enjoying. 'Ms Binang, I don't remember asking you for an opinion about how long it'd take for you to do what I asked; I remember distinctly asking for your opinion about substance, not procedure. Do you know the difference? Now get cracking.' And with that, he hung up, having considered the matter closed.

However, Naledi phoned gain, and stood firm. As a result, Mount V extended her deadline to 4.30 the following afternoon. She was proud she'd stood her ground. Unbeknowns to her, Mount V was also impressed, at having a new lawyer who had some spirit in her. He was looking forward to experiencing a bit of fireworks between them.

Linky overheard the call as he was leafing through an inquest docket. 'You don't know how to keep away from a fire now, do you?'

'Shut up,' Naledi retorted.

'I can do that – I've been known to do it.' Linky wasn't in the least offended by Naledi's command: it took more than that to get him agitated.

Now, relieved she had a more humane deadline, Naledi started to read the contents of the docket. She decided she'd read it as she would a book: from front to back. Once she started reading, she became so absorbed she failed to notice that time was flying by.

At 4.30, Linky, who'd as usual been playing solitaire for at least half an hour, gathered his deck of cards and prepared to leave. He'd calculated that if he stole thirty minutes of government time every day until he took his optional retirement at age forty-five, he'd have been paid the equivalent of about sixteen months' wages without having worked for it. He'd decided it was brilliant that it was actually possible to pull off the rort. Pausing at the door, he looked back at his office mate and said, 'The beauty of all this is that when they promote you, they'll promote me too. In tandem we'll rise, and in tandem we'll be stalled as the road narrows. Isn't it brilliant? Then, one day, you'll get fed up, and leave to test your skills somewhere else. And then, *viola!* I'll become attorney-general: the Attorney-General of the Republic of Botswana, Mr Lincoln Mapetla! Don't you just love life? The good thing is that unlike a teacher or a nurse, I can't be transferred to some small vil - lage somewhere, like, say, Mabutsane or Rakops. Isn't a lawyer's life great?' He closed the door behind him, and Naledi could hear his laugh bouncing off the long corridor. He laughed even as he passed Mount V's door, and rather than gently close the door that led to the stairs, as almost everyone else closed it, he banged it shut.

Naledi stayed on, reading. She thought about taking the file home, but decided against it: she didn't know the procedure for taking a docket home, but thought there might be a register for recording dockets removed from the office. She was in her seventh month as a lawyer, and still had more to find out about in the area of office procedures before she could simply open her briefcase, stuff in it an official docket about a girl's disappearance and take the docket home: what if she were to lose it? And she was nervous at the thought of having the docket with her on the bus.

When she'd finished reading the material, she read it again: something wasn't right about it, but she couldn't put her finger on it. She finally left the office, having promised herself that when she got home she'd jot down some notes about what was bothering her. By the time she left the office, the April sun had disappeared and left in its wake yellows, blues, purples, greys and reds. She hurried to the bus stop and travelled home in a pensive mood.

From what she'd read, Naledi discovered that Neo had disappeared five years ago. From the witnesses' statements, it was clear that the villagers believed Neo had been killed for the purposes of what southern Africans call *muti* and what in the Setswana language is called *dipheko*. The villagers believed that some 'big men' had wanted to 'harvest' human parts in order to either strengthen the men's business or maintain their position of power. Naledi couldn't remember hearing or reading any media reports about the case, but what puzzled her more was why the docket had been unearthed now. She deduced that something was afoot, because only yesterday Boitumelo Kukama had phoned her and asked vague questions about a five-year-old ritual-murder case. Boitumelo was a good friend, and they occasionally played basketball together. Her phone call had been strange in that she'd tried to make light of the matter even as she was asking for information. Then there was the docket itself: Naledi was sure it was incomplete, and sensed that some of the statements in it contained inconsistencies. The statements also contained crudely executed alterations.

In the small, cramped bus, music blared out, the fare collector shouted at the passengers to make room for others, and passengers liberally offered their opinions about what was wrong with this and that minister. Naledi continued to think about the docket in the office. She always found the bus's passengers to be the best source of news; tonight, though, she was so preoccupied with thinking about the file she'd just left behind that she was hardly listening to the conversations. By the time she got off the bus, she'd resolved to call Boitumelo in order to find out more about 'CRB 45/94'.

CHAPTER 17

B oitumelo was just as anxious as Naledi to make contact. She was the first to get to the phone, and when Naledi answered it, Boitumelo suggested they discuss their business over dinner rather than over the phone.

A few hours later, the two friends were chatting at their favourite restaurant, the Grill and Papa. After they'd finally ordered their meals, it was Naledi who brought up the business they were there to discuss. She opened with 'What's your interest in this old case, anyway?'

'What's yours?' Boitumelo countered.

Naledi looked seriously at her friend. 'You made the first call, remember? And you're not a criminal lawyer. So, what's your interest in a five-year-old case about an alleged ritual murder?'

'I'll be honest with you,' Boitumelo replied; 'I don't know. I'm asking the questions on behalf of a friend who tends to get herself deep into messy issues. She's asked me to find out, and I'm trying to do it – so far, with few results! Two days ago, the responses I got were honest, blank faces; now, they're cagey expressions. So, you tell me: what's going on?' She looked at Naledi to determine whether she'd get an expression of blankness or caginess.

Instead, she got an expression of puzzlement. 'I don't know how much I can tell you; all I can say, at this point, is that the file – no, not "file": "docket"; apparently in our chambers we have no files, only dockets! Why are you lawyers so arrogant? My word!' Naledi let her first response remain unfinished.

Boitumelo chuckled. 'Does that large elephant still think he's king?'

Naledi replied, 'No one's had the guts to disabuse him of that belief, so yes. But to get back to the point, he pulled out this old docket and told me he wants an opinion – just like that – so I spent the afternoon reading it.'

'And?' Boitumelo queried.

'And wouldn't you know?' Naledi was glad to finally deliver the punchline. 'It turned out to be the same case you were asking about only yesterday! And I can't tell you any more, because I don't know where you're coming from. So, unless you level with me, this is all you're getting from me.' They might have been friends, but they were also members of an adversarial legal system.

Boitumelo decided to try another tack. 'But you know I'm not a criminal lawyer: why would telling me be a problem?'

It was clear, however, that Naledi wasn't about to budge from her position. 'Mount V has given me instructions not to talk to anyone – that's one good reason. Second, I have a bad feeling about this. Until I know more, and that includes about your interest, I'm saying very little – even to you, girl friend.'

'Okay, then,' Boitulemo conceded; 'let me give you what I have. But you have to promise to keep it confidential. I know I can trust you.'

However, before Boitumelo could go on, Naledi interrupted. 'I haven't made any promises yet – let's make that clear between us. I don't know where this is going, therefore I can't promise not to pass it on or use it. I'm a prosecutor, remember? Or at least I'm trying to be one.' She smiled: it was a bit of an exaggeration to call herself a prosecutor.

Boitumelo now tried to suggest that the two women belonged to the same camp: the 'justice and truth' camp. 'It might well be that our interests are the same – so hear me out. My friend believes there was a police cover-up five years ago. Something's happened recently – perhaps new information's surfaced. But she's con - cerned that another cover-up will take place unless people who care about justice and truth do something.'

Naledi was intrigued. 'Why does she think there was a cover-up five years ago?'

'I don't know,' came the honest reply.

Naledi asked the next obvious question. 'Why does she suspect another cover-up's planned?'

Boitumelo's reply was identical: 'I don't know.'

Naledi pressed on. 'What's brought this case to light again?'

'I really don't know,' came the next honest reply.

'You don't know much, do you?' Naledi couldn't help herself.

'No,' Boitumelo shot back; 'do you?'

'No.' Naledi let herself flash a little smile.

The two women returned to their food, and ate in silence for a while.

Naledi finally broke the silence. 'You know, you're considered bad news in government circles: you expose a lot of rot that many would rather leave buried. But the criminal area isn't where most would expect to see you; Mount V would positively erupt if he knew you were sniffing around his sacred ground.'

'Actually,' Boitumelo began, 'you're wrong: we *are* interested in criminal law; it's just that our area of interest hasn't been classified as criminal law – yet! I think wife beating's a crime, as is marital rape! as is refusing to care for your offspring! as is abuse of power! as is closing women out of the army and customary courts! as are many other discriminatory practices no one wants to even name, let alone tackle! But that's another discussion altogether . . . My friend, Amantle: you remember Amantle Bokaa, don't you?'

For Naledi, Amantle's reputation preceded her. 'That's the girl who caused all that pain for the riot police two years ago, no?'

'No! No! No!' Boitumelo corrected her friend. 'Why does everyone say that? Amantle caused nothing: *she* suffered the pain. As for the police pain, it was self-inflicted: the system "looked the other way" for years, and Amantle just forced it to look at its ugly secrets – that's all.'

'Okay!' Naledi conceded. 'Don't bite my head off! I didn't mean it like that – but is she the student responsible for the commission of inquiry into police brutality? The fallout from that's still causing a lot of angst in the riot-police section – what with you making all kinds of demands! Yes, my friend, the word is you're to be avoided at all costs; you're poison.'

'So, what are you doing talking to me?' was Boitumelo's reasoned question.

'Because we're friends,' Naledi replied; 'because I think you're doing work that has to be done. Go on: tell me why Amantle has this great sixth sense that a five-year-old case, which has been deliberately covered up, according to her, is being covered up again. Why would she know all that? How would she know all that?'

Boitumelo could only tell what she knew. 'I honestly don't have the details. But my sense is that a major news story is about to break. Amantle's a TSP in Gaphala, where the little girl disappeared. She's made some discovery, which, if no one moves fast enough to suppress it, will mean the case is reopened. She suspects that by tomorrow, something big will have happened – perhaps a riot in the village, unless someone uses good sense in handling whatever the discovery is.'

'Why is she keeping so much from you?' Naledi asked.

'She doesn't trust the phones, of course,' Boitumelo explained. 'We both know that Big Brother listens in more often than most people think – especially on my phone: it must've been tapped and re-tapped so many times they're tripping on themselves!' She'd long suspected her phones were being tapped.

'I don't know whether I believe that,' Naledi remarked. 'But anyway, it's better to be safe than sorry.'

Silence again ensued for a while.

Then Naledi asked the question to which she wanted an affirmative response. 'Will you promise to tell me what's going on? That's hardly asking you to divulge state secrets. You don't believe in all this secrecy, do you? I mean the public's entitled to inform - ation: this is a democracy! We're not in one of those sorry African countries now, are we?'

Boitumelo went for balance and fairness. 'All I can promise is that I'll meet with you again tomorrow. I know this is a long drive for you, so we can meet earlier – say, after court tomorrow, before you go back to Kanye. What I'll tell you or not tell you will depend on my sense of where all this is heading. Just trust my judgement, okay?'

And with that, the discussion was closed. For the rest of the evening, the two friends talked about lighter matters of mutual interest.

Boitumelo asked, 'So, how's Mount V?' Nary a lawyer existed who didn't know about 'Mount Vesuvius' and his tendency to erupt. 'Has he attacked you yet?'

'Actually, no,' Naledi replied. 'But I wish he would so at least he got it over with: the suspense alone is killing me. It doesn't help to have Linky for an office mate: he couldn't care less about anything.'

Boitumelo knew about the Linky factor. 'But he was always like that . . . What colour are Mary's fingernails these days?'

'They were red at 12.30, when I last saw her; they've probably changed colour many times since then. Come on – let's not be mean: I feel kind of sorry for her.' However, anyone seeing Naledi's smile wouldn't have been convinced she was indeed sorry for her workmate. Mary was a beautiful woman who was always winning beauty contests. She was always worried about how she looked, and carried a mirror everywhere she went: it was almost as if she expected that one day she'd look in it and find that her beauty had been stolen by some malicious witch. She was forever checking and rechecking her features to make sure all the essentials were in place. Another method she used for cross-checking was to jump into bed with any boss who 'popped the question'. So far, though, judging by her numerous beauty-contest wins and the line of bosses impatiently waiting their turn, general consensus had been reached that the distance between her breasts, the position of her belly button, the shape of her behind, the shape of her head, and the shape and position of other important body parts were perfect. However, Mary never failed to worry that something might sag, shift, shrivel or balloon.

'Vain is what Mary is,' Boitumelo remarked.

'Insecure is what I'd say,' Naledi added.

'And how is Agang?' Boitumelo asked. 'I haven't seen him for months.'

'He's doing fine,' Naledi replied. 'He's actually one of the more welcoming of the older lawyers. He's been very nice to all of us. Of course David's still a pompous ass: that guy's so full of himself he makes me want to throw up – all over him!' Her voice had risen so much that the couple at the next table looked up.

'He has unresolved issues,' Boitumelo mused; 'always has had, the poor, pimply guy!'

'He's a nasty cake of cow dung, if you ask me.' Naledi's take was one of vehemence.

Boitumelo objected. 'Hey, girl, don't get worked up over David – he's not worth it! So, how's Michael?' She asked the question with a smile: Michael was Naledi's boyfriend.

However, when Naledi responded, her face clouded over. 'Don't open that door: there's nothing there.'

'Well,' Boitumelo persisted, 'let me take a peak: I think there *is* something there. Come on: what's going on? You've been rather "mum" about what's happening for months now – and perhaps a bit sad as well? What's up?'

Naledi, though, decided not to 'go there', and closed the discussion. 'Let's get the bill: it's getting late, and we have, according to you, a story ready to explode. The least we can do is meet the challenge with fresh minds. I'll tell you about Michael – or the lack of Michael – when all this shit's settled: it's a long story.'

Boitumelo decided to lighten the mood. 'Aren't all men "stories" – good ones, bad ones, long ones?'

However, Naledi was already signalling for the female waiter. It was clear to Boitumelo that thoughts of Michael brought her friend sadness. The waiter sauntered over. She was a pretty child trying desperately to be a woman – and succeeding, if the glances she was getting from the male diners were any indication. Or perhaps she was just being a kid, and the glances told more about the male diners than about the child.

As the two women walked out of the restaurant, Boitumelo suddenly asked Naledi, 'Has it occurred to you that you're too junior to be assigned this case?'

Naledi let a frown appear on her face. 'I haven't been "assigned" the case; I'm just to read it and give an opinion.'

'Even so,' Boitumelo remarked, 'don't you think it's strange you've been allowed to see it at all?'

'No,' Naledi answered; 'I didn't think it was strange. It's only strange if you believe in the "cover-up" story – and you don't have enough facts to support that theory.' She was still frowning.

Boitumelo elaborated. 'I think Mount V's going to start

thinking he made a mistake in assigning you this file when he starts getting calls from high up. I think he dug it up because word got back to him that we've been asking questions. He doesn't realise the file's alive again. Didn't you say he wanted an opinion today? If he really thought the assignment was important, do you think he'd have given you such a short time to respond?' She was really thinking out aloud and inviting her friend to work out her theory with her.

Naledi was finding it difficult to dismiss Boitumelo's thinking outright. 'And you think the file's going to be yanked back as soon as he realises his error?'

'Naledi,' Boitumelo began, '*you* have the file: copy it; make a copy before the file gets taken from you – *please*.' She was standing in front of Naledi, and her tone was one of urgency.

Naledi checked her friend. 'Come on: that's not going to happen – the Attorney-General's Chambers aren't like the police. We're lawyers: we don't disappear files! We don't participate in cover-ups! This is Botswana! We're a democracy, the last time I checked!' She was trying to be indignant, but little power was evident in her voice. She was remembering a whispered story about a rape docket that had disappeared years before. She'd never met anyone who had all the details about the case, but the story had been that a big man had been about to be charged with rape when the docket suddenly disappeared and the witnesses started having memory problems. It had been rumoured that the victim lost her cleaning job, only to get it back when she, too, failed to remember whether or not she'd given consent for the sexual encounter to take place. Her absence from work had then been converted to leave, and documents had been prepared and backdated in order to regularise matters. According to people who'd known the woman before the alleged incident, she'd acquired a rather quiet personality after it.

Boitumelo pushed the point. 'And how do you know it won't happen? How long have you been working there? All I'm saying is "Take a precaution." Copy the file first thing tomorrow morning.'

Naledi's response was mixed. 'Do you think I can just walk into the copying room, hand the file to Joseph and say, "Hey,

Joseph, copy this old file so Mount V doesn't lose it down the drain,'"? She was trying to convince herself that Boitumelo's concerns were nonsense, but wasn't succeeding.

Boitumelo then made a bold offer. 'I'll come to your office tomorrow morning. I'll take the file out and copy it round the corner from your office: there's that copy shop there.'

For Naledi, that decided it. 'No, I'll do it myself. If I believe it has to be done, I'll do it myself. I'm going to need a good reason to leave work a minute after I get in. But yes: I'll do it – but don't think I'm going to hand you a copy!'

'I haven't asked you to,' Boitumelo responded. 'All I ask is there be a copy in case someone decides to conveniently misplace the original. I'm positive that if anything ever happens to the original, you'll have the courage to do the right thing.'

Naledi looked hard at her dinner companion.

The friends parted knowing they'd be talking again soon. Naledi, a new lawyer who had very limited experience, felt as if she were losing control even before she'd gained any.

CHAPTER 18

It wasn't surprising that the Conference Room in the Ministry of Safety and Security was large and tastefully furnished: people knew the Permanent Secretary to be a man of good taste – not necessarily expensive taste, but definitely good. What the government wouldn't pay for he paid for from his own personal funds. And so it was that conference delegates never failed to comment on the room's features such as the oil paintings on its walls, the fresh flowers in its vases and the rugs on its floor.

Today, six people were sitting around the conference table. Two of them were the Minister for Safety and Security himself, Mr Mading, and the minister's Permanent Secretary, Mr Rolang. It was a badly kept secret that the two men hated each other. As a result of recently held general elections, the government had reshuffled the Cabinet and created a new and powerful ministry, the Ministry of Safety and Security. An especially ambitious assistant minister had ended up being appointed head of the new ministry. Another man, who'd been minding his own business within another, tamer ministry, counting the years till he retired, had been promoted to the position of Permanent Secretary to the minister. It had therefore fallen to him to move his tasteful paintings and other odds and ends to a bigger office located on the fourth floor of a 'brand spanking new' building. As a result, Minister Mading and Permanent Secretary Rolang, who'd gone to school together and who knew too much about each other, were brought under the one roof. And the 'too much' they knew about each other they didn't like.

The third person at today's meeting was the Chief of Police, Mr

Selepe. He was an imposing, uniformed figure, and the front of his jacket was almost completely covered in medals. On the table, to his right he kept his baton, to his left his hat.

To the right of Mr Selepe was seated the fourth person: the Director of Tirelo Sechaba, Mrs Molapo. She had a charming, round face, but its agreeable features masked a stubborn personality – some people would even have called it a disagreeable personality. She mistrusted the police in general, and always assumed a deeper story lay behind the story they were telling. And she probably had a good personal reason to mistrust them: several years before, her nephew had died in a mysterious shooting incident. The young man had been a police officer, and the official story had been that some robbers who he and his fellow officers were pursuing shot him. However, how the robbers had shot him in the back as he was pursuing them was a mystery the police hadn't been able to explain.

Directly across from Mrs Molapo was the fifth person: the Deputy Attorney-General, Mr Pako – 'Mount V'.

And seated next to Mr Pako was a State Counsel, Naledi Binang. She'd never been in the presence of so many important officials, nor sat at the same table with a minister, a permanent secretary or so high ranking a police officer. To disguise the fact she was nervous, she kept her eyes focused on the contents of her notebook, although there was actually nothing of interest in it. Her plan today was to fill the book with notes at the earliest opportunity. Mr Pako had made it very clear he'd be expecting her to provide full and accurate minutes of the meeting: he could already see a sensational case in the making, and was preparing himself.

As the six delegates waited for the Minister for Health, Mr Gape, to arrive, they exchanged greetings. Naledi learnt from the other delegates that the minister's tardiness was a well-known peccadillo; nevertheless, murmurs of disapproval could be heard from them. Mr Pako wasn't used to being made to wait, and suggested they start without the minister. However, Police Chief Selepe suggested they wait. He looked at Safety and Security Minister Mading, who was technically his boss, for approval, and got it. Mr Pako decided to pull out a packet of cigarettes and smoke a few minutes away. Ignoring the 'NO SMOKING' sign on the wall to his left, the 'LUNGS AT WORK' sign on the wall in front of him and the 'THANK YOU FOR NOT POISONING ME TO DEATH' sign on the wall to his right, he lit up. He continued to puff away and blow smoke ahead of him, across the beautiful table.

Mrs Molapo frowned at the recalcitrant smoker. He chose to ignore her. She coughed in protest. Still he ignored her. She stood up and opened the windows, thereby inviting in hot air and prompting Mr Selepe to object. She fixed a stare on him and muttered, 'Deal with the problem, mister police chief, not the consequence.'

All eyes then swivelled round to Mr Pako. He dragged hard and long on his cigarette, then stubbed it out on a spoon that happened to be resting on a tray full of teacups.

Finally, half an hour later than the meeting's scheduled commencement time, Health Minister Gape walked in. He was a big, lumbering man who had a faint smell of cologne about him. The smell was to remain, because someone called in a cleaner to close the windows.

Police Chief Selepe began. 'I think I can now call the meeting to order. But before we do, may I know the position of the young lady sitting next to you, Mr Pako?'

Binang looked up, startled: she'd been expecting to quietly take down the minutes of the meeting as per Mount V's instructions.

'Why,' Mr Pako replied, 'she's a State Counsel: she'll be my assistant if this case ever goes to court – that's how we lawyers work.' He seemed peeved that the Chief of Police would dare question his actions.

'I'm sorry, sir,' Selepe responded, 'but the young lady has to go. I should've explained when I called you about this meeting. You'll understand why once we go into this matter. But she must go; I'll explain later.'

Then, without waiting for Mr Pako to reply, the chief directed his next comments to Binang. 'Ma'am, you're excused from this meeting – but before you go, can you pour the tea, please? Let's get that over with, lady and gentlemen. Can you let the young lady know what you'll have? And I'll have coffee, with milk and two sugars. Young lady, please hurry up: we don't have all day.'

Fuming, State Counsel Binang served the delegates their tea and coffee, and promptly left the room. She'd been surprised at Mr Pako's invitation to attend the meeting anyway – but then he hadn't known the full story about the Criminal Records Bureau item marked '45/94'. Binang had found out enough to know that the docket wasn't destined to remain old for long – unless the people who had the power were able to bury it once more.

When the meeting commenced, Police Chief Selepe was clearly in charge. However, at the start, he occasionally looked in the direction of Safety and Security Minister Mading: Selepe knew he wasn't really the boss, although he'd have loved to be. He got the ball rolling. 'Thank you, lady and gentlemen, for attending at such short notice. And I want to thank the Minister for Safety and Security and his Permanent Secretary for making this room available for this meeting. First things first: why are you all here? The Minister for Health is here because there's a crisis at a health clinic. The Director of TS is here because one of her TSPs reckons herself to be Sherlock Holmes – a most disagreeable girl, indeed; we'll get to that in a minute. The Minister for Safety and Security isn't just the host today; his ministry dealt with the same girl two years ago. Of course, there was a reshuffle, and the minister who initially dealt with this matter isn't here today. But, still, we trust we can expect a full report from them about that case – especially why stern measures weren't taken against her. Why was she left to run around loose like this? That's a question we'll get to. The Deputy Attorney-General has been invited for obvious reasons.'

Police Chief Selepe had never wanted the Ministry of Safety and Security to be established, and had never quite accepted the fact he was a junior officer to the minister. He longed to return to the days when he'd been the chief of his own turf and been answerable to the Office of the President itself. Now, he was having to deal with 'soft' civilians who didn't have a clue about true policing; he wasn't surprised at all that two years before, a mere girl had run circles around them.

Today, he gave the delegates what he called relevant back - ground information. As soon as he stopped speaking, each delegate intimated that he or she had a question to ask him. However, he explained that he wouldn't let them go to the questions yet: first,

142

he wanted each person to brief him, whereupon each person did. Finally, he fielded questions.

The first question came from TSP Director Mrs Molapo. 'In your assessment of the evidence before you, what would you say happened to the child?'

Even in the short time the Chief of Police and the Director of TS had been in the room together, they'd reached the same conclusion that they didn't like each other. Police Chief Selepe now used Mrs Molapo's question to put her in her place. 'That, director, is confidential police information. This isn't a trial; it's a briefing to enable the police to resolve a potentially volatile situation peacefully. What I need from you is information to assist in that resolution. I hope I'm making myself clear.' He looked away from her to invite a comment from someone else.

However, Mrs Molapo hadn't finished. 'No, sir, you haven't made yourself clear at all. I'm a government official.' She didn't say, but implied, 'like you'. 'If you expect me to be involved in a resolution of anything, I believe I must know the full details – I'm not just a "spanner boy". I don't know what everyone else thinks, but I don't think it's proper procedure for the Chief of Police to use us and at the same time withhold information from us.' She looked around, hoping to find agreement. As a director, she was the most junior official in the room, and was aware that even if only one word were uttered against her, her views could be thrown out the window; she could even be told to leave.

Police Chief Selepe implored her. 'Director, director, please be professional: there's no need for emotions in this room. No one's being used. You must appreciate that I'm trying to do my job – I wouldn't interfere in yours, so I expect you to extend me the same courtesy.' He knew he was being condescending; he meant to be: he'd believed for a long time that the best way to rile a woman was to suggest she was being emotional.

And Mrs Molapo was, naturally, angered to hear him patron - ising her. 'So, you wouldn't interfere in my job – is that it? Then how do you explain the call I received from your station com- mander in Maun directing me to transfer the same girl – the one you find so disagreeable? Wouldn't you say that was interference?' Her voice was loud, her anger apparent.

143

Mr Pako decided to intervene. 'Lady and gentlemen, let's slow down for a minute. Let's review what we know, and then we can decide what can or can't be shared with other departments. A young girl caused an investigation into alleged police brutality in Kanye last year. Since then, a soldier has been dismissed and two police officers have been suspended. And, of course, we're told that the Ministry of Safety and Security is working on a policy for riot control. That's an impressive feat for this girl; that lesson tells us something about her. Let's not forget that as we decide what we're doing next in the case before us.' He looked around the room to make sure he had everyone's attention before he continued. 'Now, this same girl is a TSP in Gaphala. By some strange circumstance, she goes and unearths a box of exhibits from a storeroom in a health clinic she's working at as a TSP. Rather than run home crying and declare she's not going back there, she stays put, and from what the director here is saying, she even refuses an offer by the police to be transferred to another village. Any teenager would've seized on the opportunity for a re-assignment: it's no secret, in fact, that her posting's one of the least attractive places; I wouldn't be surprised, in fact, to find out that the Ministry of Safety and Security was instrumental in having her sent to that remote village in the first place.' He held up his hand to prevent the Minister for Safety and Security and the Director of TS from interrupting. 'Okay; okay: let's leave that one alone. Let's assume she was just unlucky enough to be sent to that edge of nowhere. Now, we have a five-year-old case, closed because it was decided the child had been killed by wild animals. We can all argue about the reasonableness of the decision, but that's what the official police line is.' He looked at Police Chief Selepe to ascertain whether he was going to contradict him on that point – but he got only a non-committal look from that quarter. He continued. 'Now, we have a Ministry of Safety and Security's nemesis, holding a box that suggests something else. We also have two nurses held hostage, with the knowledge and, perhaps, assistance of the same girl. We also have a village ready to riot. It seems to me, chief, that everyone around this table is entitled to full information: only then can we agree – guided by you, of course – as to what part of the information can be made public. Surely you appreciate there's going to be tremendous public interest in this case. The press is going to roast us, whatever the story; the least we can do is come up with a common line – perhaps even a press statement. I'd advise that you answer the questions put to you as fully as possible – and then you can advise as to what's for this table only and what's also for public consumption. And of course the president will have to be briefed – and soon.' He reached for his cigarette packet, but stopped short when he registered a look from Mrs Molapo – mercurial as he was, he knew when to keep his eye on the ball.

Health Minister Gape decided to throw his hat into the ring. Frowning, he addressed both Police Chief Selepe and Safety and Security Minister Mading. 'Why can't you just storm the place – just send in the SSGs and surround the village? It can't be that big!' He was finding it totally incomprehensible that the authorities could fail to recognise so obvious a solution.

Minister Mading gave the response. 'We can't do that for various reasons. To start with, the villagers are so remote they can hear vehicles coming from kilometres away: they'd just melt into the bush. Second, we need to get those clothes; we need to negotiate a settlement to get them back. If we storm the village, people might get killed, and the clothes are proof that the villagers were right to start with. That girl will get them out somehow – then we'll have a dead girl whose investigations we botched and dead villagers whose deaths we caused while botching the investigations! We're in a bind – that's why we need to negotiate. And don't forget: this girl is associated with this new breed of upstart lawyers who are setting up shop all over the place: Kukama, Badisa and Co. are part of that human-rights nonsense. They're her lawyers in this case I've inherited, and she even worked for them before going for TS. They're linked to these human-rights people, who seem to think the only people with rights are the bad ones – I guess *we* have no rights, as far as they're concerned! They'd hap - pily open all prison doors! Recently, some of them have even been saying that prisoners should be allowed to vote! They'd happily spend taxpayers' money setting up voting booths in prisons! Crazy!' He looked at Police Chief Selepe and then, seeming to regret his outburst, nodded to indicate that the chief could go on with the meeting.

Health Minister Gape had a frown on his face as he posed the next question to the group. 'What's the relevance of the clothes anyway – they won't tell us who killed her, will they?' People generally knew him to be the reason why the monthly meetings of ministers went for one hour longer than was absolutely necessary.

Minister Mading gave the response. 'No, they won't – but they're proof that the police were wrong to conclude the child was killed by lions.'

Mrs Molapo asked, 'And how, and why, did they have to come up with such a ridiculous conclusion?'

Police Chief Selepe addressed the Deputy Attorney-General. 'Mr Pako, is it still your advice that I answer this question?'

'Yes, chief,' came the reply.

The police chief decided to lay the cards on the table. 'My opinion is that the police officers were in a hurry to close the case out of fear of the men behind the murder. I think we all know that people who murder for *dipheko* use *dipheko* to harm the people who try to find out the truth. The police were afraid of dying or going insane. Of course, behind these killings there's always a big man or men: powerful people. These people can, and have, in the past – although we don't want to admit it – influenced police investigations.' He paused to look around: he knew he was swimming in dangerous waters – it wouldn't do for anyone to repeat that he'd suggested a powerful hand had steered the police from the truth.

'What are you suggesting?' Minister Gape asked.

Minister Mading moved from the suggested to the concrete. 'Can we go back to the main purpose of today, please? I believe we're here to develop a strategy for engaging the villagers of Gaphala in negotiations – can we discuss that, please?'

Mrs Molapo, however, wasn't about to let the issue get away. 'But I do think the chief has raised an important point. This Gaphala problem isn't unique. It's true that very few ritual-murder cases are actually solved. Children, especially girls, disappear or die under very mysterious circumstances, and no one's called to account. And when the villagers demand answers, we, the government, are the very ones who try to shut them up. This can't go on forever: the problem must be dealt with head on, otherwise it seems like we're siding with the killers.'

Police Chief Selepe was becoming exasperated with Mrs Molapo. 'We don't side with the killers – but we can't allow villagers to design and execute their own brand of justice. You know what's happened in some villages: public floggings of suspects and burning of private property! We can't allow that to happen: there must be law and order!'

Mrs Molapo had picked up on the key word. 'And since you mention suspects, were there no suspects in this case? Not even one? I can't believe no one saw or heard anything.'

The chief answered the question. 'I'm not prepared to disclose the names of the suspects at this point – even if the Deputy Attorney-General here advises otherwise. There's just nothing supporting the suspicions about the two people who were questioned. Reputations can be ruined over something like this. Sorry, but no: I'm not disclosing the names – not now, anyways.' He looked at Mr Pako, knowing he'd have to say something.

And say something he did. 'I agree with the chief on that one: based on what I've read, there's nothing to justify calling any of the persons questioned by the police a "suspect" at this point.'

Mrs Molapo refused to be appeased. 'That's assuming you have everything from the police; the size of your file, compared with the chief's, would suggest you don't.'

Mount V, who'd by any standards remained reasonably calm, looked long and hard at Mrs Molapo, but said nothing in response. What she'd just said hadn't been lost on him; he'd already planned to get everything from Police Chief Selepe after the meeting. He hated the fact it was going to look as if he hadn't thought of the idea himself.

Minister Mading, who'd been fully briefed by Police Chief Selepe before the meeting, decided it was time to go to the next topic. 'Can we go back to why we're here? This is my proposal: hold a *kgotla* meeting in Gaphala tomorrow morning. I propose that the following people attend: everyone here today.'

He then addressed Minister Gape. 'And minister, can you arrange for the head of the Forensic Science Laboratory to attend? She'll have to attend as well. I believe she's at this moment doing a job for your ministry – I need her back ASAP.'

'Why?' the minister shot back. 'Are you planning to do some

bush tests out there?' He'd meant the question to be a joke, but no one laughed; Mr Pako even huffed in disapproval.

Minister Mading then took over the chairing of the meeting from the chief, who had no choice but to slink back into his chair to let this man, who was new to policing, run the show. 'No, minister, we're not planning any bush tests. I believe we must show the villagers we come in good faith. We must ensure every player is at this *kgotla* meeting. We must show them we've nothing to hide.'

Mrs Molapo directed her next question to Minister Mading. 'After you've had everything to hide for five years, why do you think they'll believe you this time? Wasn't there a *kgotla* meeting five years ago, at which you claimed you were telling the whole story?'

Until about two years before, Minister Mading had been an assistant minister in the Ministry of Rural Administration and Welfare. Before then, he'd been a bank teller, driven only an old van, and struggled, with his wife, to support their five children. After that, his wife had lost her job, having being convicted of forging a payment voucher and obtaining money by fraud. She'd gotten off with being charged a fine and incurring a suspended sentence. Having free time and meagre resources as her propellers, she'd campaigned hard for her husband. Now, he was a full minister, they lived in a big house that had a swimming pool, and the children were going to expensive schools. The children spoke English with an unidentifiable accent, and said 'Hello,' and 'Hi there,' instead of '*Dumelang.*' Mr Mading had become rather ambitious and taken to switching tactics according to the situation – his eye was always on the big result.

Mr Rolang, his Permanent Secretary, was today surprised his boss was showing an attitude of conciliation: he'd rather expected him to want to send in a 'swat' team in response to the crisis unfolding in Gaphala. Two years before, when Mr Mading had assumed the position of Minister for Safety and Security and taken over the case of the National Stadium march against the army, he'd had to be held back by his colleagues, who were advising him to choose restraint.

Minister Mading now took it on himself to justify his previous

148

actions. 'I wasn't part of that sham: I took over a newly established ministry, and spent two years just trying to build a team. During those two years, the chief here held on to the power. Of course, as the minister, I'm ultimately responsible for all that's happened. And some would say our friend here, the Chief of Police, is the one at whose feet this whole mess should be laid – but that's not how government works: "Collective responsibility" is my motto. But things are going to be different this time; that's why I'm deter-mined that this time there'll be full disclosure – or at least as full a disclosure as possible. My concern, of course, is that the villagers are going to expect miracles. After five years, we can't possibly expect to pick any leads. We're going in with the main aim of defusing a potentially explosive situation, but the villagers will agree to meet only if they can be convinced that investigations will be revived.'

TSP Director Molapo still didn't feel like she was a team player in the game at hand. 'So,' she said, 'we have to lie to them to secure a meeting.'

'Yes, ma'am,' Minister Mading replied.

'And you have no problems with that?' A sneer accompanied the director's question.

The minister retorted, 'I have a bigger problem with the possible shedding of the blood of two nurses. I have an even bigger problem with a riotous mob clubbing every government worker who attempts to enter that village: understand?'

'May I say something, minister?' Permanent Secretary Rolang was opening his mouth to speak for the first time, to ask his minister for permission to speak.

His boss nodded; the animosity between the two was apparent, even from this short exchange.

'If Amantle, the TSP girl, is indeed with the villagers, I don't believe the nurses will be harmed. I mean, she's one of these human-rights people, and it'd hardly look good if she were mixed up in a murder – two murders, for that matter. I think the hostage thing's a bluff. I had to interview her on several occasions after the Kanye incident; she's not that type of person.'

Health Minister Gape gave the response. 'Thank you, PS, but you're talking about a girl who thinks she's some kind of hero.'

'Heroine,' Mrs Molapo muttered.

'Like I was saying,' the minister continued, 'we're talking about a girl who thinks herself a hero: would you say it's like her to be involved in a kidnapping?' He wasn't about to be corrected by a director – after all, she was a junior. It was beginning to irk him that she thought she could just interrupt when her superiors were talking. However, people knew him to have been involved in many scandals, the most recent of which was his connection to a doctor who was selling medical certificates of unfitness to parents who didn't wish their TSP children to be placed in a remote village. It was rumoured that Minister Gape was taking a percentage of the hefty fee charged for issuing the medical certificates.

Mrs Molapo knew about the scam, and knew that the minister was involved; however, she had no hard proof of it.

Minister Gape knew that Mrs Molapo knew about it, and therefore now decided not to demand so junior an official be ejected from the meeting. He was sure that the only way out of the festering situation the six delegates were now finding themselves in was to stage a show of force. 'The girl might do something silly, ending up in results she hadn't even planned or contemplated. I say an urgent intervention by the police is called for. Storm the village; arrest people; arrest this girl; throw her in gaol – that'd help her think straight. Softness doesn't get anyone anywhere in situations like these. If she'd been treated seriously two years ago, do you think she'd still be giving us trouble? Of course not!'

Police Chief Selepe wished he could concur: he was all for displaying toughness, but thought that because the village was remote, it would be foolish to mount that kind of response. 'I've already explained why we can't just storm the village. Remember that the public's just now beginning to forget what happened in Mahalapye and Bobonong three years ago – we can't afford a repeat of that. These ritual-murder cases aren't easy to handle. I'm not convinced that brute force is the answer to the problem at hand.' Although he hated agreeing with Safety and Security Minister Mading, he was a practical man.

What Minister Mading wasn't telling the other delegates was that the idea of holding the meeting in the village wasn't his. The Maun police-station commander had made it very clear that a *kgotla* meeting had to take place within the next twenty-four hours and that specified individuals had to attend. Minister Mading had passed on to Police Chief Selepe and Permanent Secretary Rolang only the information he'd considered they needed to know: he wasn't about to disclose that the order for the meeting and its attendees had come from the girl and the villagers. He now had to pretend he was the convenor of the meeting. He was therefore the unlikely architect of a negotiated settlement, whereas the other delegates had been expecting him to want to 'go in', ready to 'lock horns' with the villagers.

Mrs Molapo thought to herself, *Perhaps he isn't a stupid brute after all.*

CHAPTER 19

'Thanks, Daniel, for agreeing to do this.' Amantle was peering into the night, on the lookout for a flicker of light. It was a rather dark, star-filled night: a perfect night to be stealing away. Even so, she and her fellow TSP Daniel Modise both knew they were in one of the wildest parts of the country: hungry hyenas, jackals and lions were no doubt on the prowl; in fact, the two companions had heard the grunt of antelope and occasionally the cry of hyenas. As they drove further and further away from the village, they expected to hear more wild-animal sounds and to perhaps even glimpse some animals.

'Thank you!' Daniel replied. 'I wouldn't have missed this for anything: it's the most exciting thing that's happened to me in this Godforsaken place since we got here. Now, are you going to tell me what's going on? Why are we stealing away in the middle of the night? I believe the minimum mandatory sentence for car theft is five years – that's a long time, and exciting as all this is, I'd like to know why I'm risking sitting in gaol for five years.' As 'show-offish' young men are prone to doing, he was driving using only one hand.

Noticing his poor motoring skills, Amantle demanded, 'Keep both hands on the wheel, please! My, must we show off even in the middle of the night, in the middle of nowhere? And you'll find out soon enough. Just keep your eyes open for some kind of light signal: a torch, perhaps the headlights of a car – I'm not sure we agreed which it'd be.'

Daniel was finding it difficult to be patient and couldn't help joking around. 'Aren't we edgy tonight?! Relax! Who are we meeting – am I taking you to a secret lover? I'm curious!' He hit a button on the console, and music filled the cab of the vehicle – the Gaphala Clinic ambulance.

'Turn that off!' Amantle roared. 'And no: I'm not meeting a lover. You'll know soon enough – that was the deal. Now, stop making me more nervous than I already am, and drive – and slow down: you have to be careful on these roads!'

'Relax!' Daniel repeated; 'a bit of music can't hurt.' Nevertheless, he reached over and turned the radio off. They agreed that the music was awful anyway, and that any music would be hard to enjoy because the reception in that remote part of the country was bound to be poor.

Daniel drove on, humming to himself. Amantle continued to peer into the night, hoping to see a sign. Sometimes their headlights caught the eyes of an animal, and half a dozen times a steenbok jumped out, seemingly from nowhere, whereupon their Toyota Hilux almost smashed into it.

Then, all of a sudden, Amantle shouted urgently, 'I think I see a light! Right there: to our left! *Left! Left!* A fire! I see a *fire*! No, it's a *torch*! Flash your lights and find a way to drive over there – *now! Now!* Her voice betrayed her excitement, and she seemed to be ready to push the vehicle along to make it move faster.

'Okay! Okay! Okay!' Daniel yelled in return. 'My, aren't we in a hurry! I have to find a place to go up the bank – hold your horses, ma'am!' He chuckled as he found a place to ease the vehicle off the road and up the bank.

Daniel drove towards the light, but the other vehicle's passen - gers didn't immediately get out to show themselves; instead, they waited until Amantle had called out to them in order to identify herself. Boitumelo then switched off her car engine, and she and two other passengers emerged from the vehicle, in which they'd clearly been ready to take off at the first sign of danger. The three women – Boitumelo Kukama, Naledi Binang and Nancy Madison – had had a long day of driving, first through the desert and later through lush country. They'd seen all sorts of game, including impala, giraffes, wildebeests, gemsboks, cheetahs, bat-eared foxes and all kinds of birds. It'd been an exciting day for them, and although they were now tired and looking forward to having a

shower and some hot food, they'd enjoyed the journey enor-
mously. However, they hadn't yet had the chance to register the
reality of why they'd gone on the trip in the first place.

Boitumelo hugged Amantle excitedly. 'My, Amantle, only you
could've come up with this setting – this place is so beautiful! You
won't believe the animals and trees and birds we've seen. The
sunset today was spectacular! And we drove along a water channel
for a good part of the last ten kilometres. My God, the beauty! I
could live here – it's amazing!' She was standing at one of the
vehicle's doors, clearly waiting for a sign for her and her companions to drive on.

'Thanks for coming, Boitu,' Amantle responded, 'but who are
these people – what are they doing here? Is this some kind of
trap?' She'd been expecting the rendezvous to be with two of her
friends: the lawyer Boitumelo and the journalist Milly Samson.
Instead, Boitumelo was accompanied by Naledi Binang, a woman
Amantle knew to be a lawyer in the Attorney-General's Chambers,
and a white woman Amantle had never met. She was agitated now:
perhaps she'd gone too far with this thing – it seemed that with
every step she took, she got herself deeper and deeper into trouble.

'Slow down, Amantle,' Boitumelo began. 'I'm so sorry – I'm
too excited to think straight. Of course you know Naledi. And this
is Nancy Madison; she's a law student from Britain, working with
us at the office – an intern. Milly couldn't come – a death in her
family. You know how it is these days: this AIDS is going to wipe
this country clean, I tell you. And Nancy here's great with cameras
– or at least that's what she says. I can testify she's a good driver.
My, it's been a long day! But first things first: we're tired and
filthy – so lead the way, girl friend. I hope we don't have too far to
go: we really are tired. A shower and some hot food would be
great.' She stepped back to her vehicle, expecting Amantle to head
for hers as well.

Amantle, however, had other ideas. 'What way? We're
spending the night right here. And this is Daniel – he's a TSP, like
me. He was kind enough to drive me here – as you know, I can't
drive. Let's set up tents; then we can talk.' She walked towards the
back of the ambulance vehicle and started pulling out a bag.

Boitumelo was incredulous. 'What do you *mean* we're

spending the night here?' She ventured away from the vehicle door, just enough to face Amantle under the glow of the torch she'd used as the light signal.

Amantle paused and looked at her friend. 'That was the plan, Boitu: we set up camp here; we work tonight, away from the village and the police; and we drive into the village tomorrow morning. Let's set up tent first; then we can sit down and discuss our plans – please?'

Boitumelo was in need of more persuasion. 'And what do you mean he's a TSP? He can't drive a government vehicle! And it's an ambulance – a BX! Don't tell me you people *stole* that vehicle! Amantle, please tell me you didn't steal this vehicle – I'm out of here; I really am out of here! *Maria, Mma-Jeso!*' Her voice rose in unison with her agitation.

Fiddling with his earrings, Daniel asked, 'Can we put up the tents, get the chairs out, fix something to eat – then shout at each other?'

Boitumelo turned to face Daniel. The night was dark, so her glares were wasted on him. Nevertheless, her voice came through loud and clear. 'I'll shout when I decide to shout! And I'm *not* staying the night here! I'm *not* staying the night in this bush, with hyenas howling and elephants trampling the earth! And there are *lions* here! I'm not – positively *not* – spending the night in a tent in this place: *no way!*'

Amantle approached her friend and placed a hand on her shoulder. 'Boitu, please listen. There are no elephants in this area. We're only thirty or so kilometres from the village – so we're safe. But we can't go there – not tonight. We need to work tonight in private, and away from the police. I don't trust them not to sneak into the clinic to scuttle our plans – maybe even storm the village, after promising not to. Can we just set up the tents now, and then discuss all this afterwards?'

Reluctantly, Boitumelo relented. The group of five set up the tents, and the collective mood somewhat improved. The *al fresco* dinner menu was limited: fruit, bread, tea and wine. When Daniel brought out some meat to barbecue, Boitumelo put her foot down: she was afraid they'd attract some wild animals to their camp. 'Okay, Amantle,' she began, 'shoot! Why are we offering ourselves to lions and other wild beasts in this way? I honestly hope you're just being dramatic; I can't handle any more excitement tonight.'

Across the flickering fire, Amantle looked at Naledi, who hadn't said very much all evening. She addressed the group. 'Can we talk in front of this State Counsel here? No offence, but I still don't understand how she can be here.' She'd met Naledi a couple of times before, and she actually liked her; however, it seemed to her that Naledi shouldn't be accompanying Boitumelo on a mission such as the one at hand.

Naledi looked back at Amantle and responded, 'I understand you're concerned. I came here on an impulse. I didn't tell anyone at the office where I was going – and I'm pretty certain if I'd told my boss my plans I'd have been fired promptly. And I probably *will* be fired as it is, anyway. But Boitumelo convinced me she was on the side of truth – and here I am.'

Amantle turned her attention to Nancy, who was busy looking at the sky as if it held a magic she couldn't quite understand. 'And you, Nancy: why are you here?'

'For adventure?' Nancy asked rhetorically. 'And Boitumelo said she needed a cameraperson. So here I am, and it seems to me we're having an adventure already! No – seriously – I've done a bit of research into this case, and I find it fascinating. And it sounds to me as if you're completely crazy to pit yourself against all these powers, both bureaucratic and supernatural! And all this on the edge of the Okavango Delta? Only a fool wouldn't have wanted to come. Beauty and horror are what pulled me here.' Her expression was one of bemusement.

Amantle then proceeded to tell the group what had happened over the past few days. She ignored everyone's interjections and questions until all four listeners gave up and listened.

However, when Amantle had finished speaking, Naledi decided to assert herself. 'Are you telling us you've taken part in kidnapping two people – two nurses? And that as we speak they're being kept captive in the village clinic? Is *that* what you're telling us?'

Amantle hoped that in being firm she'd maintain some kind of control over the situation. 'Don't use that tone of voice with me, please – I'm not one of your witnesses. And I don't think you can call it a kidnapping exactly: the villagers needed some kind of leverage over the police.'

Naledi blurted out, 'I'm a lawyer, and I call that a kidnapping! Oh, my God – I never thought . . .' She was perhaps envisaging not only joblessness but imprisonment for aiding and abetting in a whole host of offences. 'Mount V will definitely erupt all over me! This is heavier than I thought! My, my, my: I sure can pick 'em!'

Boitumelo stood up. 'And you've fled the village in a stolen ambulance! And as if that isn't enough, your assistant here doesn't even have a driver's licence! What do you think you're doing, Amantle? This is too much – way too much!' She was about to march away from the fire, but when she saw a pair of yellowish-green eyes watching the group, she promptly sat down. 'And now, as if that isn't enough, we'll probably be eaten and gone long before we're put in prison. What the shit is that animal peering at me – can someone tell me, please? I can't handle this.'

'That's just a hyena,' Daniel offered. 'They're fairly harmless. And I doubt it's you it's peering at – I doubt it's actually peering.'

Boitumelo wasn't mollified. '*Fairly* harmless? *Fairly* harm - less? What the shit's *that* supposed to mean: we only get half eaten, or what? And when did you start being an expert on hyenas, anyways – aren't you from down south? From the way you speak, you have to be from the south!'

Daniel kept his cool. 'I've been out in the bush a couple of times since I've been here, and I was told that hyenas are cowards – really: if you wave your torch at it right now, it'll run off. It's hoping to pick up some bits of food from this camp – that's all.' He went back to piling more wood on the fire to make the fire bigger.

Naledi held on to the issue. 'I don't know about all that: hyenas hunt in packs and tear their victims apart, from what I've seen on TV – and they're messy eaters, too.' She looked around at the darkness surrounding them, and swept her torch across the grass plain. She wasn't too happy to encounter the eyes of some more wild animals.

'What do you think, Nancy?' Amantle asked. 'You're really quiet.' She was hoping she could defuse the situation by shifting the focus away from Boitumelo; she didn't think Naledi was helping by providing graphic images of hyenas' eating habits – and it wasn't as if she herself wasn't feeling apprehensive.

Nancy replied, 'I have no experience with any of this: if you tell me we'll survive the night, I have to believe you. I'm assuming you're not suicidal. The stars are beautiful, though; amazing – look at that Milky Way! And that's the Southern Cross, isn't it? Beautiful sky; just amazing. But I'd suggest we move into the big tent; that way we won't be confronted by all these eyes every time we turn around – I'd rather not see them at present, actually.' She stood up to prompt the campers to move into one of the tents.

Naledi thought it a good idea. 'I say we do as Nancy suggests: we have lots of thinking to do – and work, by the sound of things. And I can't work with so many animals watching.'

Amantle was getting angry with Naledi for her tendency to indulge in the use of graphic images. 'Do you have to be so descriptive? You're making other people nervous: my God, Naledi, stop it!'

'Okay; okay,' Naledi responded. 'Just give me another cup of wine; I'll be okay – I just wasn't expecting to end up in the bush, in the company of novice campers, surrounded by predators ready to eat me!'

Boitumelo stood up and had to restrain herself from dashing to the tent.

Nancy asked her reluctant colleague, 'What did you think you'd be using the camping gear for, if I may ask?' She had the ghost of a smile on her face.

'I don't know!' Boitumelo replied. 'I was expecting camping grounds with other people – and showers! and toilets! I didn't expect to spend the night in the company of howling jackals; I didn't expect that my friend here would have broken every con - ceivable law in the book: kidnapping! *Maria, Mma-Jeso!* Kidnap - ping's serious – very serious! I just can't believe I'm sitting here in the company of kidnappers! Amantle, what the hell did you think you were doing?' Her nervous energy was bubbling over for all to see.

Amantle answered, 'I didn't do anything – things kind of happened around me!'

Boitumelo turned on the drama. 'A great defence indeed: "No, judge, the kidnapping just happened around me – and the car-theft charge? That just happened around me as well. I'm this innocent little girl, and things just happen around me." Yeah, my friend, stay with that line of defence: it sounds really great!'

Amantle had had enough. 'Boitu, stop it; just stop it! You're not helping things the way you're carrying on. We're here; we've all risked a lot already. The question is "What's next?" And let's move into the tent – *please*! – and *now*!' She was hoping that in being firm she'd help jolt Boitumelo out of her spiralling anxiety.

Once the five withdrew to the tent, they felt more secure within its thin, vinyl walls. Boitumelo became less agitated and more focused on the purpose for which Amantle had summoned them all.

It soon became very clear that Amantle wasn't clear about what she expected Boitumelo and the other aides to do: she was writing the script as they were going along. She'd hoped Boitumelo would arrive charged with the desire to help develop the script. 'You're the lawyers,' she stated. 'I've told you the problem; it's up to you to propose a solution – a plan! I just know I have the items of clothing, which the police want very much. The villagers want the investigations to be reopened. I think you should act as the villagers' lawyers to make sure things don't go the same way they went last time.'

Nancy chipped in. 'Can I ask a question? What do you mean you "have the items"? You mean here, with you?'

'Yes,' Amantle replied; 'the box is in the ambulance.'

Before Boitumelo could let go another explosion of anxiety, Naledi raised her hand to stop her. 'All right, Amantle,' Naledi said in a calm voice; 'what else haven't you told us? Running away with police exhibits is probably an offence – but we won't dwell on it at the moment. Is there anything else we need to know before we continue?' She was slowly reconciling herself to the fact she was unemployed and that at some point she'd probably have to face Mount V about the whole thing. She shook her head in order to erase the memories of her last prison visit; however, she found it impossible to ignore the picture of a young woman knitting shapeless sweaters in order to while away her three-year prison term.

'No,' Amantle responded; 'I think I've told you everything. And the way I see it, the investigations were closed five years ago; these clothes aren't, technically speaking, exhibits in continuing investigations. In any event, the police say this isn't a murder case – so how can I have broken any law?' She didn't quite believe what she was saying.

Naledi put forward a proposition. 'May I suggest you leave the law to us for a little while? Is there anything else you think we need to know? For example, do you have the petition the villagers have signed? Perhaps we should review its language before you and the villagers stand in front of the entire nation tomorrow admitting to all kinds of crimes.' She extended her hand to Amantle to prompt her to give her the petition. 'And you might want to tell us, as accurately as possible, what you said to the station commander – they probably taped the conversation.'

Amantle asked Daniel to accompany her to the ambulance in order to retrieve both the box and the petition. As they were walking, Daniel said to her, 'You got guts, sister. Don't mind all that from Boitumelo – you wouldn't have to know her to see she wouldn't trade this for anything. *I* wouldn't trade it for anything – I'm loving every little, exciting minute of it; it makes the whole TS experience worthwhile.' He grabbed her and hugged her. However, she wasn't feeling as relaxed about what was going on, so the hug she gave him back was rather lukewarm.

Back in the tent, the group looked at the unopened box solemnly, but no one made a move to open it. They talked for a while; then Amantle put on a pair of gloves and opened it. She lifted the crisp items out for everyone to see; she'd estimated that no one could see the pathetic items, caked in dried blood, and not be angry – angry and charged up. And anger and charging up were exactly the reactions she got.

Then, in a calm voice, Naledi declared, 'I have something to show you guys as well.' Until now, she hadn't made up her mind whether she'd offer the file to Boitumelo; now, she made up her mind to do it – she'd worry about the consequences later. 'I have a copy of the case file with me – and a bit more: is anyone going to accompany me outside to get my briefcase?'

Nancy stood up and picked up a torch.

Silence ensued again until the two returned. Naledi then handed over three bulging envelopes to Amantle, who quickly looked through their contents, which were secured in coloured folders, without really taking much in.

Naledi explained, 'The thick, blue folder is a copy of the file the police sent our office five years ago. The green one's my own notes, an assessment of the evidence. The red file you have there is stuff I shouldn't have at all; it wasn't part of the original file, but if you read it, you'll get a sense of what probably happened five years ago, leading to your finding this little box at that clinic. May I suggest we use the next two hours to read the materials we have? I'll read the petition. The big file can be conveniently split in two, so we'll each have two pieces for something to read. After we finish, we'll pass on the materials. Once we're all finished, we can discuss what to do next. What do you think?' With every word she was uttering, she was putting a greater distance between herself and her old office.

The other four participants agreed it would be a good plan, and quiet soon ensued as they settled down to read. The task took a bit longer than the estimated two hours, though, and Daniel and Amantle ventured out four times to make coffee and tea for everyone. Each time they ventured outside, they had to use one of the torches to create a flickering circle of light in their path. It seemed that all kinds of eyes were watching them – eyes that probably belonged to harmless impala grazing away in the night; still, it was disconcerting to be surrounded by non-human beings.

During their first foray outside, Daniel remarked, 'Let's hope we don't hear a lion for quite a while – I don't think Boitumelo could possibly handle it.' He piled more wood on the fire.

'Yeah,' Amantle responded; 'I hope so too. I also hope elephants don't choose to pay us a visit.'

Daniel commented, 'I heard that little lie you told about there being no elephants in this area – even if our mates don't see any, surely they'll see the dung tomorrow. I imagine the whole area's full of elephant dung; I'm surprised they didn't see any when they were driving here.'

'I guess I shouldn't have lied to them,' Amantle agreed, 'but my hope is that by tomorrow, Boitumelo won't be as afraid as she is tonight. She's making everyone nervous; we can't concentrate unless she calms down.'

Inside the tent, Boitumelo called everyone to the centre. 'Okay, guys, I know we're not all finished, but we don't have too much time. We'll start with you, Naledi: what do you make of what we have?'

Naledi calmly stated her summation. 'No doubt we don't have all the pieces, but it seems to me that this is what happened. The child went missing on the afternoon or evening of the fifteenth of April 1994. A search party of both police and villagers worked almost round the clock for five days, but found no trace of the child. On the sixth day, a man by the name of Shosho showed up at the police station carrying a bundle of clothes. They were bloodstained. He'd been part of the search party, so he was certain the clothes had been placed where he found them after the search of that particular place. A police officer placed the clothes in a box, properly labelled the box and placed it in the exhibits locker. Now, from information that doesn't form part of the police file, I've found out that that same night, there was a car accident in Botane, a village not very far from here. The rest is conjecture, based on records I've been able to get from a nurse at Maun Hospital. Somehow, things must've gotten mixed up. Three injured people from the accident were transferred to Maun Hospital in a police vehicle. On arrival, one of them was already dead. In the confusion, the box must've been sent with the vehicle – and perhaps, in the confusion, someone thought it came from the vehicle. Perhaps the box was never placed in the exhibits locker; perhaps it was, and was then taken out in error – that isn't clear. Someone, perhaps a nurse, came across the box, and without thinking, or perhaps thinking it belonged to a patient, sent it to the clinic, in the ambulance. Now, it's quite possible the ambulance driver didn't even read the label: his job is to transport people, their personal effects and medicines – not to read. What I'd assume happened is the box was put in the storeroom and has been sitting there ever since. Now, five years later, Amantle here finds it, and all hell breaks loose.'

It was definitely food for thought. After a collective pause, Boitumelo said what was on her mind. 'What I don't understand is why what you've just found out wasn't found out five years ago. Why all the cover-up? – because there *was* a cover-up, no matter what else you'd like to call it.' She wasn't so much challenging Naledi's assessment as trying it out in her own mind.

Naledi paused before responding. 'I think the lion story was created out of fear; there's nothing to really suggest collusion between the killers and the police – at least not with the *entire* police force. You have to see this whole thing from the point of view of the people who were in charge. There could never have been a doubt in anyone's mind that the child was the victim of ritual murder – that was clear. These police officers were frightened from the word go. They had to search for the child; many of them were too far away from their family traditional doctor to protect themselves from the girl's slayers; they were afraid. Then, when the box of clothes mysteriously disappeared, what were they to think? Of course they assumed the worst. And of course the lion story gave them a chance to abandon the investigations. Children disappear all the time, and frightened police officers are sent after the killers. They come back with nothing, because they're not too keen to catch anyone. They were doomed to fail, as happens in most of these cases – *doomed to fail!*' She glanced at the box containing Neo's clothes.

Nancy then cleared her voice and asked Naledi, 'Could you be wrong that the cover-up was out of fear, as opposed to a deliberate attempt to shield the killers? What I mean is can you imagine that kind of collusion in the system, as you know it?'

Silence reigned before Boitumelo answered. 'I have to say that what Naledi's saying makes more sense; I wouldn't, however, rule out the possibility that a police officer or two was directly involved in either the killing or the protection of the killers. I can't, however, imagine lower-rank officers deliberately protecting the killers; "being afraid" makes more sense. And if an officer in a powerful position was involved, he could really work it to make sure they stayed afraid and totally ineffective.'

Amantle was trying to process all the information she was receiving. She thought the story still had too many holes in it. 'None of this answers the question of why or how the clothes ended up where they were found – or even why this particular child was targeted. *How* was she selected? It seems to me the killers would've had to know her habits beforehand. If we assume a vehicle was used, and if we assume the killers had planned the whole thing, we have to assume they weren't just riding around different villages hoping to find a lone child. This leads me to believe there must be a village link to it all; that was one of the reasons I decided we shouldn't meet in the village tonight: I sense someone from the village must be involved.'

'I hear you,' Boitumelo responded. 'But, we must accept we're not going to try to solve this murder tonight: what we need to do with this information is to come up with a plan for tomorrow's meeting; we need to decide what we hope to accomplish tomorrow. As you suggested, Amantle, I passed on information about the meeting to all the major papers – but what is it we want to pass on to the public? What is it we want to accomplish?'

Amantle replied, 'No doubt we'll have to hand over the clothes to the police; we want to do that at the *kgotla* so at least that part can't be covered up again.'

Daniel now took a turn to speak. 'And the villagers have a set of demands, as they've stated in their petition – but I think that might be where the lawyers come in.' He looked around for some indication he was on the right path. 'Boitumelo, and perhaps Naledi – I don't know about the ethics of Naledi's involvement in this – might have to publicly identify themselves as lawyers acting for the villagers. Does that make sense?'

Nancy answered the question. 'I think that *does* make sense – and don't we need to prepare . . .' She left her sentence to trail off as she and the other four listened to an indeterminate sound outside the tent. 'What was that? Did you hear that?' she asked.

At first, no one answered. Then Daniel cast a sideways glance at Amantle and finally responded. 'That was, of course, a lion – but before anyone panics and derails the very good progress we've made so far, I want to assure you that that lion was at least ten kilometres away. And there's plenty of game outside, there: there's no reason whatsoever why a lion would desire any one of us in this tent – none at all.'

Boitumelo had found another opening. '"*Assure*" us? Did you say "*assure*" us? Ten kilometres my ass! That lion's no further than *one* kilometre away – and even if it *were* ten kilometres away, who says it plans to stay that far away? It has legs, no? Four powerful legs, with powerful paws attached to each one of them! It can roam these plains as it pleases. Amantle, why couldn't you have chosen a more civilised place to find this box? *Really!* Do you have to be so damn adventurous? I mean there were how many TSP positions in this entire country? And you had to draw this one! And you just *had* to drag us out into this place. We have lions roaring down our ears, and hyenas staring at us, and all manner of animals howling at us – and you think this is *fine*? You think it's *regular*? You think it's just Boitumelo being *unreasonable*? *Maria, Mma-Jeso!*' She was standing and almost shouting. However, when no one said anything in response, and the lion outside roared without a care, she sat down and admitted, in a small pathetic voice, 'Guys, I'm not handling this thing too well; I know that. I just don't "do bushes" too well – not lion-infested bushes, anyway. Just give me a minute to calm down. Can't we move into the vehicle? I think metal's much safer than this thin material! Those *Americans*: they can go to the moon, but they can't build a claw-resistant tent! It's almost as if they *want* us to be eaten! Let's move to the car – *please*?

Naledi corrected her about the tent's country of origin. 'This tent was made in China.'

'*Shut up!*' Boitumelo responded vehemently.

Amantle wasn't sure whether to be stern or gentle with her friend: Boitumelo was usually so self-assured and in charge, but tonight she was falling apart when her colleagues needed her to be focused. 'No: you know the car would be too cramped to work in – and just think how many cattle posts are in this area: people live around here, and I bet you're more likely to die from a car crash than be killed by a lion. Lions don't like humans: a lion has to be old or injured and desperate to go after a human.'

Boitumelo countered, 'And who says the lion outside isn't old or injured and desperate?'

'She has a point,' put in Naledi.

'Naledi, why don't you just shut up?' Daniel demanded. 'Do you *have* to make everything worse?' He was glaring at her.

Amantle then gently pulled Boitumelo down and made her sit down. She offered her a cup of tea and spoke to her as if she were speaking to a child. 'You listen to the radio all the time, no? You watch TV and read the papers? Okay: how many car accidents have you read about over the past week alone – probably five? Maybe more. And we all know car accidents are so common that most don't even make the papers, right? We also know a single lion attack on a human being would make news, even if it happened in some zoo in some country we otherwise never hear about, right? *Right!* Now, when was the last time you heard, read or watched anything about a lion attacking a human being? Think about it. When was it? I bet it's so long ago you can hardly recall the details. Of course it happens – and when it does, we're shocked. But it doesn't happen often enough for us to even entertain the thought. It makes the headlines precisely because it's very uncommon. Now, please drink your tea and let us get back to work. I have big problems, and none of them include being in danger of being eaten by a lion . . . Nancy, you were saying?'

All eyes turned to Nancy, who replied, 'I was going to suggest we prepare a statement you or Boitumelo could read tomorrow on behalf of the villagers. The petition's okay, but we need to develop a document that makes it very clear what the villagers demand and expect, and what Boitumelo's role will be after tomorrow. My concern, however, is that we can't pretend much can happen after a five-year cold trail. It'd be irresponsible of us to lead the villagers to think this murder will be solved; it most probably won't – or am I wrong?' She looked up to elicit comments.

Amantle explained, 'That's what I tried to tell them as well; the thing, however, is that many of the villagers believe they can have the murder solved through divination – that would mean they take the clothes to a diviner.'

'Well, I'm an outsider here,' Nancy remarked, 'so I don't need to believe in that. But why can't they be allowed to do it if it'll satisfy them? Surely no harm could possibly come out of it. If they find the killers, that'd be great, and if they don't, they don't.'

Boitumelo put her teacup down and took a sip of wine before she responded. 'It's not that simple, Nancy: divination could well ruin the evidence. And it wouldn't be a good idea to simply sur - render the only evidence in this case to a stranger. And what if the diviner they consult is the same one the killers consulted years ago? What if divination involves killing a goat or cow or whatever and soaking the same clothes in the animal's blood? I understand why Amantle persuaded them not to consult a diviner. Tomorrow has to be mainly about getting the authorities to admit their mistakes. They must clearly apologise for the cover-up and explain why it happened. The officers involved must be punished. And we're to be the villagers' eyes and ears in Gaborone to make sure what's promised at tomorrow's meeting takes place. I wish there were a chance of meeting the villagers ahead of the meeting – is that a possibility, Amantle?'

Amantle replied, 'The meeting's scheduled to start at nine o'clock. If we start off early, we can meet the small group that's watching the nurses at the clinic; we could even round up a few more – rural people get up really early, so that shouldn't be a problem.'

Boitumelo picked up on the reference to the nurses. 'Can we talk a bit more about the nurses? I really hope you won't be facing a kidnapping charge for your role in that – the villagers too. And if the state decides not to charge you, the nurses might decide to sue you anyway. What exactly do you mean by "the small group that's watching the nurses"? What does "watching the nurses" entail?' She had a concerned look on her face as she focused on her young friend.

'Okay; okay,' Amantle responded; 'the nurses were told they couldn't leave the village – they couldn't anyway, because there was no transport out: no vehicles have been allowed into the village over the past few days. And –'

'They had an ambulance at their disposal,' Boitumelo interrupted; they could've had the driver drive them out. They *are* – or at least *were* – in charge of the clinic, the ambulance and the driver.'

Amantle explained, 'The driver fell ill rather unexpectedly; he took a week off. And government rules are very clear: only a designated officer can drive a government vehicle – so the nurses were advised to stay within the clinic compound for their own safety. They're government officers, so the villagers might have unreasonably held them responsible for the police failures in this case. Some villagers took it upon themselves to watch over them for their own safety – and at least ten villagers can testify that the driver had "the runs" and had to take sick leave. At no point were the nurses physically restrained, hit or denied food.' She looked around, a deadpan look on her face. 'Do you see kidnapping in these facts? I was hoping you, as my lawyer, wouldn't be so quick to see an offence where none was intended. Haven't you told me before that someone has to have a guilty intent as well as perform a guilty act? I see neither here.'

The other four looked at Amantle in silence for a while. Daniel broke the hiatus by clapping his hands. Using the voice of court officialdom, he declared, 'We, the members of the jury, find the defendant not guilty of the offence of kidnapping.' Smiles beamed all round.

'Not so fast, mister jury foreman,' corrected Boitumelo. 'And you, Daniel, watch way too much TV: there's no jury in this country, so her fate, if it came to trial, would be in the hands of one person. Let's hope that that one person is as easily convinced of Amantle's innocence as are the occupants of this tent.' She looked at Amantle. 'That's a good beginning, Amantle; we'll have to revisit that angle before we're finished tonight. But that's not bad, not bad at all. I'm impressed. That's not to say you're home and hosed – but I'm impressed.'

Amantle nodded in approval. She then remained quiet for some time before again raising the question of the murderers. 'Let's go back to the question of who the murderers are – not the names, but what kind of people they must be: profiles, kind of. This is a remote village, so the killers must've come by vehicle. And to cut up a child that age alive, you'd need at least three people, possibly more: the child would have to be held down.'

'I think you're right,' Boitumelo said; 'the killers would've been driving a vehicle – I mean we're not talking about poor people here: we're probably talking about politicians or business-men.'

'Why can't it be businesswomen?' Nancy wanted to know.

'Ritual murders are mainly committed by men,' Boitumelo explained, 'although not always. If a woman were involved, she'd probably be in the role of a *sangoma*: a witchdoctor – but even they're mainly men. No, I'd say we're talking about men – although that's not necessarily so. No; no: we can't discount involvement of a woman or women – especially these days, with more and more women becoming *sangomas*. What do you think, Daniel?' She looked to Daniel for some insights.

Daniel nodded and considered his response. 'I'd say men as

well. A woman might trap the child, but generally the killing's a male thing – men already successful but wanting to go even higher: an MP wanting to be a minister; an assistant minister wanting to be a full minister; a deputy headmaster wanting to be a headmaster; a businessman planning to expand his business – that sort of thing. But, then, you're correct: it *could* be a woman wanting more power – wasn't the alleged killer of that child in Sanoko a woman?'

Nancy had a thought. 'How about a minister or headmaster or businessman wanting to stay where he is – warding off a takeover, as it were?'

'That too,' agreed Amantle. 'You're right; of course you're right.'

It was Nancy again who asked, 'Would the witchdoctor attend the killing, do you think?'

'Yes, that's possible,' responded Naledi; 'the killers have to take the parts to their witchdoctors, after all. His role, as I understand it, is that he'll grind the body parts, mix them with herbs and use the concoction as *muti*, or medicine. Of course, a lot of what we know is conjecture: it's not as if you can just walk up to someone and get the details! God knows how the little that *is* known is known for sure at all! Another thing: we can't overlook the fact that killers often kill for other people – they might be messengers for the big men. And there's something else to think about: even if the killers are the big men themselves, they might also sell the body parts to other big men – the ring of actors might be larger than the four or so people who were actually involved.' She shook her head, thinking that the task before them was seemingly hopeless.

Amantle stated what was on her mind at that moment. 'It seems to me that however we look at it, the killers – or at least some of them – will be at the meeting tomorrow. They have to be people associated with this village somehow. At least one of them has to be a man who knew which child to select – a businessman who has a cattle post in these parts? a politician who's addressed a political rally in the village?'

'But,' Boitumelo suggested, 'as we've already agreed, we're not going to solve the case tonight – so let's go back to what we can do tonight.'

The group of five spent almost the whole night working on the case; none got more than two hours' sleep. When the eastern horizon reddened, Amantle and Daniel started the fire and began making breakfast – a sumptuous one, by any standards: bacon, sausages, eggs and toast. As the ingredients sizzled on the flat pan specially designed for outside cooking, Boitumelo, whose mood had significantly improved, made tea and coffee. She was proud of the night's work they'd all completed. No doubt the reddening of the eastern horizon was some comfort for her. When a lone elephant appeared, seemingly out of nowhere, she scrabbled into her vehicle, but when the elephant passed on as if it hadn't even seen the party, she came out and had breakfast.

Amantle broke into the breakfast chatter. 'Doesn't it bother you that the case was actually declared closed so soon after the child's disappearance?'

No one answered for a while. It was Boitumelo who broke the silence. 'What do you mean?' she asked Amantle.

Amantle replied, 'Isn't the usual line in this kind of case to pretend investigations are going on whereas nothing's happening at all? Who would've benefited from a definite decision to have the case closed?'

Again silence ensued. Naledi finally offered her thoughts. 'Perhaps the reason's simply that they'd decided early on to say the child was eaten by lions. Having said that, surely there was nothing to investigate?'

Amantle added another question of her own. 'But why such a definite stance so early on? Why was there no attempt to actually investigate the murder? Surely there must've been some leads: tyre tracks; an unfamiliar vehicle in the village; some herder who saw something! Even if the clothes indeed ended up at the clinic by some accident, how do we explain the fact there was no attempt to investigate this case? I don't buy the theory that fear was the only motivator here: someone pulled strings to kill the investigation – someone must have!' She was thinking out aloud.

'But who?' asked Boitumelo, who was also expressing her thoughts unedited. 'Do you think, perhaps, it was the station commander? He took over the station two years before the murder, and has been in the position ever since.'

The five had been ignoring their breakfast, and were now moving closer together. Naledi cleared her voice to speak, and the others listened. 'I think Amantle's right: someone with the power to use the clothes' disappearance to both frighten people and suggest that any more investigations would be futile did just that. If it was the station commander, his juniors would've been happy to be given a way out; if it was someone higher up, wouldn't the station commander have wondered what the reason was for the interference?' In attempting to tease out the reasons from the few facts the group had, she was being led to only ask more questions.

Amantle declared, 'I have this feeling that someone with ill motives influenced the police decision to close the case.' She couldn't let the thought go.

Boitumelo put an important fact on the table. 'We already know that big people are involved – that's a given: ritual murders aren't committed by poor people.'

Daniel interjected. 'I don't know about that: what if the killer was a diviner collecting *dipheko* for his own use? Then no big man would be involved in this type of case.'

As had happened the night before, they'd resumed their circular discussions by trading scenarios and feeling there was no hope of finding out the truth.

'Mmmm,' Amantle agreed; 'I guess you're right. But even then, he'd have to do that for someone or some people. Who are those people? They'd have to be involved in the killing too, no? Someone with power shut off this thing tight and quick and early.' She nodded as if in agreeing with herself she was converting her speculations to facts.

Daniel asked, 'Have you ever considered there's a ring of ritual murderers who operate countrywide and sell human parts to a select clientele?'

'Jesus Christ!' Amantle gasped. 'That's too scary to even imagine!'

Whenever Amantle was involved in talking about witchcraft, she was overcome by an especially sad memory. One morning, when she'd been about eight, just as she'd been hoping to have a couple of hours before the sun came up, a voice had splintered the peace of the early hours: 'Witch! There's a witch in my yard!

Witch! Help! There's a witch in my yard!' As Amantle had been springing off her floor mat, competing with her siblings to be first to the rondaval's entrance, she'd noticed that as a result of the shouts the whole neighbourhood had been woken. She'd then looked on in horror as her grandmother, who'd seemed disoriented, was frog-marched, by two women, from the neighbour's yard towards the ward *kgotla*, or meeting place. Just then, Amantle had heard her mother, behind her, cry in a strangled voice, 'Oh, my God! Oh, Mooketsi, who bore me, who now lies at Magwera graveyard! The Bakgatla who've borne me, what am I seeing now?!' It had been Amantle's mother's mother-in-law who was being dragged to the ward *kgotla*.

'*Mma, mma, what happened?*' Amantle had cried, frightened. '*What's going to happen to grandmother?*' The children's grandmother had usually shared a rondaval with Amantle and her brother Moratiwa, but Amantle had spent that night in their parents' rondaval because she hadn't been feeling well. It had been the case that her grandmother should still have been in bed, because she usually hadn't risen until almost everyone else had gotten up; in fact, it'd been Amantle's task to empty the old woman's chamber pot every morning, and she'd had to wait for her to use it one more time before she could carry it away. How her grandmother had come to be found practising witchcraft in their neighbour's yard early in the morning, when she usually hadn't had the energy to get up so early, was a mystery.

Amantle's mother hadn't answered; instead, she'd kept on calling on her parents and a long line of ancestors, all long dead, for help.

Amantle had walked towards Moratiwa and whispered, 'What happened? How did grandmother get there? Did you see her leave the rondaval?'

'I don't know,' Moratiwa had replied. 'I was asleep; I don't know – don't ask me: they'll say I'm a witch as well.' There was fear in his face.

'But grandmother's *not* a witch; *she's not a witch!*' Amantle had shouted the last words, and the crowd had turned to look at her.

'All we can say is that witches bear baby witches, just like snakes bear baby snakes!' The retort had come from an angry neighbour at the back of the crowd.

Amantle's mother had seemed to recover somewhat from the shock. She'd turned to her children and ordered, 'Get back to the *lapa* – all of you! – back into the *lapa*!'

Amantle and her siblings had scrambled back into their compound, but hadn't known what to do once they were there. On any other day, they'd have started the fire and made a breakfast of tea and *motogo*; in fact, on any other day, they'd have gone next door to get coals for the fire because theirs had gone out during the night. This morning, instead, they'd stood on tiptoes and watched the village *kgotla* from over the yard's perimeter wall.

It'd seemed as if some trial were already in progress, but too many people had been speaking at the same time. 'Last year all my chickens died, and I never thought it could be her!' a neighbour had announced. Another neighbour had said in response, 'Why did you talk to her? You should've left her there, stuck in one place for days.' Amantle had known, without ever having seen it happen, that a witch can stand stuck to one place for days if the owners of the yard don't talk to her or him. Another contribution had been 'We must try her right now – *right now!*' The crowd had been thickening as word was getting out that a witch had been caught. 'What was she doing when you found her?' 'Where are her witchcraft tools?' 'She's a witch! A *witch!*'

'Please let me explain,' Amantle's grandmother had pleaded. 'I'm not a witch. Please let me explain. I needed to go and relieve myself. Please help me; please, somebody, help me!' Tears had welled in her eyes and run down her old, wrinkled face.

'Whoever heard of a witch saying "Yes, I'm a witch?!" You think we're stupid?' someone had yelled in response.

Then, a pool that could only have been urine had spread around the old woman's legs.

'*Ijoo!* Watch out! Her powers are going! She's pissing on herself!' someone had offered.

Mma-Seeletso, a woman from a neighbouring ward, had asked, 'Is she really a witch? Perhaps the poor old woman was lost – disoriented due to her failing sight. She hasn't been well for a while.'

'People whose grandmothers were witches will excuse other witches,' another neighbour had retorted.

Mma-Seeletso had then charged forward as if ready to punch someone. 'My grandmother wasn't a witch, and if you don't hide in the crowd, perhaps I'll know who you are and I can tell you exactly what your own grandmother was! You despicable snake! Come out from the crowd! This woman is no witch, and you all know it! Perhaps she wandered into Mma-Soso's yard because she's losing her sight; perhaps she went there to ask for something – but did you give her a chance to explain? No! And you two,' – she directed her anger at the two women, sisters from another ward, who'd dragged Amantle's grandmother to the *kgotla* – 'you came all the way from Rapotsane Ward, a ward populated by nasty, spiteful people, to come and cause all this trouble! And perhaps you should be asked what you're doing in our ward so early in the morning: perhaps *you're* the witches, you good-for-nothing *mafetwa*. Now we know why you're still *mafetwa*: who'd marry such mean women?'

The crowd had then moved back as Mma-Seeletso walked towards the humiliated old woman, who was sobbing silently, her head bowed.

'Come, Mma-Meleko,' Mma-Seeletso had implored; 'let's go. Today I'm embarrassed to be a human being. I have to say that even animals would be kinder to their own! Come, mma, come.'

As Mma-Seeletso had led Amantle's grandmother home, the crowd had dispersed quietly.

Amantle therefore knew that charges of witchcraft weren't always based on solid evidence. This morning, she shook her head in order to clear out the disagreeable memories.

Naledi offered yet another angle to the scenarios the five were considering. 'Another thing, it could be that the people who closed the case were motivated by a desire to avoid riots. These kinds of murders stir up people's emotions, and innocent people end up being hurt in the process. It's happened before: people stoned; houses burnt; people accused despite there being little evidence to support the accusations.'

'Okay, people,' Boitumelo announced, 'let's move it: we need to pack up – time to face the bad guys!'

Within twenty minutes, they were leaving their camp. Even Boitumelo looked back wistfully at the mound of earth left over from the buried fire.

They drove along the river, past lagoons teaming with herds of impala, lechwe, water bucks, birds, elephants and many other animals that none of the five could name. They even came across a pride of lions, too full and lazy from the previous night's kill to be bothered by the group's obvious gawking. From the safety of the two-vehicle convoy, the five marvelled at the beauty of nature. Birds skipped on water lilies, crocodiles basked on sandy banks, hippos grunted and yawned, and monkeys hissed at everyone from the safety of their treetops.

'How can so much beauty coexist with so much evil?' Amantle wondered out aloud.

No one chose to respond.

CHAPTER 20

'The ancestors and God are unhappy today; let's hope they're on our side.' Mma-Neo muttered the words as she pulled her small shawl tightly around her shoulders. It was her best shawl, the one she reserved for important occasions such as weddings and funerals. It was bright purple and trimmed in black. She made the comment about her ancestors in response to the relentless hooting of a lone owl perched on the big *morula* tree next to the *kgotla*: owls are bad luck, and she didn't need one on this day, of all days.

'They have to be on your side,' responded Rra-Naso. 'The anger isn't directed at you – can't possibly be directed at you. I have a feeling you'll soon learn who your true friends are.' There was a certainty in his voice through which Mma-Neo was given a boost of confidence. The two had just met with Amantle and her four friends, and the five youngsters were still in the clinic office making last-minute corrections to their many documents. A few villagers had started milling around, waiting for the big day to begin.

Mma-Neo was overawed by the fact that big people from the capital were to meet in her village in order to answer a summons linked to her. She'd long lost any hope that the mystery of her daughter's death would ever be solved. She'd long accepted that compared with the death of a rich person, the death of a poor person didn't elicit as much passion for bringing the perpetrators to justice – or at least that was what all the radio broadcasters suggested. She'd become fond of Amantle. Today, she said to Rra-Naso, 'That girl Amantle must be careful: she still has her life to live after this village – I believe she's hoping for a government scholarship to go to university. You must advise her not to be too visible today: these people will be watching her, and she might be punished later. Maybe her lawyer friend should do all the talking.'

Rra-Naso had also come to admire the young TSP girl who'd shaken up their village. 'That's so kind of you to think of someone else at a time like this. Yes, you're right; I'll talk to her – but I doubt it'll make any difference: she's a driven young woman. But you're right: she needs to know when to step aside. I'll talk to her.' He, too, was worried that the youthful and exuberant Amantle might act without giving thought to her own interests.

The two sat on an old bench from where they'd be able to view the *kgotla*, and waited for the government officials to arrive. In the eyes of the other villagers, they were increasingly becoming a couple. Grief had brought them together, and the villagers hoped that if the two gained nothing else from the whole sad mess, they'd gain a lifetime relationship – that perhaps, amid the sadness, they'd find a kernel of happiness. The two sad friends watched as BX vehicles started rolling into the village.

As Mma-Neo sat there, she stole a few glances at her friend. He'd become gentle with age, especially since his wife's death. *Loneliness would do that to a person,* she thought to herself. However, she remembered a rougher Rra-Naso from days gone by – perhaps not exactly 'rough', but definitely stronger and sterner. She remembered an incident in which he'd led an effort to have his nephew Ramarago cured. It'd been a tough decision for Ramarago's family members to make, but once they'd taken it, they'd had to execute it with firmness and resolve.

Mma-Neo had found out about the plan when Neo had come home from school bearing the news she'd heard from some villagers that Ramarago, the deaf-mute man who lived in Ramasilo Ward, was going to be cured of his insanity. Ramarago was a huge, lumbering man who wore a *tshega* as if he were a little boy. Even Neo's fifteen-year-old friend Mosweu had been out of a *tshega* for close to two years: he wasn't about to expose his butt to the entire world in that skimpy piece of clothing! Ramarago, however, had torn at any trousers he was forced to wear. Although he hadn't been able to speak, whenever women or children went by, he'd made frightening, guttural sounds and lifted his *tshega*, thereby exposing himself. His family had kept him tied to a tree, and people had said he slept there, even at night. The family, Neo had heard, had engaged the services of a man from the neighbouring village of Mosilo, a man who'd had the power to cure insanity.

That day, Neo had hurriedly changed out of her school clothes, and announced to her mother that she was happy that Ramarago would soon be clean and decently dressed. She'd been wondering whether he'd subsequently remember his 'mad' days. She'd also been wondering what would be the first words he'd utter once he were cured. She'd then started to be sceptical about whether any cure were possible. Why hadn't the family found the curing man before? After all, the village of Mosilo was only ten kilometers away. 'Do you think he'll be cured?' she'd asked her mother.

'I don't know,' Motlatsi had replied. 'But they say Marekiso's cured many similar cases. They say he learnt his skills from his grandfather.'

'Why should it be public?' Neo had asked. 'Most cures are done privately – why should people watch?'

'They say insanity can only be cured publicly,' Motlatsi had explained. 'Let's go and find out.'

Mother and daughter had then hurried to Ramarago's home, and as they'd approached, they'd been able to see that a reasonably large crowd had gathered. Four men – two on each side of Ramarago – had been holding on to leather ropes looped around the patient's chest and waist. Ramarago had been doubled over, and saliva had been dripping from his mouth. Just as Neo and Motlatsi had joined the crowd, Ramarago had raised his *tshega* and let out a loud, guttural sound. Most of the children had fled as a result. Motlatsi had instructed Neo to go home: she hadn't expected to see Ramarago being restrained in that way, although she couldn't have said what she'd expected to see. Neo, however, hadn't been able to move: she'd been rooted to the spot at which she'd stopped to watch the unbelievable spectacle unfolding before her very eyes.

'Tie his hands as well,' one of the restraining men had said. Some other men had then brought two more ropes and tied them around Ramarago's hands. Two more men had then joined the original four, to provide reinforcement. A man had then come from one of the rondavals, accompanied by Ramarago's father. He'd been carrying a whip, the type used for driving cattle and donkeys. He'd then charged forward, shouting, '*Madness, leave my son! Madness, leave Ramarago!*' With every shout, he'd used the whip to lash Ramarago. On being attacked, Ramarago had bellowed voicelessly and tried to run. The six men had held on with all their might.

'Mad people are strong,' a woman standing next to Mma-Neo had informed no one in particular; 'these men must hold on tight.'

The man holding the whip had then mercilessly rained lashes on Ramarago. On contact, the whip had split the poor soul's skin, whereupon blood had streamed down his body. Many of the children had held their hands over their nose and mouth, staring in horror. Neo hadn't been able to watch any more. Motlatsi had watched her as she'd left silently, and then followed and caught up with her. As they'd passed the back part of Ramarago's compound, they'd seen Ramarago's mother with her hands over her ears, crying pitifully.

Two weeks later, Motlatsi had seen Neo creep up to Ramarago's compound: the girl had clearly been hoping that Ramarago wouldn't be at his tree, tied up as he'd been ever since anyone could remember. Motlatsi, too, had gone there. Together, they'd peeped in: the length of rope had been there, but no Ramarago. They'd looked at each other and smiled, thinking, *At least he was cured.* However, just then, Ramarago had let out his frightening sound, stepped back from the thorn-bush fence where he'd been hiding, and flipped back his *tshega*. Motlatsi had watched with dismay as Neo had run back home, and by the time Motlatsi had reached home, Neo had been crying inconsolably. When the little girl had stopped crying, she'd vomited, then lain down and promptly fallen asleep.

One of the six men who'd held on to Ramarago had been Rra-Naso. He'd only been doing his duty, even if the treatment had failed. Looking at him as they sat down together today, Mma-Neo was unable to see the strength and determination that had seemed to possess him that day: yes, grief can drain people of their strength – wasn't *she* a prime example?

Later, when Motlatsi recalled the day of the big *kgotla* meeting, what her mind seized on was the stunningly blue sky below which many low, soap-sud, white clouds had gathered. She recalled thinking that the day was the kind of scene Neo might have drawn – everything exaggerated: sky too blue, clouds too many and too white; a day on which Motlatsi had allowed a sliver of hope to enter her heart. She recalled the hooting owl and how nervous it had made her.

But that was later.

CHAPTER 21

Under the blue and white sky, someone else was watching the vehicles arrive. Lesego Disanka had told no one that she was planning to attend the *kgotla* meeting to be held in Gaphala. However, she'd had no problem getting a ride to it.

Lesego had found out about the meeting by accident: during her university holidays, she'd been an intern in the Ministry of Health and been given the task of organising transport to enable Minister Gape to attend the meeting. Her attention had been drawn to the name Gaphala, a name she'd been able to neither see nor hear without feeling a jolt of pain go through her body. When she'd examined the paperwork for the *kgotla* meeting more closely, she'd discovered its location was to be Gaphala. She'd been piqued to find out that the trip hadn't been at all planned ahead of time: none of the ministry's employees had known about it, and when they had been told, they'd been instructed to keep it a secret – there is, of course, no better way to get civil servants to tell all and sundry about something than to tell them not to tell anyone.

She'd made a few phone calls to the Central Transport Agency and found out that a few other four-wheel-drive vehicles had been ordered for a trip to Gaphala. She'd then decided she'd make herself extra-helpful to the minister's personal secretary, and being a temporary 'go-for', she'd raised no suspicions when she'd offered to help make preparations for the minister's trip. The secretary had happily given her the task of making the hotel reservations, following up on the transport arrangements and photocopying the minister's briefing notes.

Within minutes, Lesego found herself standing deep in a crowd of villagers as they filed into the little *kgotla*. Five years had passed since the fateful night on which she'd watched her father's hands as they'd wrapped little parcels under the light of her own torch – a torch she still had, a torch she'd never been able to use since that night.

She could now see her father ascending the VIP stand. She and he had had very little contact over the past five years: she'd always had a good reason not to come home during school holidays: a school trip, a church trip, a visit to a relative. Her parents had visited her a couple of times, always at her headmaster's insistence, because she'd been a very good student: he'd needed to show her off to her parents, and they'd had to come. And, under the glare of the entire school community, she and her father had touched; they'd had to touch: they'd had to have the obligatory hugs and kisses in order to acknowledge her achievements. The touches had been frosty, and welts had been left in her heart as a result of them.

Now, the past was pulling her back – or was it the other way around? Perhaps it was the present that was pushing her back to her past, demanding she confront her demons.

A few other VIPs now seated themselves up on the stand with her father. Much handshaking and smiling ensued; Very Important People patted each other on the back as everyone waited for the meeting to commence. As Lesego watched, she noticed that the Very Important People were sitting under a thatched canopy in order to shelter them from the sun. In contrast, the Not Very Important People were standing against the trees; a few had an umbrella. Her mother was sitting among the raised VIPs, dutifully accompanying her husband.

Lesego felt alone in the crowd – after all, it actually consisted of smaller groups who had interests in common. The government officials were in one group, the villagers in another, the newspaper people likewise. Her father and mother were a couple. She felt as if she were the only solitary attendee. She felt like a moth dancing around a fire, sure to be singed. Her mind went back to that night, five years before, on which she couldn't fall asleep. She recalled the details as if she were once again living those few days. Fear had squeezed out the five years that had passed, and as always happened, she couldn't recall the events if she thought of them as having occurred in the past; she could recall them in the present tense only.

What's she to do? Her father's this rich man, and they live in this nice house. She has her own bedroom – in her village, an almost unheard-of luxury! Both her parents drive, and each of them has a car. But she's not happy: something about her father frightens her. He's kind; he's not stingy with money: she wears the latest fashions, and he pays without complaining; he drives her and her brothers and sister places whereas other children have to walk. But it's as if another man is living within the man they live with – and it's the man within she's afraid of. His eyes are the eyes of someone who has deep secrets; her fear is that those secrets could sunder the family peace.

Tonight, she can't sleep: she feels a storm gathering in her head and all around her. Her father's been meeting secretly with Head Man Bokae and a man she doesn't know. She knows they've been meeting in secret because a week ago she found them in the small office in the family butchery. She had to go in there to pick up a set of keys her mother had left there earlier. The butchery was long closed, and wasn't the best place to meet: it was small and cramped. And the men had only a candle burning – at first, she thought it might have been too much trouble for them to run the generator for the main lights. However, the family house had more-comfortable spaces in which people could meet and was only a few metres away from the butchery. And she remembered that as a result of her father's furtive and secretive association with Bokae two years before, he became quiet and subdued. For weeks he seemed like a frightened man whose eyes had become searching . . . then, just as suddenly, he returned to his old self.

Now, he's meeting with Bokae in secret again. She hasn't said anything to her mother about finding her father at the butchery:

there's something sinister about the three men huddled over a candle, whispering in the semi-darkness. She knows about her father's mistresses and is sure her mother knows as well. She's aware that beneath her mother's pretended confidence lurks seething anger. She's seen a glimpse of it one morning, when her father arrives later than usual. He's tried to slink into the house unnoticed by the children, only to emerge from the bedroom minutes later sporting a rather prominent bump on his head. Around the breakfast table, the bump grows with the silence. The more the silence is ignored, the more it looms. And the bump seems to grow in prominence until her father leaves the table and returns to the bedroom. Her mother spends the rest of the day in her room while her father potters around the garden, as if in a state of confusion. The problem isn't that he's been to see one of his mistresses; it's that he's daring to flaunt the visit to his wife, his children and possibly his neighbours. He should give an excuse, such as that he had to go to the cattle post – or, better still, he should have been back before sunrise. Surely the mistress's neighbours would have seen his car leaving in the morning. If Lesego had found her father with a mistress in the little room, she wouldn't be as afraid as she is after finding him with the two men – a mistress is unlikely to threaten the peace of their home; Lesego feels that those two men do.

That's why she's sitting on her bed, watching the gate and hoping her father comes home: *Come home safe,* she prays. It's way past three in the morning, and still no sign of her father. She calls him on his mobile phone, but there's no answer. She feels that if he were at his mistress's house he'd answer for the simple reason that he'd assume it's an emergency. She can feel in her bones that something's happening tonight, something to do with Bokae and the man she's since found out to be the deputy headmaster of a neighbouring-village school.

She's almost nodding off, when she hears a car drive up. She looks up but sees no headlights. She peers through the window and can vaguely make out her father's double-cab Toyota Hilux. It has to be it – but why are the headlights off? The doors are opening, and a man's getting out. The butchery gate's being opened. She strains for the telltale squeak, but the gate makes no sound. The person opening the gate must know he has to pick up and push the heavy gate at the same time to stop it squeaking. The man's opened the gate. The vehicle slides in, and the gate's closed behind it. Why would her father be driving into the butchery with no headlights on? Why would he be driving into the butchery? Who's the man who knows not to make the gate squeak? The name Bokae rushes into her head. She's sweating with fear and confusion.

She puts on a coat over her pyjamas, then puts on a pair of shoes. She walks hurriedly through the house, making as little noise as possible. She uses her hands to feel outwards to avoid bumping into furniture. Once she's out through the main door, she darts to the back of the yard, and exits through the small gate. She walks rapidly towards the butchery, and enters the yard through the small pedestrian gate. She can see her father and two other men. She recognises them as being Bokae and the man since revealed to be the deputy headmaster. Car doors are gently closed, and the men hurry towards the back of the building. They look strange: there's wildness about the way they hurry along without speaking. She ducks back, expecting them to head for the small office in which she saw them weeks before. Instead, her father unlocks the back door to the butchery itself. The men follow silently: shadows in the night. A key turns after them.

What can they possibly be doing in there? And what are they carrying? All Lesego makes out are plastic bags. Each man's been carrying a plastic bag containing wet-looking items. The moon's not bright enough to help her see any more. And her father only briefly turns on the torch he's holding in his right hand. For a minute, she thinks they might be carrying some meat – but that wouldn't make sense: the butchery's full of more meat than they could ever wish for. It wouldn't make sense for her father to bring home small pieces of meat in the middle of the night.

She wonders what to do, then decides to look through a window. It's too high: she needs something to climb up on. She remembers a ladder's resting against the front of the building. She moves towards it, half drags it over to the window, and climbs up. Where are they? She can't see them: there's no light in there. Her father switches on the torch – her torch – and yes: it *is* pieces of meat the men are carrying. What are they doing with pieces of meat in the middle of the night? The light falls on Bokae – and is that blood on him? The men are taking off their clothes and piling them into a corner. Her father brings out clothes from a big plastic bag he pulls out of the fridge. What's he doing? Why would clothes be in a fridge? Why are the men changing in the middle of the night? What does all this mean? She's afraid. Her father individually wraps the pieces in cellophane he usually uses to wrap meat for customers. She watches his big hands, and shivers: those hands have held her and loved her. Some pieces are really small; the biggest is no bigger than a slice of bread. The other men watch silently. A hand reaches over to stop him; it's Bokae's. The men consult in whispers. She catches the word 'anus', and sees the men nod as they continue to wrap. They place the tiny parcels in a plastic bag, then place the bag in the deep-freezer. She watches her father as he locks the freezer. He collects the clothes they've just taken off, and the three men walk towards the door. She goes down the ladder, and runs home. She falls asleep almost immediately: she's so scared, her mind desperately seeks oblivion.

She wakes up to the smell of burning trash. She walks up to the front of the gate to find her little sister Morati helping their father burn the trash: a big pile that contains all kinds of stuff – old clothes, raked leaves, grass – even cans. She looks at the pile and sees a white T-shirt she remembers seeing last night. Her eyes fly up to her father's face. Their eyes meet, and something happens: he knows she knows, and she knows he knows she knows some - thing. He grabs the can of paraffin and pours on a liberal amount. The fire flares up, and Morati whoops with excitement. Lesego notices for the first time that her father's wrist is bandaged. A bit of blood is staining the bandage. She rears back as if she's been hit across the face. She turns around and runs back into the house.

A little while later, she hears Morati ask her father, 'What's wrong with Sego?' She doesn't hear her father's response. She walks past her paternal grandmother, Mma-Disanka, and almost knocks her over, then continues on through the living room and straight to the bathroom. Fear rises from her stomach, then spills out in yellow and green streaks into the toilet bowl. Her head's pounding. After what seems like a long time, she returns to her bedroom.

'What's wrong, Sego – are you sick?' she hears Morati ask. She hasn't heard her little sister come in.

'I have a headache – that's all,' she replies. She forces a smile. Bile rises to her throat. Tears well in her eyes.

'Daddy says you'll be all right if you just rest today. Here: he wants you to take these.' A fat hand is extended to her.

She looks up with alarm, but her sister is merely offering a small canister of aspirin. 'Where's mama?' she asks.

'She's in the kitchen – didn't you see her just now? Didn't you hear her calling after you?' Morati is looking at her with a mixture of concern and scepticism.

'No, I didn't,' Lesego responds. 'Can you leave me alone for a while? I'll be fine – I just need to rest for a little while.' She smiles to encourage her sister to leave the room. The little girl leaves with a puzzled look on her face.

She tries to read and listen to music – anything to distract her attention. Her mind keeps flying back to last night and two years before. Over the months, the fear has become numbed due to the fuzziness of memory. She still isn't sure what it was that scared her so much back then. She remembers Bokae; she remembers a jumpy, agitated father; she remembers a sweating father whenever the one o'clock news comes on; she remembers a cold mother around the same period. She remembers that weeks later, her father regains his strength and the family rhythm returns to normal. Now the fear is back – except that this time her father looks anything but afraid: he looks strong and towering, if anything. But Bokae, dark - ness and little pieces of meat have to mean something sinister.

Without even knowing she's been planning the move, she runs out of her room in search of her father. She finds him in the kitchen, enjoying a breakfast of eggs and liver. He likes his liver rare. As she sees the blood on the plate, she freezes. She sees the plate filling with blood. Instead of the liver, she sees little pieces, and hears the whispered word 'anus'. Panic envelops her. Fear grips her, and she backs out of the room. All eyes are on her.

'Are you okay, Sego?' her mother, Mma-Lesego, asks. 'Sit down, my child. You look scared: what's the matter?'

She feels her mother's hand on her shoulder, and shrinks back: it's the hand that bandaged the hand that wrapped the little pieces of meat locked in a deep-freezer in the butchery; it's the hand that cooked the liver that's bleeding on the plate that must've been retrieved from the freezer in which the little pieces of meat have been locked up. One thought crushes into another, and she thinks she's going crazy. 'Dad, I want my torch; I just want my torch,' she demands. Her voice is shrill. She's not sure whether getting the torch is the reason she came into the room.

'Sego, are you all right?' her mother asks. 'Is this child all right?' She reaches for Lesego's forehead.

'What do you need a torch for at this time of day?' her grandmother asks. She looks around, searching for understanding.

'Sego! Sego!' her mother yells. 'Sit down: you're scaring us. What's the matter?' Her mother pulls her down, gently but firmly.

She backs off: she's afraid of all of them; afraid *for* all of them. 'Dad,' she begins, 'please give me back my torch. Please: I just want my torch – please; please.' Her voice comes out as if she's struggling to breathe.

'Sego, come here, please,' her father implores her in a soft, familiar voice.

He extends a hand: a familiar hand; the bandaged hand. One finger has blood from the liver dripping from the end of it. That finger has tickled her. That voice has soothed her many times before. Those extended hands have loved her. That voice has made and kept promises. But now she's afraid of and for that voice and those hands: those hands wrapped and wrapped and wrapped small, plastic parcels under cover of darkness.

She jumps back, out of reach. 'Dad, if you just give me back my torch, I won't say anything else.' She says it in a whisper. Is it a plea? a threat? a promise?

'What's she talking about, Rra-Lesego?' Her grandmother wants to know.

What *is* she talking about? She's not sure she knows, either. Her father's standing up. He seems to lose some of his strength. Is that fear clouding his face? Or is it concern for a daughter who's going mad? She wants to say she's sorry, that she doesn't want the torch any more. If her father loses strength, who'll protect them all? She wants him to be strong, but she doesn't want to be part of the secret. She wants her torch back, her own personal sign that she's not part of the wrapping and wrapping and wrapping in the middle of the night.

There's silence. Her father's coming back; he's gone to get her torch from the car. He hands it over to her, silently.

She receives it, silently. 'There's blood on it.' It's a whispered challenge.

'I run a butchery, remember?' It's a whispered plea.

'Yes, dad,' she replies. Is she promising her dad something? She doesn't know what she's agreeing to. She leaves the room and heads for the bathroom. She locks the door, then proceeds to use soap, shampoo and antiseptic detergent to scrub and clean the torch. She's determined her torch will be clean. She sniffs at it and scrubs some more. She's trying to scrub off the memory of last night. She scrubs her hands, too. A blob of suds drops on to her foot. When she reaches over to brush it off, her hand comes in contact with her leg. She feels contaminated, so runs a bath and extends the scrubbing to her entire body. When she's finished, she takes her newly cleaned torch to her room. She puts it on the window sill and crawls into bed. She's exhausted from experiencing a fear the source of which she tries not to understand. She tries to push the words 'ritual murder' out of her head, but they slip in, seep into her brain, occupy it and force everything else out.

She falls asleep, and doesn't wake up until late in the afternoon. When she gets up, her father's off somewhere and her mother's in the living room. Her mother watches her anxiously, but says nothing.

She goes to the kitchen and gets herself some lunch. No one mentions the strange behaviour she'd displayed that morning. She acts as if nothing's the matter, and her mother's happy she has her back. The day after the night of the frantic wrapping of little pieces of meat therefore ends on a normal note – normal, that is, if the gauge for normality is only outward actions.

Over the radio, the announcer says for all to hear, 'A girl aged about twelve or thirteen has been reported missing in the village of Gaphala. The police and villagers have been searching for the child since Sunday morning, but there has been no trace of the young child so far. The police . . .'

It's two days since the torch-scrubbing incident. Lesego and her father have been avoiding each other in a tense dance through which the whole household has been cast in a mood of melancholy.

'Please, children,' Mma-Disanka implores; 'we're listening to the news: could you lower your voices? Please – or better still, go to the TV room.' She's hard of hearing, and she always demands total silence during news bulletins.

Disanka stands up as if he intends to leave the room.

'Dad,' Lesego asks, 'aren't you going to listen to the news? You always listen to the news.' A challenge is evident in her voice.

Before her father can respond, Mma-Disanka says, 'Please: I can't hear with everyone speaking. Listen! Listen! A child's gone missing in Gaphala. Will these brutal men never stop? How can people be so cruel and greedy? Rra-Lesego, sit down and listen.'

Disanka sits down to listen. Lesego glares at him. He pretends he's not aware of the substance of the bulletin. According to the radio announcer, a young girl's gone missing in the small neighbouring village of Gaphala. She'd gone off to look for donkeys but failed to return. The mother didn't report the incident till the next day: she'd been away, only to return the following morning to find the child missing. The police and villagers had tracked the child's movements by following her footprints but had found nothing useful so far. The police aren't yet saying what they suspect.

'These stupid police!' Mma-Disanka interjects. 'Of course the child's been killed for *dipheko* – you don't have to be a genius to know that!' She snorts with disgust at what she considers to be the stupidity of the police.

Lesego glares at her father. 'What do *you* think, dad?' she asks.

Mma-Disanka answers for him. 'Of course your father agrees with me – don't you, Rra-Lesego? A child of twelve doesn't just disappear like an over-ripe mushroom!'

'I agree,' Disanka concurs, weakly.

'Agree with what?' Lesego asks, snarling at him.

'What's with this child?' Mma-Disanka asks the other four family members who are present, including Lesego. 'You've been acting very strangely recently. You're either angry or scared. What are you afraid of? You think someone will come and hurt you like they did that little girl? No one would dare, Sego. Your father's too powerful for anyone to hurt any of you. These poor children always come from a poor family . . . But really, Rra-Lesego, you must go over there to help with the search. And those poor villagers will need people like you to make the police move. You'll see: nothing will happen – *nothing!*'

Lesego leaves the room.

Her mother follows her out. 'What's going on, Sego?' she asks. 'Why are you so angry with your father?'

Lesego feels she has to lie. 'Nothing, mama; nothing.' She wonders whether she's so evil that she sees evil when no one else sees anything wrong.

Her mother looks at her with great concern. 'No, there *is* something bothering you: what is it?'

'Mama,' Lesego begins, 'I want to go to boarding school – this term, this week – like, tomorrow – as soon as I can get in.' She's speaking fast; she must remove herself from this house or else she'll surely go mad.

Her mother feels panic setting in. 'What do you mean you want to go to boarding school? Why? Why now? I mean you've always said you wanted to stay home.'

Lesego has to think quickly. 'Just tell dad I want to go to boarding school, okay? He can arrange it: he has the power and the connections. Any school outside this district will do.'

Her mother doesn't accept her daughter's half-baked argument. 'Lesego,' she says, 'please tell me what's going on: has your father done anything to upset you?'

Lesego tries to hold back tears. 'Mama, tell dad I want to be transferred to another school, outside this district. Please, just do it. Then everything will be okay, otherwise nothing will be okay.' The tears spill out and refuse to stop.

Her mother reaches out to hold her.

She pushes her off, turns, and goes to her room. She finds refuge in sleep, until she's woken by a tentative knock on the door. She opens her eyes and peeps through the bedding. It's dark in the room. The knock becomes a bit louder, but remains tentative, hesitant. She ignores it. The knocker opens the door, turns on the light and walks in.

'Sego, Sego, will you talk to me?' a trembling voice asks, a voice that should be strong but isn't.

The curled-up bundle on the bed emits no answer.

'Sego, my child, please talk to me,' comes the second attempt. Still no response.

'Sego, you were still awake when I came in on Sunday night, weren't you?' There's fear in the question.

'Monday morning,' comes a whisper from the bed.

'I was coming from the cattle post – that's why I was so late.' Is it an invitation to be complicit, or an attempt to persuade her?

'Why are you telling me all this, dad?' The bundle remains covered. They're two people who love each other too much to confront each other, two people who are very afraid.

'You think something else,' he offers. 'Don't think anything else. Please, Sego: I was at the cattle post.' It's a desperate plea.

She addresses him, still under the covers. 'Daddy, please just find me a place in a boarding school – *please*. That's all I ask – as soon as possible: tomorrow. Surely you have the connections to do it.'

'Sego, I don't want you to go away – please don't go away,' he begs.

The bundle finally uncurls and rises. Lesego removes the bedding. A puffy, red-eyed face encounters a pleading one. 'Dad, I need to go away. You know it's best for everyone. I need to leave this place.'

The clean torch is sitting on the window sill. Father and daughter glance at it. Both look away.

There's silence.

The father approaches his daughter, seeking contact; seeking to comfort and be comforted.

The daughter shrinks away from him. 'Dad, please don't touch me – *ever*!'

CHAPTER 22

As Lesego is mentally replaying the events through which a rift has formed between her and her father, and consequently between her and the rest of the family, her father is doing the same: how could he be here, at this *kgotla* meeting, and not recall how he's lost the love of his eldest daughter? '*Ever! Ever! Ever! Ever!*' He continues to play and replay her whispered plea-cum-order every single day. He recalls leaving his daughter's room on that day she commands, 'Dad, please don't touch me – *ever!*' He recalls stumbling out of the room, tears streaming down his face. What's gone wrong? He's supposed to be on top of the world; hitherto, he was confident the police would end up chasing their own tails – that's how he and the other conspirators had designed the events to unfold.

Now, however, his elder daughter is compromising everything. He's even afraid to let her out of his sight: what if she talks to someone? What could she possibly say, though? That her father came home late, then burnt trash the following day? And in any case, would she dare jeopardise her own family? He thinks not; she just needs a bit of fixing by a traditional doctor to make her think straight again. Getting her into a boarding school will be easy – that much she's right about: too many people owe him too many favours for it to be a problem. He'll have to explain the whole thing to his wife, Rosinah, in a way through which he'll ease her mind, though.

He recalls going to the bathroom to clean and dress the marks on his face. He knows he can't repair his heart, though. He stumbles into the master bedroom, careful not to look Rosinah in the eye.

'Did you speak to her?' Rosinah enquires.

'Yes, I did, Mma-Lesego,' Disanka replies. 'I think we should find her a place in a boarding school: if that's what she wants, let her have it – she can always change her mind.' He's trying his best to sound relaxed about the crisis on his hands.

'Did she say *why* she wants to change schools so suddenly?' Rosinah asks gently.

'No, but I think it has to do with a boy – you know: she's sixteen, and thinks every boyfriend's the one. The boy likes another girl, from what I can gather.' He's still not facing her.

Rosinah is frowning. 'I don't think so: I don't think Lesego would let any boy chase her out of school – out of the *district*! No: there's something else. I just don't accept that "boy" story. Is *that* what she told you?' For her, nothing is making sense: neither her elder daughter's behaviour nor the explanation her husband is now offering. And he's been crying.

Disanka silently curses himself for being unable to come up with a better story. 'No; no; no – she didn't tell me it in so many words; I just assumed it from her behaviour.'

Rosinah is still frowning. 'That's a rather rich assumption, wouldn't you say? Where'd you get "the other girl" and the rest of the details?' She approaches her husband and touches him on the shoulder.

He whirls around and shouts, 'Listen, *woman*: if you can't discipline a little girl, don't blame others for your failures, okay? Just *shut up* and go to bed. If I hear one peep out of you, I'll *slap* you. And the decision's been made: she's *going* to boarding school; I'm arranging it first thing tomorrow morning. Now, please let me go to sleep, Rosinah – I'm tired of your *nagging*!' His voice has risen to an unusually high level; his manner is strange; his eyes are glistening with tears.

Within a week, having refused to participate in a family-strengthening ceremony, Lesego leaves for boarding school. Her sad family members stand in a group at the front door of their big house. A taxi's waiting: Lesego has refused her parents' offers to drive her – she's to take a taxi to the bus stop, then a bus for the rest of the 600-kilometre journey to her new school.

Since that day, life's never been the same in the Disanka household. Rosinah is irritable and difficult in her husband's company, and constantly blames him for driving their daughter away. First, she cries almost every night; then, the accusations start. 'It *must* be something you did!' she insists.

'Rosinah,' he counters, 'I don't know what you're talking about – *you* don't know what you're talking about!'

'Perhaps it's something one of your many *mistresses* has said to her!' she shouts.

'Why don't you stick to relevant matters?' he asks, lamely.

She challenges him. '*You* tell me what's "relevant"! You know something! You're not telling me everything! You and Lesego know something I don't know! Please tell me why she left like that!'

Back and forth they go, getting nowhere except deeper into sadness. Then they try and make up: they hug, and promise each other that things will be okay again. However, their sadness has spilt over into the whole family, and laughter is never genuine now.

CHAPTER 23

The villagers continued to gather at their *kgotla*. More vehicles arrived. Lesego ducked down when Health Minister Gape looked in her direction: although she didn't think there was a chance he'd recognise her, she'd decided to err on the side of caution. More VIPs arrived, and at the same time, even more NVIPs.

All eyes then swivelled around to a group of villagers who were approaching. First there was an old man. His movements were slow and gentle, almost a swagger – a jerky swagger, due to his slightly dragging left foot.

Next to the old man was a woman in her mid-forties. Her face was drawn: an expression at odds with her yellow dress, through which an air of happiness was superimposed on her. Her purple shoulder scarf had ridden up and was now more a neck tie than a shoulder covering. Her thin waist and 'happy' dress were bound together by a shiny, white-plastic belt.

Behind the couple walked four young women, one of whom quite a few of the VIPs were surprised to see was white: they craned their necks; offered their ears to each other's mouths; whispered questions. A frown spread over Head Man Bokae's face when his eyes met Naledi's – but only he and she noticed it. The white woman was taking photos; she was also holding a video camera. Two of the young women were each carrying three bulging envelopes; the third woman was carrying a clipboard and writing furiously as she was looking around.

As the six attendees reached the edge of the crowd, they slowed down, hesitating. The old man looked up at the VIP stand. His face clouded over. Lesego noticed his left foot do a strange twitch as he came to a stop. She wondered to herself, *Is that the father of the child? Perhaps he's an uncle. Is that fear spreading over his face, or just a squint? Perhaps his eyes aren't too good; perhaps he's considering going up on the stand; perhaps he can't make up his mind whether he's a VIP or an NVIP. The young women are hesitating as well. Who are they? They're with the mother and the man with the wiggly left foot.*

Some of the men sitting in the semi-VIP area on each side of the stand sprang from their chairs and offered them to the group of six. *Clearly these people are some kind of VIPs, even if they're not important enough to ascend the stand,* Lesego thought to herself.

A voice suddenly boomed forth from the VIP stand, whereupon Lesego was jolted out of her speculating and back into the present. 'Ladies and gentlemen, I call upon Rre-Chencha to open this meeting with a prayer.' The public-address system magnified the voice, and spread it across the village and beyond.

Lesego didn't close her eyes for the prayer; instead, she watched her father. He had his hands firmly folded and his head bowed in earnest as the reverend prayed for guidance and truth and for punishment of the people responsible for the death of an innocent child. He asked for all of it, he declared, in the name of the Father, the Son and the Holy Spirit.

'Amen,' rang out from the 2000-strong crowd.

Lesego's father had a solemn look on his face: to any onlooker, there could have been no doubt that he, too, was a man seeking the truth, guidance, and punishment for the people responsible for the death of an innocent child – or that he was asking for it all in the name of the Father, the Son and the Holy Spirit.

The voice of the master of ceremonies came back on over the PA. It droned on and on as the MC acknowledged the presence of each dignitary, one after the other. He mentioned the chiefs before the sub-chiefs, naturally, and Neo's mother before 'Ladies and gentlemen'. The voice was that of the Maun police-station com - mander. When he'd made sure he'd 'recognised' – as he put it – every VIP, he finally handed the microphone over to Safety and Security Minister Mading. As men of his status tended to be, the minister was a large man: clearly someone who ate well and often.

Except for a prominent mole that marred the shape of his nose, he was actually very good looking.

The meeting, Minister Mading declared, had been called to address certain developments in the case of the disappearance of Neo Kakang, in 1994. The meeting, he continued, had been called to give the villagers a chance to inform the police about any recent and relevant developments that might have taken place. It was notable that he chose his words carefully. He stopped, expecting to see several people raise their hands – even a stampede to the mike. However, nothing of the sort happened. It wasn't the reaction he'd expected to witness: in their eagerness to speak, angry villagers were supposed to trip over each other. When, after a pause, no one indicated that he or she was inclined to say anything, Minister Mading invited comments from the crowd. When one hand went up, he smiled with relief and invited the man to speak.

'Thank you, mister minister,' the man began. 'We see that only government people are sitting on the VIP podium. This doesn't please us, mister minister: we believe that Mma-Neo, the woman whose child was brutally killed – by lions, as you've said repeatedly over the years – belongs up there as well. Do I speak for the village people of my tribe?' He paused to look around.

The crowd roared in the affirmative.

The man acknowledged the response. 'Thank you. And in addition, we have visitors who are *our* VIPs: we want them up there as well. Last, we've called you here for you to report to us – not the other way round. We'll speak only after you've spoken – then we'll speak. Mma-Neo, Rra-Naso, Amantle, Boitumelo, please ascend the podium.'

Whispered conversations ensued among the people sitting on the VIP stand as well as among the people sitting in the semi-VIP areas. When Rra-Naso heard the invitation to ascend, he shook his head. However, Amantle propelled him forward. Not enough chairs were available on the stand to admit the newly elevated group of four. Lesego watched her father rise to give one of them his seat; however, a hand quickly pulled him down, and its owner then used it to order four other people off the podium.

Safety and Security Minister Mading thanked the speaker for the advice he'd just given. He then proceeded to say his piece. 'I agree with the speaker about a report from the police; it was just that I didn't want you villagers to think we don't want to listen to you. But may I ask who these people are? Mma-Neo and Rra-Naso I've heard about – and Amantle, I believe I've heard about her: she's the TSP who –' He broke off, to choose his words carefully. He then resumed. 'It would be helpful if you could explain her role and the role of the other young woman.'

The villager who'd just spoken now responded again. 'Mister minister, the young woman Amantle Bokaa is up there because she's been instrumental in recommending a lawyer to us. The lawyer is the other woman up there: Ms Boitumelo Kukama. The lawyer's role will be to listen to you and advise us about what to do with your information – so you may continue, please.' He'd once again refrained from saying anything to help the minister decide on a starting point.

Minister Mading had no choice but to continue. 'Okay,' he agreed; 'let's go on. Five years ago, in 1994, a young girl, Neo Kakang, disappeared from this village. There was a search party made up of both villagers and the police. But she was never found. Some people believed – and I'm one of them – that she'd been killed for ritual purposes. Others within the police force believed she'd been killed by wild animals.'

A murmur emanated from the crowd. Amantle raised a hand, and the sound died down.

The minister continued. 'I agree that that view wasn't a very intelligent one. But we all know that fear of ritual murderers often makes the police afraid to find out the truth. I want to assure everyone here that the mistakes that have taken place – and there *have* been mistakes – were due to fear, not to a deliberate cover-up. I know we're supposed to report to you, but I'd like to raise a matter of great concern to us: the matter of the nurses. Where are they, and *how* are they? I'd be failing in my duty if I didn't ask about them.'

The erstwhile respondent, who was clearly the villagers' spokesperson, cleared his throat and spoke again. 'We're not here to answer questions about government employees – so please continue.'

Minister Mading turned from the microphone to his entourage, the members of which were now busily whispering among themselves. He saw Health Minister Gape waving his hands about in order to make a strong point. He saw TSP Director Mrs Molapo seeming to be advising him, Minister Mading, to continue giving the report. He therefore faced the microphone again in order to continue. 'I'll go back to my report. As I've already said, we've made mistakes – only God knows whether we can rectify them. But the starting point is that we need – no, let me rephrase that: we *request*, not demand – *request* the village to hand over the items of clothing found at the clinic. We understand that Ms Amantle Bokaa here found them in a storeroom. Even after all these years, those items of clothing can be valuable evidence. Second, we request an undertaking from the village that we'll work together to solve this case. Last, but not least, we request the villagers to release the two nurses, unharmed. I want to assure the villagers that we come in peace. The last thing we want to happen is violence.' He'd delivered his three main points, and now seemed relieved to resume his position among the other dignitaries.

Boitumelo then took to the microphone. She and Amantle looked very out of place among the older and predominantly male government officials. In a clear, assertive voice, she began, 'I have a few questions for the minister, on behalf of my clients.'

Murmurs of approval sprang up from the crowd: the villagers liked the sound of the words 'my clients'.

She forged ahead with the first two questions. 'How do the police say the clothes ended up at the clinic? Where were the clothes before they ended up at the clinic?'

Minister Mading had no choice but to return to the mike. 'I don't think those questions belong here, Ms Kukama – I believe those are matters we can discuss later, at the office.'

Shouts of disapproval erupted from the crowd.

Boitumelo wouldn't be cowed. 'You're wrong, mister minister: these are *critical* questions, and your answers will determine whether my clients can trust you or not. We'd suggest you answer, otherwise we're back where we started a few days ago.' They were brave words from one so young and lacking in resources.

Minister Mading considered his response, then assumed the microphone again. 'I'll answer for the sake of progress. The clothes were brought to the station by a man by the name of Shosho. That's what I've been able to ascertain from reading all the relevant records. They were placed in an exhibits locker overnight, but the following day they were gone. I honestly don't understand how they left the locker and ended up here, at the clinic. I know that some two officers who were involved in the case tried to hide all this from the deceased's mother – but I want to emphasise it wasn't with the sanction of my office. Of course, I wasn't the minister then, but there's collective responsibility in government. I'm not at all suggesting I'm not responsible for the mess; all I can say is that somehow the clothes left the locker and ended up here. I'm determined to set up an inquiry so those kinds of questions can be answered. Now you have the clothes, we believe. Does that answer you questions?'

'Perhaps, mister minister,' Boitumelo replied; 'perhaps – but that doesn't mean my clients are satisfied. But I have another set of questions – on behalf of my clients, of course. Where are the police officers who falsified the records and lied to a grieving mother? What have you done as a sign of your disapproval of their behaviour?'

The crowd applauded.

Minister Mading was expecting these two questions and had rehearsed his response. 'To show our good faith, we've brought the men responsible. This is to show you we want this matter handled without any violence. I personally want truth and justice. It might be too late to get justice, but it's not too late to get truth. I have to be honest and say there are those who say we're handling this thing without the necessary toughness, that we should've just brought in the SSGs, and taken the clothes and the nurses. I don't believe in violence like that: we know it doesn't solve anything in the long run. So, I say "Let's talk and discuss." Yes: discuss. Now, Senai, Bosilo, Moruti, Monaana and Agang, please come forward.'

The five men walked forward from the back of the VIP stand. They huddled together, like cattle being driven through a narrow gate. No one wanted to lead the group, and when each man attempted to lose height, the result was colective hunched shoulders and awkward postures.

The minister looked pleased to be able to display his scalps: the

201

scapegoats he'd obviously found. 'These are the police officers who were involved in the initial investigations of the case. You demanded they come today, and that's why they're here. I ask you to remember that they did what they did out of fear, not a deliberate intention to protect the killers. Put yourselves in their positions: poor police officers, made to track killers who have traditional powers. What could they do, really? However, I agree with you: there must be an inquiry into their behaviour – and the follow-up must be proper punishment.'

As planned, Boitumelo announced, 'We demand a written statement from each one of them about their role in this sorry mess – but we'll get to that later, mister minister. First, another question: what chances of success do you foresee? Are you confident this murder can be solved?'

The Safety and Security Minister shook his head in regret and by way of apologising. 'All I can say is we'll do our best. You know, as a lawyer, that five years is a long time to pick up a trail again; however, what we *can* promise – what we *do* promise today, in the presence of this large gathering – is that we'll do our best. The clothes are a starting point; perhaps the torn sections can tell us something. I'll also make sure a new team of police officers is assembled to take up the investigations. I'll personally oversee the work of the team, and we'll report to you as much as possible.'

Lesego detected sadness in the minister's eyes as he looked at Mma-Neo: she was looking drawn, frail and defeated. Sitting beside her, Rra-Naso was looking equally so. They were two old souls bowed by a common burden. Lesego sensed that heads were turning towards her, and realised her neighbours were responding to a camera lens trained on her. She realised she was crying and that the tears were rolling down her cheeks: she'd obviously raised the interest of the lawyer's camerawoman. She ducked deeper into the crowd. She wondered whether either of her parents had noticed her, but when she caught sight of their serious, attentive looks, she realised they hadn't.

She then saw Boitumelo assume the microphone again, to ask for a short break so she and her team could meet with the minister privately. Head shakes and nods ensued from the podium. The government VIPs consulted Lesego's father, and he gave a vigorous head shake. The VIPs didn't consult her mother, but she offered a vigorous nod anyway. Finally, the master of ceremonies announced there'd be a short break. Lesego watched as Minister Mading, Boitumelo, Amantle, Mma-Neo, Rra-Naso and two other people walked towards the health clinic. She saw a few other VIPs follow to join them. She saw the other VIPs offer more head shakes and remain behind.

She watched as the white camerawoman whispered to her companion. She saw the companion march towards where she herself was standing. She had no intention of talking to her, so decided to melt into the crowd. After a short time, she was sure she'd eluded the young woman, and chose a tree to sit under, away from the crowd. Presently, she heard the soft crunch of footsteps behind her. She turned to see one of the two whispering women – the black one – looking down at her.

The black woman addressed her. 'Excuse me, may I join you? My name's Naledi.'

'Suit yourself,' Lesego replied offhandedly.

Naledi sat next to her, on a twisted tree. 'We noticed you among the crowd. You looked upset; you still look upset, and we're curious. What's your interest in this case? We couldn't help noticing that from your dress, you're from the city – that is, you're not a villager.'

Lesego felt trapped. She managed to ask, 'Does a person have to have an interest in this case to find it upsetting?'

'You're right there,' Naledi agreed. 'But still, the crowd isn't full of young people who are so upset by the case that they've left school or work to be here – so you must have a special reason to be here, some special interest.'

Lesego decided to pursue her own line of questioning. 'What about you? You weren't introduced to the crowd: what's your interest?'

Naledi looked at the young, red-eyed woman in front of her before answering. 'My interest is truth and justice. I wasn't introduced because, like you, I'm not too keen on some people knowing I'm here. I'm a lawyer for the government.'

Lesego's eyes flew up to Naledi's.

'Yes,' Naledi continued, 'and I'll most probably be fired when I get back to the office. I've decided that my friends, that is, Boitumelo and Amantle, are on the side of the truth. I'll most probably regret my decision when the rent comes due, in a week's time – but by then it'll be too late. So, what's your interest?'

Lesego clasped then unclasped her hands. 'So, you might lose your job. But you can get another one: you can go to work for your friend Boitumelo Kukama – isn't that right?'

'I guess so,' Naledi had to admit.

Lesego wasn't in the mood to disclose her interest in the case. 'I've nothing to lose by telling you why I'm here: I've already lost it all. So, Ms Lawyer, go searching some place else. I've nothing to tell you. Please leave me alone; I came to this tree to be alone.' With that, she looked away, making it quite clear the conversation was over.

'Aren't you going to tell me your name at least?' Naledi ventured, as a parting shot.

In response, Lesego picked up the torch that had been lying in her lap, stood up, and walked away.

CHAPTER 24

'What do you think?' Boitumelo asked her colleagues. 'Things went pretty well, no? The Minister for Safety and Security was so keen to avoid a riot he was pretty much taking orders from us! That's great.' Although it'd been a long day, they all felt the need to go over what had happened.

Daniel piped up. 'It helped that Staff Nurse Palaki decided she hadn't been kidnapped after all. The other nurse needed some persuading. But if they'd decided to press charges, the minister would've had to listen. Those profuse apologies from you helped a lot, Amantle: I didn't know you could grovel like that!' He was both teasing and being serious. He'd felt compelled to move from the ambulance to the clinic during the *kgotla*'s adjournment so he could be a 'fly on the wall'.

Amantle responded, 'I have to say that handing over the clothes to the lab man was really hard for me: I felt like I was parting with our only leverage – and I felt powerless once I'd let go. Do you know what I mean? Even with the public assurances and the petitions' being read out in front of the media, I feel kind of empty – kind of like they've won, somehow. We know they can't possibly do much after all these years. We can keep on hoping, and perhaps the police who botched the investigations in the first place can come up with a few pieces of evidence they were too afraid to record at the time. Realistically, though, it's a lost cause.' She was lying on her back on the only bed in the room, located in the back section of the clinic. Luggage was strewn everywhere.

Boitumelo munched on an apple as she spoke. 'I think we won plenty: you and the villagers forced their hand; you called the meeting, controlled it; and what's more, a few police are going to lose their jobs – and deserve to. And who knows? With modern techniques, it mightn't be too late to find something. Who knows? I'm happy the way things have gone.'

Naledi asked, 'What do you make of that crying girl, though? Where do you think she fits in?'

'What crying girl?' Amantle wanted to know.

Nancy and Naledi described Lesego. Naledi commented, 'She must be involved somehow; I just can't imagine how. She said something to me about having lost everything. We must find her, and find out more about her. I'm certain she knows something about the case.'

Boitumelo put her apple aside in favour of being more fully involved in the discussion. 'How old would you say she is? Perhaps she comes from this village – or was in the village for some reason when the murder took place.'

Naledi offered, 'I'd say perhaps twenty-two. She'd have been about sixteen or seventeen when Neo was murdered. But she looked too well dressed to be from this village – and if she were, wouldn't you know about it? You've been dealing with the villagers.' She looked up at Amantle.

'I don't know what to make of it,' Amantle responded; 'perhaps we can follow it up later – you have her on video, no? Good: that gives us at least one clue to follow up on.' She said the last sentence with some excitement.

Silence ensued for a while, until Daniel asked Naledi, 'What'll you do now the adventure's almost over? Are you going back to – what do you call him – Mount V?'

'Don't remind me of that!' Naledi demanded. 'I don't think I can go back there – not just because Mount V will definitely bury me but because I don't have the interest for that tame kind of work. I just can't imagine sitting in that office reading inquest dockets and listening to Linky any more.'

'You can come and work with us!' Boitumelo chipped in. 'We need fired-up people like you – what do you say?'

'Are you serious?' Naledi asked. 'Are you sure? I mean you're not just feeling sorry for me, are you?' She was obviously excited by the offer.

206

'I'm serious,' Boitumelo declared, 'but I have to warn you: there's no great money to be made with us – you know that; you can see it from the car I drive. And there's a lot of work. But there *is* excitement – I mean look at me at present: I'm in the middle of nowhere, and I spent the night with lions breathing down my neck! What law office can match that? And as long as we associate with our friend here, we'll no doubt have excitement galore.' She looked at Naledi and the others. 'She doesn't know how to live a simple life. Welcome aboard, my friend. I think a celebration's called for – where's the wine?' In sitting up, she renounced the lazy posture she'd assumed only a few minutes ago.

'What about me?' Daniel chimed in. 'I keep on being a bored TSP. If I see one more donkey, I'll throw up! At least you get time off, Amantle; you kidnap innocent nurses, steal an ambulance and order the government around – and for that you get time off? It's not fair.' He made a big show of being serious and wounded.

'Please, Daniel,' Amantle implored, 'don't go round making that kind of joke! Really, I didn't kidnap anyone. I don't want any jokes about it, okay?'

Naledi was busying herself getting the makeshift wine glasses ready. She firmly believed it was time to let the collective hair down. 'Come on, you guys: let's celebrate. What's with you? Relax! I've just gotten a new job here!' Just then, however, her mobile phone rang. When she saw the number on the display panel, she gasped: it was Mr Pako's. 'Oh, my God, it's Mount V! I know he saw me earlier today – he must have! What am I going to say to him?' She was whispering, even though there was no way Mount V could hear her.

'Let me have the phone,' Daniel demanded.

Before Naledi could make up her mind about the wisdom of letting Daniel talk to her boss, he'd taken the mobile from her. 'Hello; hello,' he said into the phone, in a mock-serious voice. 'Miss Binang? I'm sorry: you must have the wrong number . . . Temper; temper! Don't *do* that to your heart now, mister . . . Really? No need for all that anger, mister: the heart's such a delicate organ. I'd suggest you hang up before you erupt. That'd be nasty, now, wouldn't it? . . . 'Bye; sorry: wrong number. But I'd really suggest you rein in that temper of yours . . . 'Bye. Have a good day, sir! . . . O-oh: I dare say you've erupted!'

By the time the conversation had ended, the room-mates had dissolved into hysterical giggles. As a fresh ripple of giggles started up, a knock came on the door. Amantle went to see who it was.

The gaunt form of Rra-Naso was standing in the doorway. 'Good evening, my children,' he said.

'Good evening, Rra-Naso,' Amantle responded for everyone. 'Please sit down.' She looked at him puzzled: she hadn't been expecting the ailing old man to turn up, and it'd been a long day. Emotions had run high, and she'd expected he'd have wanted to go home to his family.

Rra-Naso directed his tired eyes at Amantle's companions. 'I see your bags are packed – you leave tomorrow, I'm told.'

'Yes, I leave tomorrow,' Amantle responded; 'I'll be going with my friends here. But I wasn't going to leave without coming over to see you. Not only do I want to thank you for your support; we all need to meet with Mma-Neo, you and a few other people – so we probably won't leave till tomorrow afternoon. I've just been telling my friends here how everyone says you're a tower of strength for Neo's mother.' During the *kgotla* meeting, she'd asked Mrs Molapo for two weeks off, but her real plan was to request she be re-assigned to a place closer to Gaborone: she wanted to be at the centre of the newly reopened investigations. Although she didn't believe she'd get the assignment, she was going to try.

'Before you thank me,' Rra-Naso began, 'take out a pen and a piece of paper – more than one piece of paper, in fact. And is there enough paraffin in that lamp? We're going to be here for a while. I have a story to tell. I'm laying a heavy burden on you, my child – but I think you can handle it. What you do with it's up to you. I think your friends must stay as well: they might as well hear what I have to say.' His frail body convulsed into a coughing fit.

Amantle had stopped worrying about catching Rra-Naso's TB: the past few days had been so charged that the prospect of contracting tuberculosis hadn't seemed the worst of her problems. She now tried to solicit more information from him, but he'd say nothing more until she'd checked the lamp, and she had a notepad and pen ready.

Rra-Naso then turned to face Amantle. Daniel, Naledi and Boitumelo withdrew to a corner to listen. Nancy went to get the video camera and started recording.

Rra-Naso asked that he be allowed to say his piece without interruption. He then proceeded to string his words together as if the monologue were one long paragraph. It was as if he were afraid that once he paused, he wouldn't have the energy to go on. He began in a whisper, but his voice gained strength and didn't waiver as he told his story. 'He promised me five goats if I found him a hairless lamb, a child with no sins yet. He said he wanted a girl who hadn't yet had her first period and who hadn't been with a man yet. I'm a poor man, a weak man. And I didn't want to do it, but he came to me many, many times; many nights, he came. He brought food. I was afraid to say no to his food: you can't say no to people like that. He was asking me but he wasn't asking me – I mean he was ordering me. One time, he brought a bag of sugar and milk, and tea, and a dress for my wife. Then, in winter, he brought a blanket. Still I said no. And I was afraid – very afraid. Then he brought a goat. This was at Christmas, and we killed it, and we had lots of meat. And when we ate it, I knew I couldn't say no to him any more. When he left, he said, "Four more will come." Goats – I mean "four more goats". I was afraid of him. He looked at Naso, my child, when he was leaving, and I was afraid. She was sleeping – next to the fire was where she was sleeping. He always came at night. I was afraid – very afraid – when I saw him looking at my daughter. I told him about Neo; I just found myself talking and telling him about Neo. Neo just came to my mind; I just thought of her. She wasn't in my mind before; then she came into my mind, and I told him about Neo. I told him she had no brothers, so she was always going into the bush to get goats and donkeys, like a boy. Also, she liked to be alone a lot. She wasn't afraid of the bush, like other little girls. I just told him where he could find her – that's all. I didn't catch her; no, I didn't catch her for them – they didn't need me, really, to get her. Then he gave me one more goat. He said he couldn't give me everything all at once: people would talk. But then he tricked me; they tricked me. I didn't want to be with them when they did their deed. They tricked me; they really tricked me. They came to my house one night. They told me, "Let's go outside." I said, "Why?" I was afraid. They were three; before, he'd come alone; now they were three. I said, "My wife's asleep, and she'll ask where I went." They said, "Come: a man must finish what he starts. You can't point and then go to sleep." They said that. I was afraid that maybe they wanted to kill me. I thought, *Maybe they want a man now, not a little girl any more – but no one wants old flesh: it's no use.* I was confused. They said, "Come." I followed them. I was weak. My head was full of air: no thoughts, just empty. I couldn't think. Then they pushed me into the vehicle. At first I only heard breathing; then I heard muted cries. It was like "Mmmm! Mmmm! Mmmm!" I looked, and there was the little girl: it was Neo – bound hands and feet. All three men got into the vehicle. And I drove off with them. They gave me something and told me to chew on it: "It'll take away the fear,' – that's what they said. I chewed, but the fear remained. It brought on more fear. The fear was in my head and in my heart and in my stomach and in my liver and in my knees. The girl moved, and her foot touched me, and I was afraid. She was hot; it was like a hot iron touching me. I didn't want her to touch me. I closed my eyes and prayed I'd become strong. I don't know what I said, but I just prayed and prayed. Then he said, "Shut up!" And another said, "Give him some more to chew!" And I couldn't chew: my jaws wouldn't move, and saliva was coming out, and I started to cry – to cry just like a baby. He said, "Keep quiet and be a man, or you won't come back – we'll feed you to the crocodiles." I saw we were headed for the Crocodile Pools. I tried to keep quiet, but the girl went on saying "Mmmm! Mmmm! Mmmm!" And I held my mouth with my hands so I wouldn't cry out. I pulled my feet up so I wouldn't touch the girl. After a long time, we stopped next to the river – under a big tree: the *mokgwa* tree at the Crocodile Pools. They said, "Get out." I got out. They carried the girl out. Then they said, "Touch her; hold her." I didn't want to touch her. They said, "Touch her: a man must finish what he starts." I touched her, and she was cold – as cold as a frog. And she was wet, clammy. I was afraid. I thought, *Why is she now cold?* I wasn't speaking; I was thinking these things, but I was just quiet. They took her and lay

210

her down. We all took off our clothes. They said, "You have to be as naked as a shilling for this job." She kicked a bit, but her legs were bound together. They removed the blindfold. She looked at me. It was dark, but she recognised me. She begged me with her eyes to help her. I closed my eyes, but I could still feel her eyes on me. Then they removed the mouth gag. They said she had to see and scream to release the power of the *dipheko*. Then she begged; she said, "Please, Rra-Naso, how can you let them rape me? Please, let me go: I won't tell. Leave me here, and I'll find my way home. Please; please: I could be your child – think of Naso." She thought she was going to be raped – that was her fear. I turned around to run away, but my feet were planted to the ground. I couldn't run away; they knew it: they told me they had power over me and that I couldn't run. Then I knew that the medicine they'd given me to chew on wasn't for removing fear; it was for holding me with their power. After that, I did everything with them: I was powerless; I was under their control. When they wanted to carve out the armpit, I pulled the arm with all my might. When they went for the left breast, I held the head down. I don't remember whether they cut off the right breast – I think they did; they must have: why would they leave it? And when they spread her little legs to cut out her private parts, I was still holding the head. She was strong, too. She turned her head and bit me – see: even after so many years, this small finger's never straightened up. At night, it twitches and wakes me up. The anus was the tricky part – but I was a mad man by that time. I don't know at what point she finally died; they wanted her to stay alive when they removed the parts – so they had to work fast. I didn't know how to cut, so they didn't ask me to. They said, "You have no experience – just hold where we say hold." One of them had messed up the private parts last time they'd done a similar job. He promised to be more careful this time, but the leader wouldn't let him do it. When they were all done, they licked their knives clean, and told me to lick my fingers. I did. I saw their white teeth with streaks of blood running down them – maybe I didn't see it, because it was at night; maybe I just imagined it – but no: I saw those teeth, and I saw their glee. I wasn't in my head by that time; I was out of my body, just watching them and watching myself. The little body was lying there, all bloody. It wasn't like a body; it was like a pool of blood. We went into the river to wash off the blood. I was afraid of crocodiles, but they said, "Come: you have the power now. The crocodiles won't touch you: they're our friends. We'll give them the rest of the body." They threw the body into the river, and we washed. Then, then . . . another car arrived: a big, noiseless vehicle slid out of the night. It stopped right there, near the big *mokgwa* tree. A man got out – a big man. He walked towards us, and they told me to stay behind. They walked towards the man. The pieces of flesh were in a wooden bowl. The four men looked into the bowl. I was in shock, just watching. They were choosing a piece for the newly arrived man. It was too dark, so the leader, the man who'd first come to me, switched on a torch. He reached into the bowl and selected a piece. I can still see it to this day: the light is on the man's face as he examines the piece being offered. That face has stayed with me ever since. I can still see him standing right there, under the tree. He raises his hand; the beam of the torch falls squarely on his face. Then we went back to the village . . . Now, the clothes: the clothes have caused much trouble; the clothes: I don't know why I took them – I just took them. The girl was undressed before the parts were removed. But something told me to take the clothes, and I took them. I put them in my pocket. They didn't know I took them. I think God wanted the clothes to cause trouble. Then she started screaming in my head – night and day, she screamed; she screamed and begged. I couldn't sleep; I couldn't eat. She screamed and screamed. She screamed when I joined the party looking for her. When we approached the Crocodile Pools, searching for her, she screamed loudest. She screamed when people talked about her disappearance. Sometimes I thought my wife could hear her screaming, because she'd wake me up and ask me "What was that?" Then I didn't know what to do with the clothes. Finally, I threw them away in the bush. I thought she'd stop screaming, but she won't stop. But I still can't make her be quiet. The men haven't paid me the three goats – but I don't want them. They've come to tell me that if I speak, they'll kill me. That wouldn't be a bad thing: dying would keep her quiet. She was beginning to be quieter, but you came and found the box with her clothes, and she started screaming again. I have to tell you this because although you're just a young woman, you're not afraid of their power. I think you have the guidance of God in you: God won't allow their power to touch you. I'll surely end up in hell: I deserve no better. I'm tired, my child . . . Have you written all this down?'

Amantle had written with the fury of a person possessed. She had no idea whether she had a mad man in front of her, but had put everything down. She now looked up at the frail old man: stooped, and a body ravaged by TB; a kind, sad face. She didn't have any words to respond to the story he'd just lain at her feet. She was shocked. And she was petrified. She felt the fear of the other people in the room. They'd moved towards Rra-Naso as he'd been speaking, so by the time he'd finished, four sets of horrified eyes had become fixed on him. Nancy was still shooting, spurred on by the intensity of the others' reaction. Naturally, she hadn't been able to understand a word of what Rra-Naso had said, because he'd delivered the monologue in Setswana.

He had something to add. 'Now I'll give you the names of the four men. You'll be surprised – or perhaps you won't be. There was Disanka, the businessman. He was the man who first came to me; he was the leader. He was sitting up there today – you saw him. His trucks come into this village every month. He sells goats and farm produce. Everyone thinks he's a good man, and he has respect. And of course you heard him speak at the *kgotla* today. And there was Sebaki, the headmaster of the village across the river. Of course he wasn't the headmaster then; the old headmaster died in a car crash. The third man was the head man of Diphukwi village: Mr Bokae, the one who thinks he should be chief of Diphukwi village. I dare say there are many who agree with him – that he should be chief, that is. It's not for me to say whether it's correct or not. You saw him up there today as well. And then the man who came for the piece. He, too, was at the meeting today: the Minister for Safety and Security – yes, my child, the Minister for Safety and Security. I could never forget that face – I've seen it twice in my life: that night, and today; no doubt I'll see it one more time, in hell.

'What?!' On the videotape, it would later be revealed that the utterance had come from a total of four mouths; only Nancy's had remained shut. Not only had she been concentrating on recording everything; she hadn't been able to understand a word the subject had said.

Now that every perpetrator had been named, the listeners understood that their lives could be in danger. More than anything, though, they realised they'd been tricked by the smooth-talking Minister for Safety and Security, Mr Mading.

A thought was nibbling away at the corner of Boitumelo's mind. She decided to ask the question tentatively, her heart full of fear – fear of hearing more, but also of breaking the spell and not hearing any more. She addressed Rra-Naso. 'Did you bleed into any of her clothes?' Her brain was telling her she needed to verify the story somehow. She'd concluded that if Neo had bitten him during the killing, perhaps his blood could be found on at least one item of the clothing. She was hoping, without really believing, that it was a realistic hope.

Rra-Naso replied, 'Don't worry about my bleeding, my child: that was nothing; even Disanka's bleeding, which he tried to stop by using her little blouse, was nothing. But you should've seen that coward hopping around and swearing just because a little girl had bitten him. Yes: she bit him, too – around the wrist, I think, or perhaps on the thumb; I'm not sure. He used the top as a bandage until the end; then they just left the clothes, right there. I don't know why I took the clothes – I think God wanted all this to come out, because their power didn't stop me from taking the clothes. And their power didn't stop her from screaming in my head. And their power isn't stopping me from talking to you now.'

Amantle looked at the gentle old face before her: was it the face of a man full of compassion and love? the face of a brutal killer? the face of a brave man? the face of a coward? the face of a man who'd held down a twelve-year-old girl as she was being cut up live, screaming, struggling, begging, bleeding? Was he a man who'd reached out to a grieving mother and offered her true friendship and support? Was he a monster?

Her thoughts flew about in her head as she searched for a reason. Is there a monster lurking in all of us? And if we're so paralysed by fear, if we don't dare face this evil, who will heed the screams of the innocent?

The following day, the body of the kind old man who'd been a pillar of strength to Neo's mother was found hanging from a tree just outside the village. It remained for Amantle to pass on the news to Neo's mother and the other villagers that the old man had resorted to death in order to silence not the rattling in his chest but the screaming of an innocent child that was threatening to explode in his head. And it remained to her to tell them she'd failed them, because the only evidence, the evidence they'd guarded for days, was once again in the hands of the enemy. It was a message she wasn't looking forward to delivering.

Other Titles from Spinifex Press

Far and Beyon'
Unity Dow

'To read *Far and Beyon'* is to take a trip to Africa in the hands of a knowledgeable guide, who understands your world as well as knowing her own territory backwards.'

– Keren Lavelle, *Good Reading*

ISBN 1-876756-07-1

Speak the Truth, Laughing
Rose Zwi

'Zwi is an accomplished writer . . . The lightness of her touch and her transparent desire to heal rifts between people make her a powerful advocate . . .'

– Miriam Cosic, *The Australian's Review of Books*

ISBN 1-876756-21-7

Another Year in Africa
Rose Zwi

'A tender, richly detailed and engrossing novel'

– Elaine Lindsay

ISBN 1-875559-42-6

Safe Houses
Rose Zwi

Winner, Human Rights Award for Fiction, 1994

Set against the escalating violence of the last years of the apartheid regime, *Safe Houses* is the story of three families – black and Jewish – who are inextricably bound by love and hate as well as hope and betrayal.

– Miriam Cosic, *The Australian's Review of Books*

ISBN 1-875559-72-8

*If you would like to know more about Spinifex Press,
write to us for a free catalogue, visit our website or email us
for further information.*

Spinifex Press
PO Box 5270
North Geelong VIC 3215
Australia

www.spinifexpress.com.au
women@spinifexpress.com.au